Praise for Linda Winfree's *Memories of Us*

"With sizzling sex and nail biting suspense, Ms. Winfree has yet again produced a story more than worth the money..."

~ *Rachel, Fallen Angel Reviews*

"A series not to be missed, readers can't go wrong with Memories of Us..."

~ *Melissa, Joyfully Reviewed*

"...a pleasant and well-paced romantic suspense nicely balanced with romance."

~ *Mrs. Giggles*

Look for these titles by *Linda Winfree*

Now Available:

What Mattered Most

Hearts of the South Series
Truth and Consequences (Book 1)
His Ordinary Life (Book 2)
Hold On to Me (Book 3)
Anything But Mine (Book 4)
Memories of Us (Book 5)
Hearts Awakened (Book 6)
Fall Into Me (Book 7)
Facing It (Book 8)

Coming Soon:

Uncovered

Memories of Us

Linda Winfree

A Samhain Publishing, Ltd. publication.

Samhain Publishing, Ltd.
577 Mulberry Street, Suite 1520
Macon, GA 31201
www.samhainpublishing.com

Memories of Us
Copyright © 2009 by Linda Winfree
Print ISBN: 978-1-60504-168-1
Digital ISBN: 978-1-60504-043-1

Editing by Anne Scott
Cover by Anne Cain

First Samhain Publishing, Ltd. electronic publication: June 2008
First Samhain Publishing, Ltd. print publication: April 2009

Dedication

To my Monsters, the source of all my favorite memories.

Prologue

"Daddy! No, please!"

The shrill cry cut across the still evening and assaulted Jessica's ears. She cringed as the girl scrabbled free of her captor and slipped on the wide porch, palms slapping against the wood, body hitting the boards with a dull thud. Lank dark hair clinging to her flushed face, the girl struggled to her feet and tugged against the hand wrapped around her arm. She fought with weak movements, not looking at the man holding her, eyes trained on her father's back.

"Daddy!"

Jessica leaned against the car door, a dull ache in her lower back. When the taciturn man striding toward her didn't flinch at his daughter's distress, sympathy pierced Jessica's chest. She steeled herself against it, resisted the urge to lay a hand on the swell of her stomach, hidden by a loose mandarin jacket. Sympathy was reserved for the weak, and the weak only asked to be trampled by the strong.

She'd always been strong. Always would be.

"Daddy, I'll take her and go away, I swear. You'll never see me again." Screaming the words, the teen pulled away once more, overbalanced and tumbled down the plantation-style steps. She stumbled to her feet, a bright bloodstain low on her loose gown. "Don't do this, Daddy. Please."

Her father stopped in front of Jessica, the security lights and rising moon throwing shadows on his expressionless face. Broken-hearted sobbing wrapped around them. He didn't look back. "Is everything in order?"

She nodded. "I'm meeting Danny in fifteen minutes."

His mouth tightened. "Are you sure he's the man for this?"

She bristled at his censure. The baby kicked off a flurry of movements in her belly. "He'll be fine. He's trustworthy, and he knows when to keep his mouth shut."

The girl's kicking feet thumped against the steps as the man on the porch dragged her toward the door. "Daddy, no!"

An impatient sigh racked his frame. "Roland, get her in the house."

The thick oak door closed, silencing her cries.

"Here. I want this taken care of tonight." Her father shifted the bundle in his arms into Jessica's easy hold. She glanced down at the small face in the blanket. Lashes lay against pale cheeks, a tiny hand curled along the edge of the fleece.

She turned away to fasten the infant into the carrier waiting in the backseat. When she straightened, he was too close, crowding her, his face near hers. Ice glittered in his eyes. "I trust nothing will go wrong. I can't afford mistakes, Jessica."

She smothered a spurt of fear, squashed the impulse to cover her stomach again, to protect the baby worth so much money it boggled her mind. "Everything will be just fine."

"Good." He turned away then, striding up the brick walk.

Jessica slid behind the wheel. In the car seat, the baby stirred with a choking cry but quieted under her soothing murmur. As she pulled away, the massive house rose in her rearview mirror. She shuddered.

She didn't want to think about what was happening behind

the bright windows.

Chapter One

Celia St. John sipped at a virginal strawberry daiquiri and shifted in her chair, trying to quell the low pulse of desire between her legs.

She really had to stop thinking about screwing her boss.

Being at a sex-toy party wasn't helping.

Around her, women giggled and squealed over the array of adult playthings—everything from lotions, oils and powders to vibrators and dildos. Each item she selected only fueled her fantasies about Tom McMillian.

Damn it, why couldn't she get the man out of her head?

She'd purchased a bottle of the scented warming body lotion and imagined his hands rubbing it into her skin.

She'd tested flavored body powders and envisioned her tongue lifting the pink crystals from his flat stomach.

The lifelike vibrator? Holding it, she'd wondered what he looked like in comparison.

She was obsessed. That was all there was to it. And it was a hopeless obsession. McMillian wasn't aware of her beyond her role as his lead investigator. He was still too hung up on the redhead sitting across the room, the one laughing as she wrote a check for a peek-a-boo bra and an assortment of body oils. McMillian still wanted his ex-wife—hell, the whole tricounty

12

area knew it—and that left Celia wanting a man who saw her as nothing more than a valued colleague.

Celia straightened, draining her daiquiri. She was done. No more obsessing. She'd take home her warming lubricant and one of those toys, and tonight she would *not* think about McMillian.

Her cell phone pinged its subtle tones and she pulled it from her purse. "St. John."

"Where are you?" McMillian's voice shivered over her, as if she'd conjured him with her musings. Her gaze darted to the table of toys once more.

"A party at Altee Price's. Why?"

"I need you." His voice was more terse than usual, not a good sign. "Do you have your car?"

"No, I rode with my sister."

"I'll swing by and pick you up. I'm turning off the highway now, should be there in about seven minutes."

The connection went dead. Celia gave the phone a rueful look and returned it to her purse. Typical McMillian behavior— giving orders without doubt he'd be obeyed. Maybe it was a good thing he was still hung up on Kathleen Harding. The man would be a bitch to date.

She gathered her purchases, packaged in a discreet lilac bag, made her goodbyes and stepped outside Altee's small lakefront home as the silver Mercedes purred into the drive. She walked down the steps, her stomach tightening with a tingling anticipation.

McMillian leaned over to push the passenger door open, the interior light glinting off his short brown hair. He was dressed casually, a golf shirt and khaki slacks hugging the well-defined muscles of his arms and thighs. Celia jerked her gaze from his torso to his face, set in grim lines.

"Get in. Thanks for coming." A fleeting smile, which she supposed was a concession, flashed over his thin mouth. "I should apologize for interrupting your evening."

She slid into the passenger seat, the leather molding to her body. The gift bag she laid in the floorboard next to her feet. "It's fine. What is it?"

"Crime scene." He shifted into reverse, the smooth engine barely revving. "Body of an infant discovered during a roadblock check."

Slanting a look in his direction, Celia snapped her seatbelt. The white light from the dash illuminated his expressionless face. His voice hadn't betrayed any emotion, either, but she knew cases involving children got under his skin. They had to.

"What county has jurisdiction?" She matched his cool demeanor. Please, not Darren County. Of the seven county and nearly fifteen city departments she interacted with as an investigator for the DA's office, she hated Darren County the most. Or rather, the lead investigator hated her. He still remembered what had happened with Turello.

"Chandler."

God, that was a relief. "Which investigator?"

"Cook."

Celia nodded. She liked Mark Cook, respected his expertise as an investigator. Plus, he generally wasn't a jerk about having a woman on his team. A grin quirked at her mouth. Or letting a woman take the lead, for that matter.

"What kind of party?"

Celia glanced at him, her gaze flicking over his hands on the wheel. "Just one of those hostess parties."

He lifted one eyebrow in inquiry.

She sighed. "You buy things. The hostess gets credit toward free stuff according to the amount her guests spend."

"Oh." He shook his head, a slight frown between his brows. "What kind of things?"

Pull off up here and I'll show you. She jiggled off the thought and glanced out the window, dark shapes of trees flashing by, the lights of someone's boat house glimmering on the still surface of the lake. She intended to leave behind the obsession. Starting tonight. "Depends on the party. Candles, gourmet food, jewelry, Tupperware."

She turned to study him again, a sharp, searching stare. Of course. A hint of pique twisted through her. He wasn't really interested in Altee's party itself. He had to have seen Kathleen's Jeep there. That's what was up with all the questions.

Celia narrowed her eyes. Instead of dodging and weaving about what type of party Altee had thrown, she should have told him in detail what Kathleen had purchased to use with her new husband. Except she'd seen his face when Kathleen had announced her engagement to Jason Harding, the way he'd withdrawn the weekend of her wedding.

Wonder what he'd do when he discovered Kathleen was pregnant.

He swung onto US 19. The sleek car ate the miles, the tires a bare whisper against the asphalt. Silence lingered between them and Celia stared at the darkness beyond the windows. It was always like this—he couldn't be bothered to carry on a real conversation with her. Anger trembled through her. Why was she so darned drawn to him? The man lacked basic social skills.

Or more likely, he wasn't interested in her beyond her professional capabilities.

Not knowing what to say to him didn't improve her mood. It

15

wasn't an issue with any of the other men she was acquainted with—put her in a room of cops and she could talk shop all day long.

Put her this close to Tom McMillian and the cat got her tongue every time. Too bad she wanted McMillian to get it instead.

Blue lights whirled in the distance, mixing with spotlights and casting an eerie glow on the highway. McMillian pulled the Mercedes to a stop behind the patrol cars from three counties plus the Georgia State Patrol lining the four-lane. Orange barricades filtered traffic into one lane on each side.

Operation Barbed Wire. Celia eyed the officers perusing license and insurance information as cars crept through the checkpoint. She remained a little miffed she hadn't gotten an invite to this particular party, a huge exercise in cooperative law enforcement.

A battered Toyota had been drawn to one side, and the Georgia Bureau of Investigation's crime scene van sat alongside it. The coroner's car waited nearby.

McMillian killed the engine and pushed his door open. Light flooded the interior and Celia blinked. He glanced at her. "Let's go."

She pushed her door open and met him at the hood.

He waved an acknowledgement at a state trooper who used a light stick to guide traffic forward. The beam bounced over her feet. He frowned. "Can you do this in those?"

She glanced down at the thin strap of leather peeking from beneath the hem of her jeans. The light glinted off her Pompeii Purple-polished toes. She smiled. A definite change from the sensible loafers she normally wore to the office, but no reason she couldn't work in these. "Of course."

His gaze traveled up her body, over her skinny jeans, the

green beaded camisole beneath her light corduroy jacket. She refused to shift under his cool scrutiny.

He waved toward the Toyota. "Let's go."

Her heels clicked on the blacktop. The spotlights and the waiting horror grew closer. She tucked her hair into her jacket. All she needed was to contaminate a crime scene, giving Mark Cook any reason to rag on her.

The tension emanating from McMillian didn't help. She glanced sideways at him. He remained straight faced, but the entire line of his body screamed with anxiety. Cases involving children were his special interest, hence the DA office's Child Death Investigation Task Force. She understood why his interest was so strong. What she didn't get was why he tortured himself by coming out to the scenes, instead of focusing on preparing the prosecution.

That wasn't entirely true. She did know why—the man was all about honor and duty and justice. He wasn't about to let his own emotions get in the way of what he thought was right.

He'd have made a hell of a cop.

Yellow crime scene tape twisted and crackled in the breeze. A deputy waited at the barrier, and within the cordoned area, Mark Cook snapped photo after photo, which Celia knew would become a painstaking record of the scene. She smiled and nodded at the deputy standing watch. "Parker."

He returned the nod and glanced at McMillian. "Evening, St. John. Mr. McMillian."

Cook didn't stop taking pictures. "Hey, St. John, glad you're here. Come have a look."

She stopped at the tape. "You sure?"

"Yeah. Gloves are in the kit."

She moved to the folding box holding his equipment for

17

evidence collection. Taking two pairs of gloves, she snapped them both on, one atop the other. "Coroner pronounce it yet?"

The camera flash strobed again. "Yeah."

"So what have you got?" She ducked under the tape, carefully treading to the area where he stood. Her existence narrowed to the space within that tape, everything fading to the background—McMillian, sexual obsessions, the noise and lights of the roadblock.

Cook lowered the camera. "Caucasian infant, pretty small. The guys from the Drug Task Force pulled the car, found the baby like this."

She peered at the bundle nestled in an infant seat, strapped into the Toyota's backseat. One tiny hand, curled into a fist, poked out of the folds. "A suffocation? SIDS, maybe? Where are the parents?"

He shook his head. "I don't think the driver is the dad. He's clammed up tighter than a church-going girl's legs before she has a ring."

She glanced over her shoulder at the line of patrol cars. "Where is he?"

"Sitting in Parker's car." A sneer curled Cook's mouth. "Think he's allergic to dog hair. He's sneezing up a storm."

She eyed the K-9 unit. The tinted windows made it impossible to see the man inside. "So if he's not the father, where did the baby come from?"

"Hell if I know." Cook shrugged. "That's what we have to figure out."

He'd ceased to exist.

Tom leaned a hand against the roof of a patrol car and watched Celia work the scene with Cook. He frowned. She moved with the same brisk professionalism as always, but something was different.

Maybe it was the clothes. He couldn't remember seeing her in jeans before. Hell, he'd never seen her toes before tonight. Purple-polished toes. Pretty too.

Damn, he sounded like a foot fetishist.

Her hair was loose, although she'd tucked it inside her jacket before entering the crime scene. He was accustomed to seeing the silvery blonde strands in a neat knot. She looked younger, softer somehow, with it loose around her shoulders.

He hadn't seen this Celia St. John before. She got to him.

His frown deepened. St. John was one of the best investigators he'd ever seen and his office was lucky to have her. If he had to describe her, the words would come easy— professional, thorough, disciplined, cool.

Gorgeous.

He shook his head. The physical tug buzzed within him, but he tamped it down. Letting himself focus on his attraction to her was a disaster in the making.

One, she was his employee.

Two, he didn't ever want another cop in his personal life, not after Kathleen.

The memory of his ex-wife jerked through him, bringing the expected rush of emotions—frustration, anger, pain. Simply seeing her Jeep at Price's earlier had sent the same old feelings washing over him. The strength of them had surprised him. Over the years, the intensity had diminished.

But one conversation on the golf course that afternoon and the hurt was back, strong as ever.

Kathleen was pregnant with Harding's baby. Kathleen, carrying another man's child.

He'd been trying all evening to wrap his mind around that reality. Maybe that explained why seeing Celia outside the mold he'd assigned her had him more off-kilter than usual where she was concerned. That, and a phone call telling him the Chandler County Sheriff's Department was investigating a deceased infant.

He dug his fingers into his palm, pain shooting up his arm. All he'd needed to top off a perfect day was seeing a dead baby.

"Cook, there are prints all over this car." The lyrical notes of Celia's cool voice washed over him. He glanced up, watching her as she pointed out the area.

Cook squinted. "Man, running those will take forever. And we won't have any elimination sets."

"Want me to start taking them?"

"St. John, you can take whatever you want for me, anytime you want."

"Don't hold your breath." Celia lifted the gray powder from the evidence-collection kit.

Cook peered inside the front seat before placing a crime scene marker next to the fast-food wrappers visible in the floorboard. He grinned down at Celia's head when she bent to dust the door handle. "So did you go to Price's little soirée?"

"Oh, I'm impressed, Cook. Your vocabulary's growing. And, yes, I went to Price's party. Why? You upset you didn't get an invite?"

"They were afraid I'd upstage the merchandise."

Celia laughed, the sweet sound sending a frisson over Tom's spine. He scowled. Nice place for flirting, with the baby's body mere feet away. He shouldn't be surprised—he knew how cops compartmentalized their emotions.

But he'd expected different, expected more from Celia.

Distance he could understand. Insensitivity was a different matter altogether.

Insensitive? You're standing here lusting after your investigator, and she's *insensitive?*

"How long do you think it's been deceased?" Celia was once again the consummate professional.

Cook shrugged. "Rigor's beginning to set in. Haven't checked for lividity yet. A couple hours, maybe?"

Celia frowned. "Wouldn't he notice that baby hadn't cried in a while? It's young. They cry a lot when they're little, don't they?"

Tom closed his eyes for a second, the sound of wails and snuffling cries not dimmed by the distance of time. The hollow feeling in his chest tightened.

"No clue." Cook pulled his notebook from his pocket. "First thing we'll do is check missing-persons reports. But seems like we'd have an Amber Alert for a missing child."

"I can help with running those reports." Her voice softened as she began dusting the back door panel. The spotlights picked out the darker tones of her hair.

"Great. Appreciate that." With swift strokes, Cook penned a rough sketch of the car's interior, scribbling in the margins.

Celia cast another glance at the Chandler County K-9 unit, her blue eyes gleaming in the reflected light. "I want to be in on the questioning."

The corner of Cook's mouth lifted and he returned the notebook to his pocket. "Kinda thought that, since you showed up with McMillian. Didn't figure you were dating him. He doesn't seem like your type."

Her shoulders stiffened. "Funny, Cook."

Tom glared at the back of Cook's head. Not her type? What

the hell did he mean by that?

"Know what kind of guy you need?"

"I'm sure you're going to tell me."

"Fun, no strings attached, shows a girl a good time. One who actually smiles."

"I see where this is going and it's not working." Celia's mouth curved. "I don't date Chandler County boys, remember?"

"Who says I wanted you to date me?"

"You know you're secretly pining for me, Cook."

"Oh, hell yeah, St. John. I doodle your initials all over my reports. Sheriff gives me hell about it all the time."

Irritation jerked under Tom's skin. He'd had enough. She could damn well conduct herself with the decorum demanded by his office. Tom took a step forward, shoulders tight, and stopped. The yellow tape snapped in the light breeze, a visible "keep out".

He was the outsider here. Hell, how many times had he been there in his marriage? On the exterior of the little world cops built around themselves. He folded his arms over his chest and stared at Celia.

She glanced around as if feeling the weight of his look. He kept his face impassive, hoping she'd pick up the nonverbal warning. She held his gaze for a moment, her own face expressionless, before she turned away, back to the little world where he wasn't allowed.

His cell phone buzzed at his waist and he jerked it free. "McMillian."

"What the hell is going on?" Rhett High's gruff voice filled his ear. Tom used a finger at the other to drown out the commotion around him and focused on his friend and chief assistant district attorney. "You missed the damn dinner meeting, Tom. I waited a fucking half hour for you."

Shit, he'd completely forgotten. "Sorry, man. I'm on a crime scene with Celia."

"Yeah?" Rhett sounded only partially mollified. "What kind?"

"Child death. An infant discovered during that roadblock exercise in Chandler County." He let his gaze linger on Celia, now hunched by the open back door, watching as a crime scene technician and the medical examiner folded the blanket away from the infant.

"A baby?" All irritation disappeared from Rhett's voice, a sharp note Tom knew only too well taking its place.

"Yes." He refused to give into the instinct to grind his teeth.

A pause hung over the line. Rhett cleared his throat. "You all right?"

"I'm fine." He narrowed his eyes, taking in the car, the infant seat, Cook leaning to peer over Celia's head, a hand on her shoulder. "Why wouldn't I be?"

℣

"He's not talking." Celia pulled the door to Chandler County's interview room closed behind her. Exhaustion tugged at her, tension pulling across her neck and shoulders, eyes gritty and dry. McMillian waited in the small hallway outside the room.

He rested a hand on the wall and eyed the John Doe suspect through the two-way glass. "He hasn't lawyered up, though."

From beneath her lashes, Celia looked sideways at him. "He'd have to open his mouth to do that."

Frustration sizzled through her. She'd been playing cool and bitchy to Cook's good ol' boy consideration for the last hour and a half, and they were exactly where they'd been when they started—nowhere. The guy had fear flickering in his eyes constantly, but it wasn't fear of her or Cook, of what the legal system held for him. No, this suspect was terrified of something else completely.

McMillian frowned, staring through the glass. "Keep working him."

The door opened and Cook stepped into the hall. He blew out a long breath and passed a hand over his jaw, a shadow of stubble beginning to appear there. "Oh, yeah, he's a virgin without a ring. Clammed up *real* tight."

She suppressed a smile.

McMillian shot them both a glare. "Keep working him."

Cook shook his head. "Hate to tell you this, Counselor, but the foreplay ain't getting it with this guy."

Arms crossed, McMillian failed to look amused. "Then maybe it's your technique, Investigator."

One of Cook's eyebrows angled skyward. "Never had any complaints before."

McMillian's expression bordered on thunderous, a deep vee appearing on his forehead. Cook grinned and waved a hand at the interview room. "Why don't you give it a shot?"

Tension vibrated through McMillian's body. Celia tried to tone Cook down with a quelling look. "McMillian?"

He turned those electric blue eyes on her. "What?"

She tilted her head toward the suspect. "He's not going to talk tonight. We can hold him, put his ass in a cell, and once we have the initial ME's report, we can question him again tomorrow. If we're lucky, we'll have a match on his prints. Or something we can use to get him talking."

Brows lowered, he studied the nameless man once more. "You think that's the best route?"

"I do."

"All right." He cracked his knuckles. "Remember we only have forty-eight hours before he has to be arraigned."

Cook crossed his arms. "We can always charge him with an insurance violation. That's a jailable offense."

"Do that, then. Investigator." McMillian nodded at Cook. He pulled his keys from his pocket and slanted a look at Celia. "Ready to go?"

She shifted under a strange pull of conflicting loyalties. The first forty-eight hours following the discovery of a body were crucial to a homicide investigation. If she knew Cook, he wouldn't be going home, although his shift had ended almost an hour ago, at eleven.

"Go on without me. I want to review the particulars with Cook one more time, see if we can turn up any leads."

McMillian nodded, his mouth a thin line. "You don't have your car."

Cook hooked his thumbs in pockets. "I'll give her a ride when she's ready."

If anything, McMillian's mouth tightened further. He glanced at Celia. "Is that what you want?"

She shrugged. "It's fine."

"Okay then." He stared at her a moment. "I've got to be in court at nine. I'd like you in my office for debriefing at eight."

Without waiting for an answer, he turned and walked down the hall. Cook's gaze followed him, a wicked grin playing around his mouth. "He doesn't like the idea of me taking you home."

Celia rolled her eyes. "He could care less."

"Sure he could."

"Cook, shut up and get this guy to lockup. We have things to do."

"Whatever you say, St. John." He pushed the door open. The suspect looked up, a muscle flickering in his jaw. "We're charging you tonight with failure to provide proof of insurance. You've already had your rights explained and you still have the right to exercise them at this time. Any questions?"

The man shook his head, Adam's apple bobbing in his thin throat.

Cook nodded. "All right, we'll take you to lockup for the night."

The jail was relatively quiet, the televisions and lights off, only the occasional murmur of a quiet voice rising to cut through the silence. With Chandler County's new digital fingerprinting machine, taking the suspect's prints took a fraction of the time and involved less mess. Cook placed the guy in a cell alone and slid the door closed, the lock clanging.

He held the paperwork aloft. "Won't take me long to process this."

Celia followed him upstairs to the squad room and dropped into the chair next to his neat desk. He squinted at the computer screen, angling it in her direction. "Looks like the motor-vehicle database is back up. Where's the VIN from the car?"

She picked up his notebook and flipped through it until she found his notes. As she recited the numbers and letters, he keyed them in. The screen flashed a request to wait before flipping to a display of driver information.

"There it is." Cook reached for his notebook and pen. Celia leaned forward to read over his arm. Her hair fell forward and she tucked it behind her ear. Damn, this was why she never wore it down for work.

Tillie Tyrone. 183 Miller Street, Jacksonville, Florida.

No driver history found. Vehicle not insured.

Celia clucked her tongue against the roof of her mouth. "He doesn't look like a Tillie to me."

Cook leaned back in his chair, its springs squeaking. "No report of it being stolen."

She reached for his desk phone, dialed information. Within a minute, she replaced the receiver with a sigh. "No Tillie Tyrone listed anywhere in the Jacksonville area."

Leaning over, he picked up his laptop then passed it to her. "Google her while I fill out this report."

While the laptop booted up and connected to the wireless server, she studied him with sideways peeks beneath her lashes. A sardonic laugh bubbled in her throat. He actually thought McMillian minded his taking her home. What a joke. Cook could do a lot more and McMillian wouldn't give a damn.

"Hey, St. John, you gonna do that search or just stare at the screen all night?"

She blinked. A smirk curled his mouth and he shook his head before turning back to the desktop computer. "You're not with it tonight. What's going on with you?"

God, now she was letting the crap with McMillian affect her job. That was it. The whole constantly-thinking-about-him thing? Stopped right now. And oh damn it, she was doing it again already.

She tunneled her hands through her hair and blew out a long breath. "I'm just tired."

He harrumphed, clicking the mouse to page down. "I've seen you falling-out exhausted and you weren't this distracted."

"It's your investigative prowess, Cook. I'm shocked and

27

awed."

His rich chuckle rumbled from his broad chest. "Whatever, St. John."

She returned her attention to the laptop. "Nearest Tillie Tyrone lives in Virginia. She's an aspiring romance novelist with a blog."

"Probably a fake name and address on the registration. Search the address, see what comes up." He heaved a sigh. "No Amber Alerts on a missing infant. No records at all in the database on an infant that young, custody disputes or anything. Closest thing is a parent abduction of a six-month-old from Savannah from March."

"That baby had to come from somewhere." She rubbed her fingers across her aching eyes. "Maybe he is the father."

"He's not the father."

She lifted an eyebrow at the certainty in his voice. "How do you know?"

"His kid's dead and he doesn't react at all? He's not the father."

"People react differently in stressful situations, Cook, you know that. He could be in shock." Although that didn't explain the fear she'd seen in the man's eyes earlier. "Besides, you don't have kids. How do you know how a father would react?"

His jaw tightened and he chewed harder on his gum. "Because I just do. He's not that baby's father."

She shrugged. "Fine. We'll see what the DNA test shows."

He snorted. "Yeah, six to nine months from now. Lab's still backed up. You know that."

"Whitlock owes me a favor. I'll call it in, see if we can get our labs moved to the top of the list."

"First thing in the morning, we're getting that baby's photo on the news." Cook leaned back, arms folded behind his head. "Anything on that address yet?"

"According to the tax registry, it's a vacant lot."

"Another dead end. This is going to be a fun case. I can tell already."

"Yeah." Resting her chin on her hand, she tapped her fingers against her cheek. "Pull up the VIN again. What's the title history on the car?"

The next couple of hours passed without the appearance of any solid leads. Celia could see her own frustration mirrored in Cook's face as the night deepened. Finally, he pushed back from the desk with a curse. "C'mon, St. John. Let's get out of here. You look like you could use a few hours' sleep. We'll hit it hard tomorrow morning, when we're fresh. Maybe our guy will be ready to talk by then."

She nodded, flipped his laptop closed and slid it across the desk to him. Irritation tugged at her—the urge to keep going warred with the sensibility of his suggestion. Rubbing at her nape, she rolled her head, trying to alleviate the tension sitting at the base of her shoulders. Cook slipped the notebook into its case and tucked it under his arm.

He jingled his keys at her. "Ready?"

When they stepped outside, the warm moist air of early morning wrapped around them. Frogs croaked somewhere in the distance. Celia dragged in deep breaths of the fresh air, the sleepy fuzz clearing somewhat.

Where the hell did that baby come from? Why wasn't someone looking for her?

Cook unlocked the driver's side of his ancient Blazer. "Want me to go into McMillian's office with you?"

She stretched, spine popping. "That would be great."

Her purse slid to the ground. Cook leaned down, picked it up and held it out. "You're not with it, St. John."

"Thanks." She took the clutch, and her brow furrowed. "Did you see a purple gift..."

The words died in her throat. Oh, hell.

She'd left the damn sex toys in McMillian's car.

Chapter Two

Jessica paced the length of her bedroom, cell phone pressed to her ear. "I told you not to worry. Danny won't talk."

She closed her eyes as his angry voice pounded through the line, a hammering rain of harsh, clipped words. She blew out a long breath, trying to still the irritation jumping under her skin. "Because he knows better. He knows we'll take care of him."

In her belly, the baby jabbed at her ribs and she winced, rubbing the spot with her palm. Damn brat. She turned sideways, eyeing her reflection, the grotesque bulge under the satin robe. She didn't understand why some women were so eager to do this to their bodies, why they were so crushed when they couldn't.

If not for the delicious amount of money this kid was bringing, she'd never have considered it, never considered putting her body through this torture again.

With an effort, she dragged her attention back to the man snarling at her over the phone. Best to placate him. Like it or not, she needed him, at least for a while longer. Once this baby was out of her, she was set for life. No more couples bickering over divorce and custody issues. No more court advocacy for snot-nosed minors. She'd be free, to go anywhere, do anything.

Cozumel sounded nice.

"Jessie, you damn well better make sure of him."

The first finger of fear trailed over her spine. She swallowed, shored her courage, sugared her voice. "Everything will be fine. I promise."

He tossed an expletive at her and hung up.

She tossed the phone on the bed, glanced in the mirror again and tried to suck her stomach in. Oh hell, she could have liposuction after the kid was born. She hefted her breasts. A lift too. A new face if she wanted.

She'd heard plastic surgery came cheap south of the border.

The fear tried to raise its head again and she squashed it. She didn't have to worry about him. He stood to gain as much from this deal as she did and he wouldn't risk his precious political career. As long as she carried this baby, as long as he wanted bigger and better things, she was safe.

As soon as this brat was delivered, in more ways than one, she was gone.

One could never be too careful, though. She walked down the hall to her office, flipped through the Rolodex and extracted a card. She traced her thumb over the raised black print. If he got too horsy, she'd merely give Tom McMillian a call. Tom always had had a soft spot for her, even if he'd left her bed months ago. If she gave him an inkling he might have fathered the baby growing within her...

He'd do everything in his power to protect it.

And her.

She had nothing to worry about.

ଚ୍ଚ

"Investigators declined to make a statement at this time, but if you have any information on the identity of this man or infant, you are asked to call the Chandler County Sheriff's Department..."

Tom stopped with his coffee mug halfway to his lips. On the television screen, the suspect's sullen booking photo was juxtaposed with a shot of the baby's face, still nestled in its blanket. His stomach took a slow flip and he drew a deep breath. It'd been sixteen years. It shouldn't still get to him like this. He should be ready to move on.

Kathleen had.

He shook off the bitterness. A day in court lay ahead of him and before that he had a meeting with Celia. He didn't have time for musings about the past.

The blonde anchor segued into the next story then introduced the weather. Tom half-listened while knotting his tie. His gaze fell on the lilac bag Celia had left in his floorboard the night before. He'd brought it in last night and, distracted by haunting images of the deceased child and the memories that aroused, promptly forgotten it. He frowned. She'd never said what was in it, but she'd mentioned gourmet food. Damn, he hoped they hadn't let something expensive spoil.

Buttoning his collar tips with one hand, he grabbed his briefcase with the other. The corner knocked the lilac bag sideways, its contents scattering across the granite countertop.

What the hell?

He stared at the long, thin box bearing the photo of an incredibly lifelike penis. Bubbles swirled lazily in the bottle of body oil lying next to it.

That did not look like any gourmet food he'd ever purchased.

He set his briefcase down with a thud. A bright pink

business card attached with a lilac ribbon to a spray of colorful condom wrappers peeked out of the bag. He picked it up. *"Especially for You" Personal Parties—Laci Burton.* Below the slogan, someone had scrawled in bubbly cursive—*Thanks for the purchase! Enjoy!*

A sex-toy party?

He shrugged off seeing Kathleen's Jeep in Price's drive. He wasn't going to think about what she'd purchased, how she might use those items with Harding. *Celia* at a sex-toy party? He lifted the bottle of oil. Vanilla-almond, self-warming personal lubricant. His gaze fell on the boxed dildo, images popping off in his head.

Celia, naked and spread-eagled on gold sheets, her silvery blonde hair spilling over pillows edged with heavy cord. Her lips open on a moan, skin glistening with oil, the scents of vanilla and almond heavy in the air.

Pure arousal pooled in his belly, shooting a heavy tingling to his groin. Ah, damn it, he was imagining her naked in *his* bed. His hands rubbing that oil over her skin, but her hands easing the vinyl dildo inside her while he watched...

Hell.

Sweat beaded his upper lip and he brushed it away. He was losing it. Fantasizing about the best damn investigator he'd ever hired. He wasn't going to let his attraction to her spoil that. Celia was an adult and what she did in her private life was just that—private. Her business. As long as she kept it separate from his office.

He frowned, eyeing the adult toy while her flirtation with Cook played through his head again. Maybe it was more than a flirtation. Maybe she'd bought the items to use with the sheriff's investigator. Hell, it wasn't like Tom was privy to the details of her private life.

For all he knew, she'd done more than review case details with Cook after he'd left.

More images flickered in his head...Cook's sturdy frame supporting Celia's slim body, his hands sliding over her skin, gleaming with scented oil, while she pleasured herself with that damn rubber dick and moaned the other man's name.

Tom's stomach pitched and a weird burning traveled under his skin. Primal anger fired in him, clenching his lungs, making it hard to get oxygen to his brain. What the fuck was wrong with him?

Celia could see any-damn-body she wanted. He had no control over that. Getting pissed off because she was interested in Cook was counterproductive, a complete waste of time.

But he still didn't like it. Cook was a player, known in the tricounty area for his string of one-nighters. Celia deserved better.

Maybe she didn't want more. What did he know?

He grabbed the items from the counter and slammed them into the bag. With it shoved under his arm, he snatched up his briefcase and stormed from the house. During the fifteen-minute drive to his offices, he fumed and pushed the Mercedes through its paces.

Damn it all. He didn't need this right now.

Who was he kidding? He didn't need this ever. He liked his relationships with women kept on an entirely level basis. Women who tied him in knots were not his thing. Since he'd hired her, Celia had jerked more knots in him than a Boy Scout going for a badge, so she was definitely out-of-bounds.

If she wanted Mark Cook, fine.

When he turned into the parking lot behind the office building, Celia's sporty SUV was already in her customary spot.

An unmarked Chandler County unit sat in a visitor's space.

Tom shot the vehicle a glare as he climbed from the driver's seat and locked his car. He jogged up the stairs to the back entrance and let himself in. At only a few minutes past seven, the nearly deserted offices were quiet. He bypassed his office and headed for Celia's.

Beyond her closed office door, he could hear the murmur of voices, Celia's light voice blending with Cook's deeper tones. Cook's dark chortle set Tom's teeth on edge. Without knocking, he pushed the door open.

The aroma of strong coffee hung in the air. Cook, stretched out on the sofa taking up one wall, had a file open before him. Celia sat at her desk, folders lined up in a neat row. Both heads turned in his direction.

For some reason, seeing them working didn't improve his mood. He didn't acknowledge Cook, but fixed a look on Celia. She returned his gaze, her face impassive.

"Ms. St. John, could I see you a moment please?" He turned and strode to his office. Inside, he set his briefcase on the credenza and flipped the computer on with terse movements.

Celia appeared in his doorway, eyes narrowed. "Is there a problem?"

Her hair was up in a chic knot, leaving the elegant line of her neck bare. The picture of her with Cook flashed in his mind again, the other man sliding his mouth along her throat. The irritation flared into something hotter, a primitive possessiveness. Damn, he really didn't need this. He set the wrinkled lilac bag on the edge of his desk. "You left that in my car."

She crossed the room to pick up the package. "This is why you wanted to see me?"

Settling into his chair, he flipped open the file he'd need for court that morning. The words wavered in front of his eyes, anger still jerking along his nerves. "I told you I wanted an update."

"I don't have anything for you yet," she said, voice cool, removed. "We're waiting on fingerprints and blood tests before we question him again. We need a court order for a blood sample and the judge won't be in his office until nine."

He glanced up. Her slender fingers played with the thin silver chain that disappeared into her blue blouse. Beneath her pinstriped jacket, silk clung to firm breasts. Great. Now he was able to envision the edge of her cleavage, as he'd seen it above her camisole the night before. "What is he doing here?"

She lifted an eyebrow. "We're going through cell-phone records. Doe had one of those throwaway cell phones. But we're not finding anything yet, just calls to pay phones or other throwaway cells. I put out a press release and Cook issued an Amber Alert."

He nodded. "I saw the photos on the news this morning. Good idea, there. Be ready if they want an interview later."

"I will."

"In the future, I'd appreciate more professional behavior from you on scene."

Her face froze, fingers tightening on the chain. "Excuse me?"

He clenched his jaw. "When you're working, whatever is going on between you and Investigator Cook does not need to be bandied about the way it was last night."

"Whatever is..." She stared at him, her nostrils flaring slightly with a deep breath. Her face reddened and she crossed her arms, the lilac bag hanging from her fingers. "Just what do you think is going on?"

37

"I don't know and it's none of my business, unless it affects your performance as my investigator. I merely don't approve of your flirting with Cook at a crime scene."

Bad temper crackled in her eyes. She leaned forward, resting her hands on the desk. Her blouse gaped slightly, her silver chain brushing against a hint of satin. "Is this a reprimand?"

"No." He held her gaze, his own temper rising to meet hers, his pulse thudding in his ears. "A reminder."

She leaned closer. "Just for the record," she said, her voice lowering, taking on a hint of steel, "I am not involved with Mark Cook. If I were, it would have no effect on my job performance and I resent the hell out of your implication."

"Good." He drummed the file in front of him, irritated with the relief her denial sent coursing through him. "Then we understand each other."

Her mouth thinned. "Oh, I understand you perfectly, McMillian." She straightened. "Are we finished?"

He nodded. "I'll be back in at the end of the day. I want another report then."

She smiled, the expression cold, a little feral. "Of course."

Turning, she strode from the room, the bag tapping against her hip. Tom rubbed a hand over his eyes. He'd handled that well.

Just like a jealous ass would.

The audacity of the man. The absolute gall.

Celia shoved her office door open. "Are you ready to go?"

Cook glanced up from his file. "Uh, yeah. But it's not even eight. The judge won't be in his office until at least a quarter to nine."

"By the time we drive to Moultrie, the lab will be open." She tossed the bag on her desk. What was McMillian's problem? He didn't want her, she was an adult, so what the hell did it matter who she slept with?

Not that she'd ever sleep with Mark Cook. Humorless laughter bubbled in her throat. McMillian had lost his mind.

Cook straightened to a sitting position. "Then we'll have to make a second trip over there with the blood sample."

She blew out a long breath, trying to still the fury sizzling throughout her body, shortcutting her brain. Cook was right. She wasn't approaching things rationally. And she was proving McMillian right too. Letting her emotions affect her job.

She tapped a finger against her forehead. "Had breakfast yet?"

"Does an overdose of squad-room coffee count?"

Her skin itched, feeling too tight. "Let's go get something before we meet Judge Baker."

"Sure thing." He gathered his notes and crammed them in the file folder. She ushered him out the door and toward the back exit. McMillian stepped into the hall as they passed, briefcase under his arm, keys in hand. Their eyes met and she lifted her chin, determined not to back down.

His gaze slid to Cook at her side, but he didn't acknowledge him. "I'll see you this afternoon, Celia."

Her anger pulsed, but she merely smiled. "Of course."

She continued walking, refusing to look back to see if he followed them. Cook's footsteps thudded on the metal stairs behind her and he fell into step beside her once they reached the parking lot.

He glanced over his shoulder and whistled low. "He looks pissed. What was that all about?"

"What do you mean?" She stopped at his patrol car and waited. Behind her, McMillian's Mercedes purred to life. A knot gathered at the base of her neck. Lack of food and sleep, obviously. She'd been unable to rest at all, questions about the baby bouncing around in her head. The stress making her temples ache had nothing to do with McMillian and his accusations.

Her feelings weren't bruised, either.

"All that tension and ice. What the hell did he say to you earlier?" He unlocked the car and Celia slid into the passenger seat. The strong scent of wintergreen gum blended with the disinfectant used to clean the stainless steel rear seat.

She blew out a breath and rolled her eyes while fastening her seatbelt. A harsh laugh worked its way free from her throat. "He wasn't happy about our interaction last night. He thinks we're sleeping together."

"You wanna?" Grinning, Cook fired the engine to life.

"No."

"Damn."

Her laugh this time was less abrasive. She glanced out the window as he backed out and eased into the alleyway alongside the office building. The anger gripping her chest lessened somewhat, giving way to a vague sense of hurt disappointment.

She was crazy with wanting McMillian and he thought she was involved with someone else. Damn his blind hide. Damn her, too, for wanting the ass in the first place.

Slowing for a traffic light, Cook slanted a glance at her. "Listen, St. John, I'm sorry if I caused trouble for you."

"No." She waved his apology away. "It's just McMillian being his normal self."

Wicked glee glinted in his gray eyes. "You mean an arrogant

dickhead?"

A puff of laughter escaped her. "That he is."

The light turned green and he looked at her before accelerating. "My God, you're hot for him."

She opened her mouth, closed it, shook her head. "I am not."

"You are." He laughed. "Admit it, St. John. You've got a thing for the asshole DA."

"Right." She pinned him with a cool look. "You've figured me out, Cook. He's my true heart's desire. I lie awake at night fantasizing about him. I doodle *his* initials on *my* reports."

He snickered, but thankfully dropped the subject. They killed an hour at the local diner, tossing around case theories and bemoaning the time it would take to get their lab work. Celia nibbled at a piece of toast and pushed scrambled eggs around her plate while Cook wolfed down a hearty breakfast platter. Afterwards, they walked the two blocks to the law offices that lined the courthouse square. Construction continued on the new courthouse structure, the din of hammers, saws and jackhammers filling the air.

The narrow stairway forced them to climb single file. Celia stopped on the landing and knocked at the frosted glass-paned door belonging to Judge Alton Baker.

"It's open." The judge's gruff voice wafted into the hallway.

Celia turned the ancient metal knob, the door shuddering as she pulled it open. Judge Baker sat at his desk, packing boxes scattered around the room, half a ham biscuit resting on a greasy wrapper atop a stack of files. The room reeked of old law books.

She stopped just inside the door. "Good morning, Your Honor."

He looked at them over his half-lenses, a shaft of sunlight picking out gray strands in his head of thick brown hair. "St. John and Cook. To what do I owe the pleasure?"

Smiling, she extended her warrant request. "We need a blood sample from a suspect."

Accepting the paper, he glanced at it and eyed her, his piercing gaze assessing. "This have anything to do with that dead baby?"

"Yes, sir." Cook leaned against the doorjamb. "We need to check the suspect's DNA against the baby's to prove or disprove paternity."

With a harrumphing sigh, Baker reached for a pen and scrawled his signature at the bottom of the page. "There you go. Make sure you nail the son of a bitch to the wall."

"Yes, sir." Celia took the paper back from him. "Thank you."

In the hallway, with the door closed, Cook let out a slow, audible breath and grinned. "Son of a bitch actually makes me nervous."

Celia laughed and waved the warrant at him. "Come on. Let's go make Mr. Doe's day."

They crossed the street to the sheriff's department, located behind the courthouse construction. At shortly after nine, the jail was coming to life. Celia followed Cook down the stairs to the holding area. In the hallway beyond, prisoners called to each other, and a jailer admonished them to keep it down. A lone voice groused about greasy, undercooked bacon.

On the way down the stairs, Cook flipped through the keys at his belt. "Rise and shine, Doe. We need to see you a sec."

Celia stopped dead as they entered the holding area. Doe lay sprawled, legs at an unnatural angle, his arms twisted beneath him. Blood pooled under his head. Adrenaline pumped through her, her heart rate kicking upwards. "Cook, get that door open."

"Shit." Stress vibrated in his voice. He fumbled the key into the lock and slammed the door to the side. "Son of a bitch, St. John. He did a header off the top bunk."

Memories of the fear in Doe's eyes beat in her head. They'd screwed up. She should have played on that fear last night, gotten him talking. Now it was too late. "Oh, hell."

Cook pressed a finger to the carotid pulse point. "He's dead. Damn, I gotta call the GBI. And the sheriff. Man, he's gonna have a hissy fit."

She eyed the blood, mixed with brain fluid, her stomach dropping. "Guess we didn't need that warrant after all."

Tom dropped his files and legal pad in his briefcase. Forty-minute drive to the Darren County courthouse, only to have his case placed on continuance. The aggravation didn't improve his mood.

Hefting the leather case, he turned toward the door. His gut clenched, an oddly familiar lift and fall. Just inside the entrance, Kathleen stood talking with her partner at the GBI. Agent Altee Price had been slated to testify for his prosecution. Kathleen hadn't seen him yet and he watched her. The navy polo of her GBI uniform highlighted the coppery hair framing her pale face and its fine features. She waved a hand as she talked, her thin gold wedding band glinting.

Damn, he hated the way seeing her still kicked him in the balls.

He frowned. It had been years. The marriage had died long before they'd signed the divorce papers. Those last years, he'd been the only one trying. Why did her remarriage, the news she was pregnant, bother him so badly? It was over and he needed to just let go.

Celia could help him do that.

He shook off the thought and headed for the door. All Celia was going to do was help wrap up this baby case. With his court appearance rescheduled, he could catch up with her, see how that investigation was progressing. Find out if she was still as infuriated with him as she'd been when she'd walked away with Cook that morning without a backward glance.

He strode up the aisle. Kathleen and Altee had disappeared and he pushed open the door. Small groups of people stood in the rotunda area and Kathleen caught his gaze as he exited the courtroom. A polite smile curved her mouth.

Nodding, he forced a smile in return. "Kathleen. Agent Price."

Kathleen tilted her chin. "Tom."

A small chime rang out and Altee tugged her cell phone from her waistband. "It's Botine. I need to take this. Excuse me a minute."

She walked outside, leaving him in a bubble of isolation with his ex-wife. Nerves jangled in him and Tom cleared his throat. "I hear congratulations are in order."

Her smile faltered slightly. "Yes."

"I'm glad for you."

Surprise bloomed in her dark eyes. "Thank you, Tom."

"Give Harding my congratulations." She nodded and he jerked his head toward the door. "I've got to go."

At least she couldn't tell the words stuck in his throat. Glad she was pregnant again? With another guy's baby? Yeah. More proof she'd forgotten their son. His throat tightened. After Everett's death, he'd ached to talk, to share his memories of that precious boy with her. She'd not allowed him to speak the baby's name in her presence. He'd never been able to forgive her for that.

"Tom?"

Her pretty voice stopped him. He'd always liked the way her smooth cultured tone seemed to caress his name. Wonder what his given name would sound like coming from Celia's lips?

He turned. She glanced away, then swung her rich brown gaze back to his. "I heard about the donation you made to the women's center, in Everett's name. I think...I think that was a wonderful way to honor his birthday."

At her mention of their child, his heart folded in on itself. Damn, that pain never lessened. "I think so too. Goodbye, Kathleen."

When he reached for the door handle, it pushed inward. Altee stuck her head around the door. "Kath, we need to head out. Cook called in that Chandler County has a dead prisoner."

Kathleen's lips parted. "You're kidding."

Altee shook her head. "Apparent suicide."

"Tom, it was good to see you." Kathleen moved toward the door. "And thank you."

"Sure." He frowned. "Price, you said Cook called in?"

With a wary expression, she nodded. "Yeah. Why?"

Tom shook his head. "He's working a case with St. John. Wondered if maybe it was connected."

Kathleen shrugged. "If you don't have somewhere else to be, follow us back and check on the way to your office."

He gave a curt nod. "I will, thanks."

Holding the door for her, he waited for her to precede him. He hurried across the street to the parking lot, images of blood and incredible pain flickering in his head, fading into blackness.

He had a really bad feeling about this.

Celia blew out a long breath and stared at the ceiling in the tiny office she'd been ushered into to await the arrival of the GBI. Just her luck she'd get Calvert's space, the closet with the dead fish on the walls. Cook was probably kicked back in the sheriff's leather chair. She was afraid if she kicked back, the ancient desk chair would disintegrate.

A sharp rap at the door preceded McMillian's entrance. She lifted her eyebrows, concealing her surprise at his presence. What was he doing here? Probably checking to ensure she wasn't making out with Cook while waiting to be questioned.

"I thought you were in court. Do they think I need a lawyer now?"

"Continuance." He stuck his hands in his pockets and rocked back on his heels. "Looks like your suspect found a permanent way to avoid talking."

She thought about falling six feet headfirst into a concrete floor and shuddered. There had to be easier ways to die. "He was terrified last night. I kept seeing it in his eyes, but I didn't push because I wanted the leverage of prints or blood tests or something. Maybe I should have."

"You couldn't have known he was going to take a dive like this."

Restlessness throbbed in her and she rose to look out the tiny window. "Without him, we don't have anything."

"You'll find it. I have faith in you."

She cast him a pithy glance over her shoulder. "Sure you do. You're the same man who accused me of throwing myself at Cook at a crime scene."

His mouth tightened. "I admit I didn't handle that the best

way. These cases get to me and I took that out on you. I'm sorry."

Eyebrows raised, she turned away again.

"Celia."

"What?"

"Did you hear me?"

"I did." But his sorry sounded suspiciously insincere. How many times had her mother's men said they were sorry for one slight or another? How many times had she heard it from Brian Turello? The words "I'm sorry" came awfully easy to some men. And this man was really good at bluffing in difficult situations.

Pretty damn good at manipulating people too. Turello had been a master at that as well.

"Ms. St. John?" Kathleen Harding asked and Celia spun. Her gaze jerked to McMillian's face. With Kathleen's entrance, some emotion flickered deep in his sharp blue eyes, gone before Celia could identify it.

Celia fiddled with her necklace. "Yes?"

"I need your version of events, please." Kathleen held up her notebook. She glanced sideways at McMillian. "Tom? Are you staying?"

His gaze intent on Kathleen's face, he nodded. "If you don't mind."

"No problem." Kathleen tugged a silver pen from her pocket. "Whenever you're ready."

Celia launched into the retelling, grasping the window ledge behind her. While she talked, she watched McMillian watch his ex-wife. His face remained unreadable, but that same flicker of feeling moved through his eyes occasionally. Again, the sense of irrational hurt and disappointment filtered through her. She'd known he was still hung up on the other woman. So why let it get to her?

Maybe because she'd never had to stand around and watch him moon before. Gossip was one thing. Telling herself he wasn't over the woman was too. Seeing his reaction to Kathleen was another. She released the ledge and flexed aching fingers.

What had she thought? That at some point, he'd see her as more than a cop? More than a colleague? That he'd turn to her? Talk about a hopeless pipedream. Damn, she had more of her mother in her than she thought.

"Okay." Kathleen snapped her notebook closed. "I think we're done here."

"As in, I'm free to go?"

Kathleen nodded. "Your story matches Cook's, we've already verified the time you were in Judge Baker's office and there's no evidence at this point that the John Doe's death was anything but self-inflicted. If we need anything further, I'll call. I'm sure you have plenty of work to do."

"Thanks." Celia pushed away from the window. McMillian rose from his perch on the edge of the desk and wrapped a hand around the door's edge, holding it open as Kathleen exited.

Once she was gone, he pushed it closed. Celia glanced up at him in inquiry. He folded his arms across his chest, the fine cotton of his gray dress shirt stretching over his biceps, the dove color making his eyes bluer. "So what's next on your agenda?"

She shrugged, trying to still the way her belly fluttered at his nearness. God, she was pathetic and this office was entirely too small. "A trip to Moultrie. I want to check on our fingerprints, see if the preliminary autopsy is in on the baby."

"Want some company? My calendar was already cleared for court."

"Are you sure? You want to see this baby like that?" She wished the words unsaid as soon as they left her lips. He was a criminal lawyer, for God's sake. He'd seen plenty of dead children over the past few years. She was acting like some goofy, besotted rookie, filled with concern because she couldn't imagine the horror he'd experienced personally.

"I think I can handle it," he snapped. She sighed inwardly. Yes, she'd stepped on his toes with her concern. He jerked the door open. "I guess we need to take Cook with us?"

She passed by him, the light spice of his cologne filling her senses. She glanced back at him. "He is the investigator on point."

McMillian's jaw tightened visibly as he pulled the office door closed behind them. "Fine. Go get him. Tell him we're ready to get out of here."

When she entered the squad room, Cook was seated at his own desk, phone at his ear. She rested a hand on the chair next to it and waited for him to replace the receiver. "McMillian wants to tag along to Moultrie."

Cook glanced up with a harried expression. "Can you handle that? I've got a sexual-assault call at the hospital and Calvert is God knows where. I have to take this one."

"Sure thing. Call me when you get done and I'll fill you in."

"Great." Cook pushed up from the desk. "God, I hate these calls."

She walked with him into the hallway. He waved and jogged to the side entry. With a deep breath, she turned to face McMillian, waiting by the front desk.

A session in an autopsy lab with McMillian and a deceased child.

Oh, she couldn't wait.

Chapter Three

"I haven't even done the preliminary yet." Sara Ford, the GBI lab's newest medical examiner, moved the overhead camera into position over the stainless-steel table. "We're incredibly backed up."

"You're always backed up." Celia glanced at the baby's unclothed body as Ford snapped a photo. She was so *tiny* and looked absolutely perfect. Where was her mother? Her father? An ache curled around Celia's heart. What was McMillian thinking, standing so still and silent behind her? Was he thinking of his baby, the one he'd lost so long ago? Stupid question. He had to be.

"You have no idea." Sara shook her head, her wide hazel eyes the only part of her face visible between her face mask and surgical cap. "We still have body parts from the courthouse explosion in frozen storage waiting for DNA testing."

Celia's gaze drifted back to the round little face. Dark lashes fanned over flawless cheeks. Minuscule fingers curled into small fists. Surely someone had counted those fingers and toes. "So what can you tell me?"

Sara shrugged and snapped another photo. "Female, Caucasian, approximately six pounds, probably a few hours old."

"Nothing on the cause of death?"

"No contusions, no other signs of abuse. No reticular hemorrhages in the eyeballs, so it wasn't asphyxiation or shaken baby syndrome. Other than that? Can't tell you until I open her up."

Celia suppressed a shudder. "Thanks. I need to know as soon as you have results."

Sara nodded. "I'll call you. But it may be awhile. All I'm doing is the photos and finishing the intake paperwork now. You have the murder-suicide from Montley and the suspicious death from Pavo ahead of you."

"I'd appreciate it. We'll get out of your way." Turning, she met McMillian's stony gaze and tilted her head toward the door. He strode ahead of her to the lobby and shoved the front door open, gesturing for her to precede him.

"Well, that was extremely helpful." His voice emerged as a frustrated growl, but Celia refused to rise to it.

"You didn't have to come, you know. This is the way it works sometimes—excruciatingly slow and frustrating."

He glared as they approached his car. "I'm aware of that."

"I'll put it together, McMillian. I just need some time."

"Put what together?" He tugged the passenger door open for her and stalked around to the driver's side. "The car was a dead end, your suspect offed himself rather than talk, and God only knows when the GBI will get their act together long enough to process your prints or complete your autopsy. What are you going to do with all that?"

Celia relaxed into the lush leather and snapped her seatbelt. "First I'm going to keep digging. If John Doe wasn't the baby's father, she has parents somewhere. I've already called the Florida Department of Law Enforcement and the GBI and asked for their complete listing of missing children who might fit the time or age frame for this baby. Then we'll go nationwide.

51

But you have to chill out, McMillian. Cases don't get solved overnight. You, of all people, should realize that."

His hand flexed on the wheel and he glanced over his shoulder before shifting into reverse. "Just keep me informed. I want to be apprised of what's going on, every step of this case."

"I always keep you informed."

He looked at her, his expression softening somewhat. "I know. That's why I keep you around."

Her breath faltered in her throat, somewhere between an incredulous laugh and a hurt sigh. Well. It was surely nice to know where she stood with him.

McMillian kept her around because she kept him in the loop.

God, he was a blind son of a bitch.

Which made her a hopeless fool.

ॐ

"Where have you been all day?"

At Rhett's question, Tom glanced up from the legal brief. As usual, the assistant DA strolled in without knocking. Tom rubbed at the nape of his neck, a tension knot lingering there. "I went to the GBI lab in Moultrie with Celia."

"Why?" A deep frown grooving his brow, Rhett dropped into the chair before Tom's desk. "Let me guess...autopsy on that dead baby from Chandler County."

"Yeah." Tom laid the brief aside and leaned back in his own chair, arms folded behind his head. "But they haven't done it yet."

Eyes narrowed, Rhett stared him down. Tom refused to

look away. Finally, Rhett spoke.

"Why do you torture yourself, man?"

"I'm not. I'm doing my job."

"That's Celia's job. The Child Death Task Force? Laudable as hell." Rhett leaned forward, his gaze intent on Tom's. "But it won't bring Everett back and this sick-ass obsession of yours, feeling like you have to be hands-on with any case involving a kid because you lost yours...it ain't healthy, Tom."

"What the hell do you know about losing a child?" The ice in his voice was apparent even to Tom, and he wanted to call the words back as soon as he uttered them.

Shit. He shouldn't have said that, not to Rhett, not with Amarie sick, not when there wasn't a donor.

"Nothing." A muscle flicked in Rhett's jaw. "I don't know a damn thing."

Tom pinched the bridge of his nose. "Rhett—"

"It's all right, man." Rhett's heavy sigh hung between them. "I shouldn't have said anything. It just pisses me off, you know, watching you do this to yourself."

"I'm not doing anything to myself. I'm fine."

"Sure you are." Rhett lifted his chin in a silent challenge Tom ignored.

He changed the subject. "How's Amarie?"

Rhett moved his shoulders, both hands waffling in his silent I-don't-want-to-talk-about-it gesture. A bad day, then. Probably a bad week. Tom dropped his gaze for a moment. At least he'd lost Everett quickly, hadn't had to sit back and watch him fade slowly, painfully away. Amazing to think there'd been anything close to a blessing in the rapid way SIDS had stolen his son.

"So do Celia and Cook have anything on this case?"

Rhett's deep voice pulled him back to awareness. Tom exhaled hard. "Not much. The only suspect they had committed suicide while in custody this morning. Nothing on the car, nothing on where that baby came from."

Mouth tight, Rhett shook his head. "Watch it go cold."

"Yeah." Tom grimaced. He hated the idea of that baby slipping into the nothingness of a cold-case file. Fuck, Rhett was right—he let himself grow too personally involved in each and every one of these situations.

"I'll get out of here and let you get back to—"

"McMillian?" Celia spoke from the doorway, her voice cool. He tensed, every nerve ending going on alert. A matching strain tightened her posture, as it had since they'd left Moultrie. No, before that, since he'd accused her of being involved with Cook. Her blue gaze flickered between him and Rhett. "I'm sorry. The door was open and I didn't realize you were in a meeting."

"We were just shooting the bull." Rhett pushed up from his chair. "Come on in. I've got some calls to make."

Celia shifted to allow him to pass into the hallway. Tom folded his hands on his desk. "Did you need something?"

"I'm leaving for the day. I'll be over at the sheriff's department if you need me." She met his gaze head-on, a cynical smile playing about her mouth. "I don't have anything new to report."

Something about the exchange niggled at him, almost as though she was mocking him, distancing herself. Pulling back, just like Kathleen. His spine went ramrod straight. The comparison was fucking ridiculous.

There was no comparison. One woman had been his wife, cutting him out of her life. The other was his employee, maintaining a professional distance. So the visceral reaction he had to Celia's shutting down was nothing more than annoyance with her reticence.

He pulled the brief forward again and lowered his gaze. "Let me know when you do."

At his transparent dismissal, silence pulsed in the room for long seconds.

"Of course." Her words held a distinct chill. Moments later, the door closed behind her with a soft, final snick.

Early evening shadows stretched across small, perfectly coifed lawns. With the stress of the day tugging at his neck, Tom pulled to a stop at the curb and squinted at the wooden sign swinging from chains on a large front porch. *The Bell, Candle and Broomstick.* Maybe he had the wrong place. He glanced at the other homes—colorful, renovated mill houses holding antique shops, a trendy down-home restaurant, a handful of clothing stores, a casual nightclub. He knew the area, a popular neighborhood where the proprietors lived in rooms behind or above their shops.

He just hadn't realized Celia lived here.

At least he hoped he had the right address. His nerves still jangled from being in that autopsy lab, and if he was honest, from the weird tension that had drifted between him and Celia throughout the day. All he wanted was to pick up the file his administrative assistant was sure Celia had and go home. Maybe do some laps. Have a Scotch. Read the huge brief that idiot trying to defend himself had sent over.

Is that really what you want?

No. Tom closed his eyes. He wanted to see her, away from the office, to look into those crystal blue eyes and get another glimpse of the woman beneath the cool layers of her law-enforcement capability. He wanted to let the sweet lushness of her voice soothe away the unease unfolding within.

Damn, he needed a life.

He didn't need the little thrills running over him just from the idea of being in Celia's home, getting another glimpse of the person she was away from the office.

Pushing the door open, he stepped out then walked up the brick walkway. Wind chimes moved in a tinkling rhythm at the edge of the porch, and music, some kind of metallic pinging blended with a flute, flowed from an open window in a soft wave. A bubble machine puffed sparkling spheres from the same window.

He mounted the steps, painted porch boards creaking a little beneath his loafers. Beside the leaded-glass door, a discreet sign announced the shop's hours. He grasped the doorknob, a solid, bumpy weight in his palm, and turned. A warm, sweet smell washed over him as he stepped inside. A bell jingled with his entrance.

Towering bookshelves, crammed with leather-bound tomes and colorful paperbacks, covered one wall. On tables scattered throughout what must have been a formal parlor lay displays of crystals, jewelry, stoneware, more books. He eased through the room, a frown tugging at him. Somehow, he couldn't envision Celia here. He had to have the wrong address.

From one table, he lifted a vivid box, his frown deepening. Tarot cards?

"That's a beautiful deck. The artwork is amazing." The lyrical voice wafted from the doorway behind a long counter and he did a double take. For a moment, he'd thought the woman was Celia—they looked and sounded that much alike. But something about this woman's face was softer, more serene, where Celia's eyes held the edge most law-enforcement officers' did. That edge had softened somewhat in that autopsy lab this morning and he'd gotten a glimpse of the woman inside. By the time she'd left the office that edge had been solidly back in place.

He'd liked what he'd seen though, of that softer Celia. After she'd disappeared to God-knew-where to work with Cook, the insight had haunted him at the most damnable moments— arguing a motion in chambers, trying to strategize with Rhett. Hell, he'd even found himself looking for her at the end of the day, and not just for an update. He'd wanted to see *her*.

Celia St. John was driving him certifiable.

The Celia look-alike stared back at him. "Oh. It's you."

"I'm sorry, I think I have the wrong house. I'm looking for Celia."

The clear green eyes—another difference—shuttered. "She's not here yet. Would you like some tea?"

"Please." He stepped forward, indicating the shop with a nod. "Nice place."

"Thank you." She moved to the end of the counter and set two china cups on the polished wood. "I'm Cicely, by the way. Celia's sister."

"A pleasure. I'm—"

"I know who you are." She lifted her head, her sea-green gaze piercing through him. "Cee lives and breathes her job. Or maybe you hadn't noticed."

"I—" He smiled at the nickname and shook his head, taking the delicate cup she offered. He didn't know enough about Celia beyond the office to realize she might share his workaholic tendencies. "Thanks. Honestly, I hadn't."

One of her plucked eyebrows winged upward. "I bet there's a lot you don't notice."

Tom took a sip of the dark tea, the taste of cherries and cinnamon exploding on his tongue. Cicely regarded him steadily. She gestured at the box he'd dropped back on the table. "Are you interested in the Tarot? Would you like a reading?"

He stiffened. "What? Oh, no, that's fine...I don't—"

She leaned forward, a mocking glint in her eyes. "Don't what? Believe?"

Somewhere behind her, in the long dim hallway, a door opened and closed. Familiar footsteps sounded on hardwood and the tension gripping him relaxed.

"Cis?" Celia's voice wrapped around him, sending a rush of warmth through him. His hand tightened on the cup and he glanced toward the hall, anticipation settling heavy in him. This was ridiculous. He was reacting like a teenager catching a glimpse of his crush. The self-recrimination didn't lighten the tightness in his chest any.

"In the shop," Cicely called back.

Moments later, Celia appeared in the squared-off entry. She stopped, staring at him, her face unreadable. An uncontrollable smile quirked at his mouth. God, she looked so different at home. He'd gotten a glimpse of her other fashion side at the crime scene and here was another one—a white cotton camisole top, snug jeans, leather thong sandals with beads and stones. Her hair spilled over her shoulders and he wanted to wrap it around his hand, experience the softness of it, pull her in and cover her mouth with his. A surge of arousal joined the anticipation low in his abdomen.

She moved forward and he shook himself free of the sensual haze. Sadness seemed to drag at her features. Where had she gone after leaving the office, to put that expression on her face? Or was it left over from what they'd witnessed in the autopsy lab that morning? He hadn't been able to shake the images of the baby's body all day.

He set the cup aside. "Hello."

"Hey." She brushed her hair back, tucking it behind her ears, and joined her sister on the other side of the counter. "Why are you here?"

"I..." The thin silver chain she always wore dipped between her breasts, whatever lay on the chain nestled between them. He tugged his gaze upwards, to the smooth curve of her shoulder then to her eyes, as shuttered as her sister's. "I needed the file on the Finney case. Raquel thought you might have it, but you'd already left the sheriff's office and weren't answering your cell." My God, he was rambling. *Get to the point, man.* "I thought I'd run by and pick it up on the way home."

She nodded. "I didn't have my cell with me. I've got the file next door. I brought it home to review for my testimony."

A smile slid over Cicely's face. "We were just having some tea and a chat while he waited."

A look passed between the sisters and Celia lifted her eyebrows. "Bet that was interesting."

"Definitely." Tom tucked his hands in his pockets. He felt like he was outside some inner secret here, almost as if the sisters had some kind of in-joke at his expense. "The file?"

Celia tilted her head toward the hall. "Come on back."

He followed, eyeing the sway of her hips encased in dark denim. God, she had beautiful curves, from graceful shoulders to her firm breasts, to gently rounded hips and the sweetest ass he'd ever seen. He was bordering on obsession here and she was oblivious. In the dim light, silver winked at him above the low waist of her jeans. Body jewelry. Did she wear that under her pinstripes and silk at the office? A buzz of arousal rippled through his groin. He swallowed hard. She was his employee and he was ogling her behind her back, conjuring up salacious fantasies.

"So you live with your sister?"

"It's a duplex." Halfway down the hall, she swung a door inward and stepped through. "We converted it a couple years ago when she opened the shop. She got the big room up front and the right side, I got the left and the attic loft."

He entered the room after her and immediate peace settled on him, releasing the sensory overload he'd experienced in the shop. "Why the Bell, Candle and Broomstick? Is that symbolic or something?"

"Cis's tongue-in-cheek sense of humor." She crossed the room and pulled open a pine armoire, revealing a television and several baskets. She rummaged through one. "I think she actually has an antique brush broom over there somewhere."

He glanced around. Plush couch, comfy chair, an ottoman—all in rich, touchable fabrics and earthy colors. A collection of photos shared space on a table beneath the window with a large clear globe. He wandered over, eyeing the pictures. Celia and her sister together at various ages, sometimes with a woman who had to be their mother. The glass ball sat on an ornate stand, and he rubbed a hand across the top, his fingers tickling with the contact. "Why a broomstick?"

"She's a psychic who gives readings and runs a new-age shop. Around here, that translates to 'witch'. Please don't touch that."

He jerked his hand back and whirled, a flush heating his face. "Sorry. I shouldn't—"

"No, I didn't mean to snap. It's been a long couple of days and I shouldn't take that out on you." She hugged the folder to her chest, an array of expressions chasing over her features. For a slow moment, he sensed she struggled with a silent decision then she relaxed. "It was my mother's. I'm a little protective of it."

He glanced back at the globe, remembering the Tarot deck, then looked at her once more. "Do you...ah...I mean, are you..."

"Able to see into the future? Discern what the stars might hold?" A wicked smile lit her face and she laughed, the genuine sound relaxing him all over again. She had a beautiful laugh, one he didn't hear around the office all that often. "No. Why? Did Cis make you nervous?"

A puff of laughter escaped him. "A little."

"She has that effect on people sometimes. I think it's the eyes. She has this way of—"

"Looking inside you." He'd seen Celia do the same thing with suspects, though, reading them, reading the situation.

"Exactly." She shook her head, her grin turning conspiratorial. "And by the way, she's not a witch. So no worries that she cursed you with her tea or anything."

He edged a finger along the wrought-iron table. He should take the file and go, not continue standing here, looking at her, feeling relieved that the tension between them had diminished, wanting this conversation to go on and on. Not delve into her mysteries the way he craved. What he should do was keep everything on a professional footing before he got himself into major trouble.

His impulses refused to listen to his rational brain. "You're very close, aren't you?"

She caressed the edge of the folder, a winsome expression on her face. "We are. Can't imagine my life without her."

He nodded. "It's good that you have someone like that."

Her hand drifted up to fiddle with the chain about her neck. He followed the movement with his eyes, wondering again what hid between her breasts at the end of the delicate links. She tilted her head to the side, hair shifting over her bare shoulder. "What about you? Any siblings?"

"No, I'm an only child." This was getting too personal, too much like first-date-getting-to-know-you talk. Time to make an exit. He moved forward and extended his hand. "I should be going. I've taken enough of your evening."

"Of course." Her expression closed, her eyes going cool again. She held out the folder. "This is what you came for."

"Thanks." He took it, fingers brushing hers in the process, a prickling warmth spreading up his arm. Yep. Definitely obsessive. Definitely time to go. Swallowing, he saluted her with the folder. "See you in the morning."

He strode to the door, intent on showing himself out.

"McMillian." Her voice, soft and a little strangled, stopped him.

He glanced back. She leaned against the plush armchair's back. Silver glinted at him again along her narrow waist. "Yes?"

She pushed her hair behind her ear again. "Have you eaten?"

"No, not yet."

"Would you like to stay for dinner?"

Dinner followed by breakfast tomorrow morning. He passed a hand over his hair. "Celia, it's not a good idea for us to—"

"Do you take the high road in everything you do?" Her chin tilted in clear challenge.

No. He possessed gray areas even he didn't want to admit to. "We work together. Any kind of involvement would be...difficult."

"It's a simple dinner invitation, not a lifelong commitment. And working with you now is beyond difficult," she muttered.

He frowned. "What does that mean?"

Her knuckles whitened where she gripped the edge of the chair back. "It means..." Her eyes slid closed and opened, something he'd never before seen in her gaze burning in the blue depths when she looked at him. "*I want you.*"

The words slammed into him, a punch to the gut, and he tried to process what she was saying. "Celia..."

"I want you and it's driving me crazy." She blew out a long breath and ran her hands through her hair, mussing it. "Obviously. God, I can't believe I'm saying this."

He couldn't either, but damn if he was going to blow this. Holding her gaze, he advanced on her to stop inches away. He dropped the folder on a side table and it slid to the floor, papers spilling across the polished wood. He wrapped his hands over hers and leaned in, close enough to see her pupils dilate. She smelled clean and uniquely female—no perfume, simply a mingling of her soap with the pure scent of her skin.

Desire pulsed through him, a buzzing ache starting in his groin and beating out along his veins. "I'm glad you did."

She stared at him for a long heartbeat before lifting her chin once more, fitting her mouth to his. Sensation exploded in him, awareness of the warm suppleness of her lips, the fine bones of her hands beneath his, the incredible heat of her form along his. She kissed him, a soft brush of lips, followed by a firmer caress. He held her hands tighter and kissed her back, teasing the line of her mouth, coaxing her to open to him.

With a soft exhale, she did, the tip of her tongue slipping along his mouth. He pushed closer, hips fitted into hers, trying to assuage the throbbing below his belt. He groaned. "God, I can't believe the way you taste."

She arched into him, her fingers flexing below his. "Kiss me again."

He did, dipping his tongue into her sweet depths, pressing her against the chair. His growing erection strained along his zipper, a literal ache coursing through him. The only thing that was going to soothe that was being inside her, thrusting into her wetness, feeling her close about him.

Maybe being with her would help him forget the memories haunting him—the ones aroused by Kathleen's pregnancy and dealing with this case.

A fantasy flared to life in his brain while her tongue tangled with his—opening his fly, sliding those tight jeans of hers down just enough to bare that beautiful ass, bending her over the plush chair, driving himself inside her.

Her hands fluttered beneath his palms and she pulled her mouth free, her head falling back. "God, yes," she moaned. "I want that too."

Too? He blinked, some of the desire-laden fog clearing from his brain. "What do you mean?"

She smiled, eyes closed, absolute abandon on her face. "Over the chair."

How did she *know* that? He released her hands and stepped back, his gaze darting to the crystal ball by the window. The matter-of-fact way she'd announced her sister was a psychic beat in his head. Unease slithered through him. "I'm sorry."

Her lids snapped up. "For kissing me?"

He took another backwards step, his desire extinguished. A familiar chill gripped him, raising gooseflesh on his arms. "This was a bad idea. We can't do this."

"McMillian—"

"I'll see you in the morning." He needed to get out of here. He bent to gather the file and its myriad reports scattered on the floor.

"Are you even going to tell me what went wrong?" Uncertainty hovered in her voice.

He didn't look up. "It's just not a good idea."

With a snap, he tapped the papers against the floor and shoved them into the folder. He glanced at her as he rose and wished he hadn't. She worried her swollen bottom lip with her teeth, watching him, her eyes soft and bruised. He tucked the file beneath his arm and nodded. "I'll show myself out."

The door closed behind him. Celia dug her fingers into the thick upholstery and swallowed against a wave of hurt and disappointment. What had she done wrong? He'd been as into that kiss as she'd been. She'd felt every inch of his erection pressed into her, had restrained herself from rubbing against him to ease the desire flowing through her. There'd been such a strong connection between them. Hadn't she seen what he wanted to do to her—

Seen?

She froze. No, it couldn't be. She didn't...she wasn't...

No. Absolutely not. She hadn't been seeing his fantasy. It had to have been her own, where she wanted that kiss to go. Lord only knew what she'd done to scare him off. Come on too strong. Or maybe...oh hell.

That wasn't her fantasy. She'd clearly seen it from his perspective, not her own. Maybe she was just going crazy. The sexual frustration, the wanting him, had finally pushed her over the edge.

She'd propositioned her boss.

Her lungs stopped working. She'd risked everything—her position, her professional reputation—with that stupid *I want you.* What the hell had she been thinking?

She hadn't been.

That was the problem. She'd been feeling, lost in the absolute incredibleness of actually touching him, kissing him, arching against him.

She had to face him in a staff meeting tomorrow morning.

With a groan, she covered her eyes with trembling fingers. Damn. This was worse than the freaking sex-toy debacle, than having him think she was involved with Cook. She needed a drink. A strong one. Maybe more than one. Pushing away from the chair, she walked through to Cicely's side of the house.

She found her sister sitting at the counter, closing out the shop's paperwork for the day. Celia folded her arms on the counter edge and sighed. "Hey."

Cicely slid her an inquisitive glance. "Your guy hightailed it out of here like the hounds of hell were after him."

Oh, that made her feel better. "He's not my guy."

"Need to talk?" Cicely made a neat stack of ones and began counting.

"Not right now." Celia levered away from the counter and walked along the wall, perusing the books. She knew she'd seen a volume on it here somewhere. A red leather cover, faded gilt lettering. "Maybe later. You want to go get a drink when you're finished?"

"Sure."

Celia floated her fingertips over the spines. She frowned. It wasn't here.

"Cee?" Cicely's soft voice drew her attention and she glanced over her shoulder. "What are you looking for?"

Celia shrugged as a spurt of foolishness filled her. "You had a book on the Gift."

"Sold it two days ago. It's out of print and I'm watching eBay for a replacement." Cicely wrapped a rubber band around the bills. "Why are you looking for that, anyway?"

Celia smiled, feeling sheepish. "The weirdest thing just happened."

"With McMillian?"

"Yes." She rubbed the links of her necklace between her thumb and forefinger. "I kissed him, and I thought, well, I thought he was as involved as I was. I swear I could see what he was thinking about us." She laughed. "I was thinking about you and Mama, wondering if maybe I picked up a little of the Gift after all."

"It's not you."

"What?" Celia frowned. Not her?

"It's him."

Celia laughed. "Come on, Cis, be serious—"

"I am." Cicely shrugged and stacked the money in her bank bag. "I felt it when he walked in."

"But then how could I see—"

"He projects." Cicely locked the bag away in the safe. "He's got a strong aura too. A dark one. Lots of stuff he's still carrying around with him. Be careful of that one, Cee."

Celia stared at her sister. It couldn't be. It simply couldn't. McMillian was the most logical, practical man she knew.

Not to mention, the most intuitive. The possibilities boggled the mind. However, nothing changed the fact that he'd pulled back and walked away. So he'd had a taste and he wasn't interested in anything further. She straightened her shoulders. She could deal with that.

After a couple of Summer Solstices, heavy on the vodka, and maybe one of her sister's vanishing spells.

Tom slammed the driver into the ball, the satisfying *thwack* vibrating up his arm. The ball veered in a wild arc to the right, hitting a marker four golfers down, and he bit back a curse. The other men scowled his way and every muscle between his shoulders tightened.

He couldn't hit for shit tonight.

Kissing her had been a bad idea. What he should have done was walk away when she asked him to dinner. Hanging around to hear her say she wanted him? Massive mistake. Because now the words pounded in his head, turning his drive to crap.

He had a strange feeling he'd be listening to them for days, probably turning his performance in the courtroom to crap too.

The memory of her mouth under his invaded his mind again. His gut tightened. He whacked another ball.

It cut to the left. He was screwed.

No, but you could have been.

Yeah. Literally. All he needed was a sexual-harassment lawsuit and the resulting publicity. He shrugged that off. Celia wasn't the type to set him up. She'd proved to be unfailingly honest.

But he'd never figured her for the type to blow a guy's mind with a simple "I want you".

He shouldn't have kissed her.

Hey, pal, she came on to you, remember?

And like an idiot, he'd walked away.

How the hell had she known what was in his head? Coincidence. They were just thinking along the same lines. That's all, with her back pressed into that chair and the absolute fire of that kiss between them. She'd said she wanted him. Why wouldn't she be picturing the possibilities?

He set another ball on a tee and frowned, remembering the way her sister had seemed to see into him. And that crystal ball. He'd witnessed for himself the way Celia could read a suspect. Maybe she'd just been reading him too.

He'd overreacted. What might have happened if he hadn't? If he'd followed through on her "God, yes"? Images tumbled through his head, Celia beneath him, legs resting on his shoulders while he sank balls-deep into the blazing heat of her body—

The ball sliced freakin' sideways.

Damn it.

"Man, what is wrong with you tonight?" Rhett set his bag down beside Tom's. His empty bucket dangled from his left hand. The lights gleamed off the dark butterscotch of his shaved head, picked up the glimmer of his wedding ring.

"Hell if I know." Tom jerked a hand over his hair. One of his wild drives had sent a ball into Rhett's zone earlier and his friend had been giving him odd looks ever since. "Maybe I need a different driver."

"Somehow I don't think a different club's going to do it. You only hit like that when something's weighing heavy on your mind. I wouldn't have to look far for that something."

"Yeah." Tom slid the driver into his bag and slipped the cover over the metal head. He jerked his chin at Rhett's bucket. "You ready to get out of here?"

"I take it you need a drink."

"Hell, yes." Maybe a good Scotch—or a couple—would get her off his mind, help him sleep.

They shouldered the bags and dropped off their buckets. Frustration lingered in Tom, wrapped up with the oddity of that interlude with Celia. "Rhett, do you believe in psychics?"

Rhett groaned, rolling his ebony eyes skyward. "Did that woman from Valdosta call again? I told her we weren't interested in hiring a staff psychic."

Tom chuckled. "No. I mean, do you think one person can pick up another's thoughts?"

"Mind reading? No." Rhett glanced at him, their feet crunching on the loose gravel of the parking lot. "Why do you ask?"

"Just curious."

"I think some people are highly intuitive and just really good at appraising others. They can seem like mind readers. But actual psychic ability? No way."

"Yeah." Tom rubbed a hand over his nape. That was it. Celia was reading him. That was all. It had to be. "Neither do I."

She ached, a deep hurt settling into her chest. Celia lifted her glass, sipping at the fruity concoction. One drink and two guys hitting on her hadn't lifted her spirits and she didn't have high hopes for the second Summer Solstice or the cute blond at the other end of the bar. She picked the cherry out of her drink and chewed while the blend of embarrassment and disappointment swirled in her.

Why couldn't he have turned out to be a lousy kisser? She could have moved on then. But no...sweet heaven, the mouth on that man.

"Stop obsessing." Cicely sucked at her slice of orange, her voice muffled. "It causes wrinkles."

"I know." Celia sighed and rested her chin on her hand, eyeing the crowd in the mirror behind the bar. Packed as usual, even on a weeknight, the Cue Club held people laughing around the pool tables, couples wrapped up on the dance floor, friends sharing a late evening meal. "God, what was I thinking?"

"Cee, stop being so hard on yourself. You made a move and you crashed. Big deal. It happens."

"He's my *boss*. I have to see him every day—"

"Fine. So you look him in the eye and you move on. There are a ton of other guys out there." Cicely pursed her lips and dug in her small bag. She withdrew a tiny vial—old wavy glass with a cork stopper. "Look, if you want it, there's the answer to your problem."

"Cis, God! Don't do that!" Celia palmed the vial and glanced around. It didn't look like anyone had noticed them. "The rumor mill will have it that you're dealing drugs. Or that we were doing drugs. Or that—"

"You know, you really spend too much effort worrying what other people think."

Celia glanced down at the powder in the vial. "What is it?"

A smile tipped the corners of Cicely's lips. "What do you think?"

Celia traced a finger over the tiny glass bottle, old memories turning over. So many times she'd seen her mama press one of these into the shaking hands of some desperate woman, her soothing voice whispering advice. "Is it one of Mama's?"

Cicely nodded. "Sprinkle it here in the mornings," she said, rubbing a finger between her breasts, causing the blond to light up at the end of the bar, "and whisper for him to be still. Before you know it, you're ready to move on." She paused for a long beat. "If that's what you really want."

Of course it was. Wasn't it? She tucked it into her pocket. "Thanks."

"You're not going to use it." Cicely tossed her hair over her shoulder. A knowing expression lifted her lips, crinkled the corners of her eyes.

"I might." Celia sipped at her drink once more. Would her mother's charm help her forget the humiliation of what had happened in her living room? Too bad she didn't hold with such. As a little girl, she'd believed in her mother's "magic", but later she'd figured out that mostly her mama had simply been a master at evaluating people and helping them find a way through their problems. She really needed Mama's help getting through this mess she'd made with McMillian.

How could she have misread him so badly? He'd said he was glad she'd told him how she felt, he'd seemed awed by the power of that kiss, as much as she'd been. She tunneled a hand through her hair. Maybe he was right. Maybe it was just a bad idea. Who was she kidding? It was the worst idea ever and she should have thought it through before she'd thrown herself at him. Her cheeks warmed and the sick emptiness of remembered embarrassment twisted her stomach.

"He just walked in the door," Cicely said. "I won't bother to tell you not to look."

Celia cast a casual glance over her shoulder. Sure enough, McMillian made his way to a vacant booth with Rhett High at his side. Her face burned hotter. Certainly, McMillian wouldn't share his version of her foolish behavior with the assistant DA.

She downed the remainder of her drink. "Let's get out of here. Maybe get a coffee or something."

"Sure." Cicely slid from her stool and finished her drink as well. "But, Cee? Running away isn't going to solve anything."

Maybe not, but tonight, it might help, at least until she had to face him in that damn meeting tomorrow.

They wove through the crowd and Celia carefully kept her gaze averted from McMillian's booth. She had to cope with him and her own stupidity tomorrow. Tonight she could lick her wounds.

"Hey, St. John!"

At Cook's voice, she spun to see him winding his way toward her. She sighed, wanting nothing more than to just get the hell out of here. She forced a smile as he reached them. "Cook. What's up?"

"I tried to call you earlier."

Sometimes a cell phone was a curse. People expected everyone to be available 24/7. "I left my cell at home."

His gaze darted over her shoulder. She glanced back at Cicely and shrugged. "Cicely, this is Mark Cook, with the sheriff's department. Cook, my sister Cicely."

He nodded and reached for Cicely's hand, recognition lighting his eyes. "We've met. Yoga instructor, right?"

"Right." Cicely flicked a hand between them. "Will you two be a while? If so, I'm going to get another drink."

"Wait a sec." Celia turned to him. "What's up?"

His gray gaze glimmered and he lifted his beer to his lips. "Wouldn't you like to know?"

"Cook, I've had the day from hell, okay? I'm not in the mood. Tell me or die."

"Blood tests are in."

Excitement trickled through her. "Really? Do tell."

Cicely rolled her eyes. "I'm going for that drink."

Celia waved a hand, her attention still focused on Cook. "So?"

He grinned. "Doe wasn't the father."

"We know that for a fact?"

"Baby was type AB negative and Doe was type O positive.

73

No way he fathered that baby."

She pushed her hair behind her ear. "So the question is—"

"Who are the parents?"

"And where did that baby come from?"

Chapter Four

When Tom arrived at work, the parking lot was empty, save for one familiar SUV. Frowning, he whipped into his spot. Beginning his workday a little after seven was part of his routine because he was assured some time alone in the office. He was usually the only one there this early.

He glanced at Celia's Xterra as he jogged up the stairs. A fine layer of dew coated the steel blue paint. How long had she been here?

Quiet lay over the offices. He dropped his briefcase on his desk and headed down the hall for Celia's office. His belly tightened with each step, the blend of tension and anticipation he connected with seeing her.

The door stood open and he paused in the doorway. Papers littered Celia's desk, her laptop open on the blotter, her coffee mug on the corner and the aroma of stale coffee heavy in the air. Eyes closed, she curled into her chair, cheek against her shoulder. He frowned again. She was still wearing her jeans and camisole from the night before.

Had she been here all night?

He stepped into the room and lifted one of the papers from the desk. An Internet printout, a news report on the abduction of an infant from a Mississippi hospital three days before. Another on a woman murdered in Maryland, her unborn child cut from her womb.

He dropped the papers on her desk, his gaze straying to her face. With her features relaxed in sleep, she looked younger, more vulnerable. He followed the line of her mouth, remembering the lush fullness moving beneath his, opening to him. Ah, damn it, how could one kiss ruin everything? How the hell was he supposed to work with her now? Every time he looked at her, memories of the feel, the smell of her, would plague him.

She stirred with a murmuring sigh, dark lashes lifting to reveal a dreamy expression. They fluttered down again, a smile lifting the corners of her luscious mouth. She stretched, camisole pulled taut over her breasts. He tightened his hands into fists, palms itching to fit to those curves.

Her eyes opened again and recognition trickled into her gaze. The line of her body stiffened, her features tensing as she came fully awake.

"What time is it?" Sleep husked her voice. Rumpled hair fell about her as she leaned forward to pick up her desk clock.

"A little after seven."

She moaned, the little sound sending a tingle of awareness through him. Great. Now he was associating everything she did with sex.

She rubbed a hand over her face. "I have to go home and change."

"Have you been here all night?"

Irritation darkened her eyes. "Obviously."

"Why?"

"Blood-test results came in. Cook was right; John Doe wasn't the baby's father. And that child came from somewhere. I just need to figure out where."

So that's what the deep conversation with Cook had been last night in the bar. He'd watched her laugh with the other man, hating the primal jealousy stinging him. He'd walked away from her after that mind-altering kiss. For all he knew, she might consider turning to Cook. That was all he needed—those pictures in his head again, of her long legs wrapped around the investigator, his hands and mouth on her skin.

Shrugging off the frustration, he nodded. "I appreciate the work you're putting into this."

Her eyes cooled further, her mouth tightening. She pushed up from the chair. "I really don't want your appreciation, McMillian."

Irritation stung him, bristling through him. Why did women have to turn everything personal? "Is this about what happened between us last night?"

Eyes narrowed to slits of glittering blue ice, she looked at him. "Nothing happened *between* us. That was a momentary lapse of sanity on my part—which you can bet your ass will never happen again—and male curiosity on your part. It was meaningless and has nothing to do with this case. And just for the record, I'm not putting these hours in for you. I'm doing it for that baby's mother."

"She has a father somewhere too." He folded his arms over his chest. His male pride smarted at her easy dismissal of the kiss that had led to his repeated dreams of her the night before. "And you call that nothing?"

She gathered the papers on her desk and stacked them with a smart snap against the desk before laying them aside. A cynical smile twisted her mouth. "What would you call it?"

The hottest kiss he'd had in recent memory. "Interesting."

"Right." Her laugh bordered on a disgusted snort. "That was interest that had you running for the door."

He scowled at the picture she painted. "It wasn't like that."

She pinned him with a cool look. "Why are we even having this conversation? You said it was a bad idea and you were right. Exactly what do you want, McMillian?"

That brought him up short. He opened his mouth, closed it. What did he want? He wanted her to acknowledge the intensity of that kiss, to admit it was more than nothing. He wanted to know how she'd known what was in his head. More than anything, he wanted to kiss her again, to see if it would be just as strong the second time around. A twinge of arousal flared.

"That's what I thought." She shook her head, slung her purse over her shoulder and stepped out from behind the desk. "You don't have a clue. I'm going home to shower and change. I'll be back for the staff meeting."

"Wait." He reached for her arm, sensation prickling up the nerves in his arm from the contact. Her sleep-warmed scent wrapped tendrils around him. She glanced at his hand on her bare skin then up at him, her expression mutinous. He sighed, resisting the urge to shift his fingertips over her softness. "You're right. I don't know what I want from you."

A cold smile played around her lips. "Sure you do. You're a guy. You just haven't figured out how to pretty it up yet, even with your law degree and silver tongue."

Annoyance shot through him, made him edgy. He released her but stepped between her and the door. "You think that's all I'm interested in? Sex?"

She arched an eyebrow. "Pretty much, yeah." A harsh laugh bubbled from her throat. "And I can't blame you for it. I put the damn idea in your head."

Put the idea in his head? He remembered how she'd seemed to know what he was thinking. A frisson moved down his spine. "What do you mean?"

78

"With that stupid 'I want you' last night. So don't worry, McMillian, I'm a big girl, plenty old enough for my wants not to hurt me. This little interlude or whatever is over—"

"The hell it is." He stepped forward, thighs brushing hers, and she stepped back, surprise flaring in her gaze before her legs collided with the desk. He leaned into her, resting both hands on the desk edge, either side of where she gripped the fine cherry wood.

She sucked in a breath, chest rising near his. "Back off."

Uncertainty trembled in her voice. He eyed her, picking up unmistakable signs of attraction—the way her pupils dilated, the slight flare of her nostrils, the tip of her tongue flirting along her upper lip. "Is that really what you want?"

Her lashes dipped and she worried her bottom lip between her teeth for a moment. When she opened her eyes, he caught a glimpse of the bruised look he'd seen there the night before. A cold lump settled in his gut, wistfulness for something lost or carelessly thrown away curling through him.

She straightened, staring him down. "I really need to go home and change if you expect me to make your meeting on time."

He stepped away, ran a hand over his hair. "Celia, I'm sorry. I shouldn't have—"

"No." A pensive smile curved her mouth and disappeared. "I'm the one who's sorry. I'll see you at nine."

Head high, she walked by him into the hallway.

With the knot still holding residence in his belly, he closed his eyes. God, he was a stupid son of a bitch.

Stupid. Stupid. Stupid.

Celia rested her forehead against the shower wall and

pounded her fist on the tile. Stupid to tell him she wanted him. Stupid to let him get to her all over again. Stupid to be this wound up in a man.

Any man.

"Enough." She lifted her head, water streaming over her, and wiped her face. And why the vague sense of disappointment? What had she expected? She'd dangled sex in front of a man. How was he supposed to react? Ask to get to know her better before she spread her legs for him? Jesus above, she was so incredibly stupid. Like a naïve virgin, expecting more.

She didn't *want* more.

She swallowed, the humiliation twisting and striking in her belly like an angry snake. Was this what her mother had experienced, over and over and over again?

When would she finally get the idea that men were all alike? A woman couldn't trust them and they only wanted one thing. If her mother's men hadn't proved that, Turello certainly had. How many times did she have to have proof of that before it sank in?

What was wrong with her? The worst part was, pressed against that desk, looking up into his hungry gaze, she'd still wanted him. Wanted to strip off his jacket and tie, peel away her jeans and let him have her, right there, screw the consequences. She closed her eyes.

Damn it all.

As far as her self-respect balance went, she was seriously overdrawn.

She still had to sit in that meeting, listen to him, look at him. Face him. Tears welled and she sucked them down.

Pushing her hair from her face with one hand, she turned

off the water with the other. A handful of drops pattered onto the tile floor and she swung the door open, grabbed a towel and stepped out.

Her phone was ringing.

Hell, like she wanted to talk to anybody right now. With the towel wrapped around her dripping form, she hustled to the bedroom and grabbed the cordless phone. "Hello?"

"What took you so long?" Cook's voice rumbled against her ear.

She dropped on the side of the bed. "I was in the shower."

"Really?" His tone turned to wicked glee. "What are you wearing?"

"A chastity belt. And I threw away the key." She closed her eyes, disgusted. More proof that all men were the same. "What do you want?"

"We have autopsy results. Message was on my desk when I got in this morning. Ford's a damn tease, so there weren't any details."

She couldn't find any level of excitement. "Great. Are you going to Moultrie?"

"I thought *we'd* go to Moultrie, as soon as you got your lazy ass in gear."

"Can't." She pushed up from the bed and crossed to her closet. "I have a staff meeting."

"Play hooky."

"Don't tempt me."

"Temptation is my middle name, St. John."

An unwilling smile tugged at her lips. She pulled her navy suit from the rail. "So that's what the T stands for."

He chuckled. "Come on, you know you'd rather hang out in

an autopsy lab with me than sit around listening to McMillian talk."

He had no clue how right he was. She sighed. "Can you wait an hour and then go?"

"I really didn't want to. I have warrants to serve later. Tell you what—I'll even buy you breakfast at El Toreo's."

She smiled again, the ache around her heart not lifting. Too bad she didn't want him. He'd be a fun date. She shook off the musings and reached for her spectator slingbacks. Besides, what was more important right now? Finding out where that baby belonged, giving a parent closure, or following McMillian's office rules?

She lifted underwear from its basket. "You're on. Give me twenty minutes."

The GBI office was relatively quiet. They picked up visitor badges at the reception desk and ventured back to the autopsy lab. The heavy disinfectant didn't quite mask the smells of blood and decay.

Cook pushed the door open. "Ford?"

She emerged from her small office, already clad in scrubs, a surgical cap printed with dancing dinosaurs covering her hair. "Figured I'd see you two this morning."

A tingle of anticipation ran through Celia. "So?"

Ford crossed to the table which bore a small sheet-draped figure and pulled the fabric away. Celia cringed at the Y-shaped incision on the baby's tiny chest, the stitches raw and angry. Ford passed Cook a sheet of paper. "So you don't have a homicide."

"What?" His gaze jerked to the report. Surprised, Celia glanced over his shoulder.

She looked up at Ford. "Natural causes?"

Ford nodded. "A congenital heart defect."

Cook frowned. "And with medical intervention?"

"Barring a transplant, that baby would have died within days of birth, just as she did. This is interesting, though."

Celia followed Ford's finger, eyeing the baby's navel, a remnant of the umbilical cord still attached, tied off with white cotton string. "What?"

"I think you have a home birth. In fact, it has to be, or this baby would never have been allowed to leave the hospital. The umbilical cord? Cut with scissors."

Cook shrugged, unimpressed. "What else would you cut it with?"

"Surgical scissors. This was cut with an instrument much less precise. See how jagged the edges are above the clamped area?"

"Yeah." Cook sighed and rubbed a hand over his neck. "How does that help us?"

"Find the scissors, find the roll of string, and I can tell you if it was the instrument that did the cutting."

He held the report aloft. "Mind if we take this with us?"

Ford waved a hand at him. "Your copy. Be my guest."

Celia followed him outside. The morning already held a sultry promise of afternoon heat to come. She ran a finger along her necklace. "We're not any closer to the answers, Cook. What was Doe doing with that baby? Where did she come from?"

He tugged a pack of gum from his pocket and extended it in her direction. She shook her head and he popped a piece in his mouth. He chewed, brow wrinkled in a thoughtful look. "Well, we have a couple of possibilities."

"What?"

Her cell phone pinged, forestalling her answer. She tugged it from her waistband, stomach falling when she glanced at the display. McMillian's private line.

Oh hell. She really didn't want to talk to him.

Celia lifted the phone to her ear. "St. John."

"Got your message from Raquel." Papers rustled behind McMillian's terse voice. "What did the ME say?"

With a suppressed sigh, Celia slid into the passenger seat. "The baby wasn't murdered. She died of natural causes."

"SIDS?" His voice tightened and she didn't miss the pain winding through the single syllable. She steeled herself against a spurt of sympathy. She didn't need to feel any soft emotions for him.

She glanced at Cook as he settled behind the wheel and fitted the key in the ignition. His jaw remained as taut as her nerves felt. The radio beeped, static crackling. "No. A congenital heart defect."

"All right." More paper rustling, and she pictured him standing behind his desk, phone propped under his chin while he pulled court papers together. "I'm headed out to Darren County. I'd like to see you this afternoon before you leave."

Her stomach plummeted. "Sure."

"Good. We need to talk."

The line went dead and she snapped the phone closed, letting her head drop forward with a muffled groan. Cook laughed. "Let me guess. You've been summoned to the principal's office."

Worse. She could just imagine what McMillian thought they needed to talk about. Her face burned. She straightened and blew out a long breath. "You're a bad influence, Cook."

"You're just now figuring that out?"

A strand of hair, escaped from her loose knot, tickled her cheek, and she brushed it away. "You said something about why Doe had this baby in his car? Which, by the way, we still don't know *was* his car, because it belongs to a nonexistent person. God, we'll never sort this case out."

"Are you done?" He pulled into traffic. "I've been thinking about that, you know, possible reasons why he'd have the kid if it wasn't his. The most unpalatable? Kiddy porn. Or the sex trade."

She shuddered. That possibility had occurred to her as well. "Give me another option."

"Black market for human organs."

"I think that one's an urban legend, Cook."

He shrugged. "Still gotta consider it. And there's always adoption."

"Like he was the adoptive parent?"

"Like an illegal baby ring. Gray market adoptions." He glanced over his shoulder before changing lanes. "White newborn, desperate parents with lots of money. Tick and his wife are looking at adoption routes and the process is huge. I can see someone wanting to buy their way around that."

She tapped her phone against her lips. "That's a possibility. So if there are no legal adoption papers, what do they do about a birth certificate?"

"I don't know. Buy one? Call it a home birth? You're the one who works for a shyster. Ask McMillian."

"I will, this afternoon. Maybe the Florida Department of Law Enforcement will have something on a missing baby, since the GBI hasn't turned up anything—"

"Ford said something about a home birth, remember?"

"Yes. Why?"

"Somebody has to supervise that, right?"

She laughed. "You're asking me? How would I know? Besides, if I ever have a kid, it'll be in a hospital, with a doctor and lots and lots of drugs. But I think most women who do a home birth have a midwife or something similar."

Cook nodded. "We find that midwife…"

"And we find our parents."

℘

"McMillian?"

Celia's voice washed over him and Tom glanced up from the case-law update. The cascade of relief at her appearance startled him. It was late, after six, and with the office empty and quiet, he'd almost given up on seeing her.

He pulled off his reading glasses and laid them aside. "Come on in."

She took two steps inside and stopped. Her fingers edged along the fragile links of her necklace. "I'm sorry to leave this so late. I've been tracking down birth records for the counties bordering the state line."

Arms crossed behind his head, he leaned back in his chair. "Any luck?"

"Not yet." A tight smile flitted across her mouth. "Cook thinks we might be looking at an illegal adoption ring. Parents desperate for a baby, willing to do anything."

He nodded. "Makes sense."

She waved a hand toward the door, looking everywhere but at him. "Well, if that's all, I'm going—"

"Celia, wait." He rose and came round the desk to stand

before her. She lifted her eyes to his, but the blue depths revealed none of her emotions. Tension coiled in him, tightening the muscles along his shoulders. He had to do something about this situation between them, and he couldn't afford to screw up again.

"I have—"

"Listen to me. Please. I value you as a member of my team." He ran a hand over his nape, tendons bunching under his fingers. "You intrigue me as a woman. I'd hate to lose the former because of the latter. This morning, I was completely out of line. Professionally and personally."

"Fine. Apology accepted." She folded her arms over her midriff, the line of her body screaming of stress.

His hands itched to grasp her shoulders, rub down her arms. "I'd also hate to miss the opportunity to discover who you really are."

She stared at him, cynicism washing her eyes. "I see you found a way to pretty it up. Admit it. You want me in your bed."

"I'd be insane not to." Probably insane for pursuing this, but doubly insane not to explore the possibilities vibrating between them. "Admit you want to be there."

"I already did." Pursing her lips, she glanced away. "Let me guess. We should have a one-night stand, get the sex out of our systems."

"No, that's what your buddy Cook would suggest. I prefer a monogamous relationship of limited duration with the terms understood by both parties upfront."

"You're such a damn lawyer." She turned those crystal eyes, narrowed and calculating, on him again. "You mean you like short, no-strings affairs, as opposed to Cook's one-nighters."

"Exactly." He tucked his hands in his pockets, making sure he couldn't touch her. If anything came of this, it would be her decision, not because he'd influenced her. If she said no, that was the end of it. He'd just go quietly insane with sexual frustration. "We're attracted and it's getting in the way."

She tilted her head, the movement exposing the tiny pulse beating in her throat. "We *are* mature, consenting adults. There's always the option of exploring that attraction."

An irresistible smile pulled at his mouth. "When it's over, it's over. We go in with our eyes open and no one gets hurt."

She watched him a long moment, until the urge to shift under that steady gaze filled him. "Do you really think we can do that?"

He nodded. "I do."

Her soft exhale sounded suspiciously like a snort. He frowned. Shit, she was going to say no. He rolled his shoulders under a sudden wave of tension. "What?"

"There's no such thing as eyes-wide-open and no-one-gets-hurt. Someone always gets hurt, even if it doesn't show."

He refused to give in to the desire to lean toward her, to kiss her until she acquiesced. "I won't hurt you. Let me prove it to you."

"I don't know." She passed her thumb over her lips, gaze darting to his and away. "I need to think about it."

Muted satisfaction rushed through him, like striking a deal on a particularly difficult case. He had her on the hook. He forced himself to appear as removed as possible. Being too eager was never a good thing. "That's fine."

He allowed himself to run a finger along her jaw, the skin smooth and soft beneath his touch. "If you decide this is what you want, we can have dinner tonight. My place, about seven-thirty. Bring your swimsuit."

She'd crossed the line from stupidity to insanity. Celia killed the Xterra's engine and reached for her sequined net bag. The bad part was she didn't care. Well, almost. But with her desire for him outweighing the risk to her emotions, she was ready to dive into the craziness, her entire body buzzing and tingling with eagerness. All she had to do was keep her eyes open as the relationship closed over her head.

He wasn't hers, this wasn't about flowers and forever, and she could climb out and walk away before she got in too deep. No problem.

Bag slung over her shoulder, she slid from the SUV. His house was what she'd expected—a tall cedar contemporary on the lake, clean, modern, no frills. A small Honda sat in the drive, the silver Mercedes nowhere to be seen. Probably protected in the double garage. She followed the concrete walk to the front door, rang the bell and waited. Nerves jumped and she squashed the anxiety.

Deep breath. Eyes open. She just had to remember that.

The door opened to reveal a woman in her midforties, thick dark hair pulled back in a ponytail. She carried a tote of cleaning supplies. She fixed Celia with a perfunctory smile. "Ms. St. John?"

Anxiety jabbed at her stomach. "Yes."

The other woman stepped outside, holding the door with one hand. "Mr. McMillian is in the pool. He asked me to tell you to go on back."

She pointed across the foyer, toward the rear of the house, and Celia smiled. "Thanks."

She stepped through the doorway and the door closed

behind her. Italian tile swept through the foyer, segueing to polished hardwood floors in the living room. She eyed the glass doors at the back of the house and shook her head. So like McMillian. How many times had she seen him do the same thing to a defense attorney?

Make them come to you.

The man was a complete control freak. She'd let him have this one. The next shot would be hers.

She drifted through the living area, ran her fingers along the back of a butter-soft leather couch. The large room was beautiful and professionally decorated. Nothing here said it belonged to Tom McMillian. She couldn't find a single personal touch.

The glass doors opened onto a wide deck, steps sweeping down to a concrete patio surrounding the Grecian-inspired pool. Beyond the pool area, thick St. Augustine grass flowed to a covered dock. A handful of ducks floated between tall cypress trees. The rushing buzz of cicadas filled the air and a light breeze carried the earthy smell of lake water.

As the other woman had said, McMillian was in the pool, swimming laps. Celia paused at the top of the steps, watching him cut through the water with powerful strokes. Tight muscles rippled beneath his skin and the nervousness fluttering in her stomach shifted, morphed into a liquid stab of anticipation.

Forget the deep breath and open eyes. She was ready to be in over her head with him.

Ready to drown in him.

She descended the steps. Ferns waved in cedar planters, and the setting sun cast blue shadows on the patio. Stainless steel lights spilled pools of gold here and there.

He hadn't noticed her. She stopped by a lounger and laid her bag aside. Tendons stretched and pulled in his back. She swallowed. The man was absolutely beautiful. Agonized expectation swirled through her, a rush of wanting and unadulterated lust, settling into a warm ache low in her belly and between her thighs.

No, he wouldn't be *hers*, but he'd be her lover. And at this rate? All he'd have to do was touch her and she'd be a puddle at his feet. She needed to get a grip.

He reached the deep end and stopped, holding on to the concrete apron with one hand, pulling goggles off with the other. He wiped water from his face and grinned at her, short dark hair plastered to his head. "Hey."

"Hey, yourself."

"I'm glad you decided to come." He released the apron, treading water. Water trailed down his neck to the tight muscles of his shoulders and biceps. "You should come in. The water's great."

Said the shark to the fish. She shrugged off the whimsy and toed out of her skimpy sandals while pulling her camisole over her head. She slanted a quick glance at him. His grin had died, male appreciation sparking in the cool blue of his eyes while he surveyed her plain black bikini top.

She pulled the clip from her hair and shook it loose about her shoulders. A wicked smile tugging at her lips, she half-turned from him. Men were such simple, visual creatures.

Make her come to him? He was trying it again. Well, she'd make him wait for it.

She slid her chain over her head and dropped it into her bag. "I thought we were having dinner."

"We are." His voice was nearer and she looked over her shoulder to find him at the side of the pool, the strong point of his chin rested on his crossed arms. He was eyeing her legs and his gaze traveled up her body to her face. He grinned again, the expression purely male and predatory in nature. "But I thought you might want to cool off first."

"It's not that hot yet." She turned her back, biting her lip to hold in a laugh. Taking her time, she slid her khaki shorts down her legs and stepped out of them. Not looking at him, she folded them neatly and laid them beside her bag.

"Oh, I don't know. From here, it's pretty damn hot." His voice sounded a little strangled. She turned to face him and unclasped her belly chain, coiling it atop her shorts. He met her gaze, his face taut. "That bordered on cruelty, Cee."

She liked hearing the nickname on his lips. With a sultry laugh, she took a running start and dove. The cool shock of the water closed in, enveloping her body. She surfaced, gasping a little at the sudden chill, and slicked her wet hair from her face.

He remained in his prior location, leaning against the pool wall, watching her. She blinked away water, the faint aroma of chlorine filling her nose. "You're right. It is nice."

That prowling grin curving his mouth again, he pushed away, doing a slow crawl to the other side. "It could be a whole lot nicer."

God, he was all ego. And damn if she didn't like it. She treaded water, cool waves lapping at her but doing little to soothe the heat spiraling under her skin. "Patience, McMillian. Good things come to those who wait."

"Maybe I'm not a patient man." He swam to her, stopping scant inches away. She stared into his eyes, droplets clinging to his dark lashes, falling free to follow the slashes by his mouth. His white teeth flashed in a shark's smirk, one that sent heat pooling in her abdomen. "Sometimes great things come to those who make it happen."

A heavy expectancy filled her, a stinging rush that tightened her breasts and sizzled along her skin. "I like the way you think, Counselor."

She closed the minuscule distance between them, threading her fingers into the short hair at the back of his head. Her chest bumped his, stomachs rubbed, treading legs tangled. She saw the flare of surprise and desire in his eyes before she took his mouth.

The kiss was no tentative exploration. Instead, he opened his lips immediately, their tongues stroking, teasing, dueling. An arm clamped around her waist, dragging her against him and she closed her eyes before they sank beneath the surface. Excitement flashed in her, the intensity of sensations zinging along each of her nerve endings.

She moaned into his mouth and wrapped her legs around his waist, giving herself over to his strength and the cushioning hold of the water. He pulled her closer, dipping his tongue deeper into her mouth.

They broke the surface and she pulled her mouth from his, filling her lungs on an exhilarated laugh. He chuckled, finding his footing on the pool's sloping floor, still holding her with one arm, smoothing her hair from her face. She held his gaze, finding her own reflection in the desire darkening his eyes.

He lowered his head and kissed her again, slow nips along her lips rather than the all-out ravaging they'd shared before. Surging closer, she explored his shoulders and arms, loving the play of muscle beneath her fingers.

His hands eased up and down her back, circled her waist, smoothed up her ribcage to the edge of her bikini top. His lips held hers, clung, let go. He smiled, stroking his thumbs along the line of her ribs.

Satisfaction cascaded through her. Tonight, he'd be hers. Fantasies and images kicked off in her mind—her head tossing on golden pillows, her body arching into his as he thrust into her.

She blinked. Not her fantasy. His. What he wanted, in her head again. She didn't understand how, but she wasn't in the mood to question. She wrapped her arms around his neck, pressed her breasts into the hard wall of his chest and brushed her mouth over his. She'd just have to make sure every one of his fantasies came true.

She was sure he'd satisfy hers too. An arm hooked around his neck, she traced the line of his lips with a finger.

"I love the way you taste." He pressed a kiss to her fingertip. "You're incredible."

Oh, he had no idea. She was going to be his dream come true, tonight anyway. She tilted her head back, the better to see into his eyes. Hunger blazed in the dark blue depths.

Make them come to you.

She released her hold on him. "Didn't you say something about dinner?"

"Um, yeah, but—"

"No buts. I'm hungry." She swam to the side of the pool and leveraged herself out. She lifted a towel from the stack on a glass-topped table and turned, watching as he followed her lead. His biceps bunched when he pushed out of the water, and once he stood on the apron, rivulets raced from his chest to his rippled abdomen. Dark hair clung to toned calves beneath his olive board shorts. Oh, yum. Yes, she was definitely hungry.

Smiling at him, she rubbed at the ends of her damp hair. "So, McMillian, what's cooking?"

Chapter Five

Oh God, she'd screwed up.

Jessica backed away from the computer screen and the brief message refusing her latest demand. Her pulse thudded a sick tattoo in her ears and she fumbled for the business card atop the desk with numb fingers. The ivory rectangle tumbled to the floor, fluttered under the desk. A curse on her lips, she slid from the chair, her distended belly an awkward hindrance as she reached for the card.

The baby punched at her ribs and stole her breath. Hatred washed through her. Why had she ever agreed to the stupid pregnancy idea in the first place? No money was worth this. She should have gotten away early on. Now she'd ruined everything.

He would kill her.

"Stop it." She leaned back on her haunches, the card clutched in her hand, and pressed her fingers to her burning eyes. "Just stop it and get it together. He's not going to kill you because you aren't going to be here."

She pulled the cordless phone from its charger and turned the card to read the number scrawled on the back. With shaking fingers, she punched in the numbers and listened to one, two, three rings.

"Come on, Tom, answer the fucking phone," she whispered, fear tightening her throat. On the fourth ring, the voice mail picked up, his smooth courtroom voice directing her to leave a message.

"Shit." Message, hell. She tossed the phone against the wall. Fury joined the dread burning through her. Damn it, she was depending on him and he couldn't answer his phone?

Why was she sitting around here anyway? Pressing her hands against the chair seat for balance, she pushed to her feet. Her head swam, vision blurring for a moment.

She'd give Thomas Everett McMillian III a message all right. She'd present him with her pregnant belly, on his fucking doorstep. She wasn't dying for this baby.

Or anyone else, for that matter.

"Aren't you going to answer that?"

A chill ran over Tom's skin, but he shrugged it off and leaned back in his chair, his gaze on Celia. She'd pulled her damp hair into a knot and tossed on her shorts, but eschewed her camisole and sandals. He'd followed her lead, tugged on a polo shirt with his trunks and stayed barefoot.

He glanced up the steps toward the house, the distant ringing of a phone wafting to them. Another frisson tried to work over him, but he shook his head. "Voice mail will get it."

Celia tilted her head, a quizzical smile curving her lips. "What if it's important?"

"Not as important as this." A breeze whispered in from the lake, making the candle between them waver and dance. The dinner salad Lora had put together before she left had satisfied one hunger; the one Celia had inspired with her little striptease still burned. He didn't find himself in any hurry to hustle her up the stairs and lay her across his bed, though. Instead, he was content to sit here, listen to her laugh, watch the expressions chase across her face.

The soul-deep pleasure bugged the hell out of him.

He liked the way she looked at him too, her crystalline gaze flickering over him. She was hungry for him and she watched him as if trying to figure out where to start. The mere thought resulted in a shudder of sensation down his spine.

She popped a piece of tomato, dripping with Lora's homemade vinaigrette, in her mouth. Her lashes fluttered down and she sighed. "That's fantastic."

He eyed the sublime satisfaction on her face. Maybe he wouldn't wait to take her upstairs. One of the chaise lounges would work—he could peel the damp bikini away, slide his mouth and tongue along her skin, teasing and tasting until *he* made her sigh and moan like that.

Her eyes flew open and her fork clattered to the plate.

"Oh." A slight flush washed her cheeks with color and she fumbled with her napkin. "Sorry."

He shook his head and extended a hand for her plate. "Are you finished?"

She rose, her movements easy and graceful. "Let me help you clean up."

He tried waving her back to her seat. "Not necessary. I'm just sliding them in the dishwasher."

"Maybe I want a tour of your house." With a smile, she trailed a finger along his arm as she passed. The simple caress left a quiver in its path. A grin quirked at his mouth. Who'd have known a tease lurked beneath her cool professionalism?

And who'd have guessed he would enjoy every second of it?

He jogged up the steps after her. In the kitchen, she helped him scrape and rinse the plates. She ran a palm over the marble countertop, an appreciative smile lighting her face. "Cis would die for this kitchen. She's a gourmet nut."

He lifted the open bottle of wine in silent offer and she nodded. Pouring two glasses, he glanced at her. "Do you cook?"

She laughed, accepting the glass he proffered. "I can, but why should I when Cis will?"

"Good point." He swirled his wine, watching her sip. The moisture made her lush mouth glisten and renewed desire punched him in the gut. He wanted to kiss her again, wanted to taste her sweetness mingled with the tart wine. "How about that tour?"

She slipped an arm about his waist, surprising him. The rounded firmness of her breast pressed against his ribs, heat sparking along his skin from the point of contact. "Let me guess...ending in the bedroom."

He brushed his thumb over her lips. "Maybe."

Smiling again, she lifted her glass. "Lead the way, Counselor."

A showing of the downstairs took only a few minutes. He loved watching her move through his home, soaked in the way she took every opportunity to touch him—brushing against him in doorways, sliding her fingers over his arm, feathering them over his spine. By the time they reached the stairs, she had every molecule in his body alive and buzzing.

Upstairs, she paused in the doorway to his office and laughed. "I don't believe it."

"What?" His face and neck warmed, and he folded his arms, leaning a shoulder against the wall behind her. Here it came—she was going to give him a hard time. He could see it in the devilish tilt of her mouth, the teasing glow in her eyes.

"You have clutter," she teased.

He eyed the boxes of legal journals and stacks of sheet

protectors holding his baseball-card collection. He was going to put them in binders, some day. "It's just stuff I haven't found a place for yet."

She arched an eyebrow at him. "How long have you been living here?"

"Four years."

"It's clutter."

"You were a Boy Scout?" She gazed at the photo of his Eagle Scout ceremony, hanging in a grouping of college and high school pictures by the door. The startled surprise in her voice caught him unaware.

"Yeah. Why?"

"Because Boy Scouts are supposed to be...fair and honest and all that jazz." She bit her lip, devilment glinting in her eyes. "You have gray areas, McMillian."

He didn't move, watching as she peered into the third bedroom, which held only his treadmill and home gym.

Back on the landing, she grinned. "Told you we'd end up in the bedroom."

Anticipation settled heavily in his groin. "I suppose you want to see mine?"

Her smile widened. "I can't wait."

He pointed at the slightly open door. "Be my guest."

She pushed the door open and walked inside. He stepped to the doorway. She stood in the middle of his room, arms folded across her midriff, gaze darting about. She tilted her head toward the bed, the comforter folded back, the pillows mounded at the headboard. "Nice sheets."

A laugh rumbled in his throat. "Egyptian cotton."

She walked to the bed, tracing a finger along a pillow. His skin vibrated, as if she touched him instead. "They feel great.

Fantastic color, too."

"I'll tell my decorator you approve."

She eased that finger up her thigh to the waistband of her shorts, popped the button free. His mouth dried, his pulse kicking a notch higher. This was really happening. Celia St. John, undressing before him. A male fantasy come to life.

She slid the zipper down, let the shorts fall to the floor, stepped out of them. Standing before him in only the brief black bikini, she brushed her hair back, a naughty smile on her face. "I suppose if I were coy or shy, I wouldn't tell you how long I've waited for this."

He lounged against the doorjamb. "I don't think either word's in your vocabulary."

"I've wanted you for a long time, McMillian." Her hands moved up to untie the string top. She caught it with one hand before it fell away. "Thought about you. Dreamed about you. Fantasized about you."

What man didn't want to hear that from a woman? She let the scrap of fabric fall to the floor. He sucked in a breath, riveted to the beautiful roundness of her breasts, cinnamon nipples tight and puckered. He dragged his gaze up to hers. "Were you thinking of me when you bought the toys?"

"What do you think?" Her sultry laugh tickled his ears, resonated through him, ended in a rush of sensory stimulation.

"I sure as hell hope so."

Her hands slid to the bikini bottoms, fingers tucking inside the waistband. "Were you thinking of me when you found them?"

"Most definitely."

She inched the waistband down, wiggling her slim hips a little. "Too bad I didn't bring them tonight."

He rubbed a finger over his lips, every cell tensed with anticipation. The images of her pleasuring herself in his bed, while he rubbed oil into her skin, flared in his head. Arousal settled in a heavy weight below his belt. "Would you have put on a show for me, Cee?"

"Would that turn you on, McMillian?" The bottoms moved lower, giving him a glimpse of blonde curls between her thighs. A tiny tattoo lurked above those curls, a design in blue and black he couldn't quite make out. "Does watching do it for you?"

"You're doing it for me right now, sweetheart."

The black fabric slithered to the floor and she straightened, meeting his eyes boldly. He let his gaze trail over her—the graceful line of her shoulders, high breasts, the gentle curve of her waist and hips, the lean muscles of her thighs and calves, pretty toes tipped in gleaming pink polish.

She made no move to cover herself, but stood still under his visual exploration. "Like what you see?"

"As I said, you're incredible." His voice emerged a hoarse rasp. He lifted his gaze to hers. "Beautiful."

Tossing her hair behind her shoulders, she turned her back on him and sauntered the few steps to his bed. He watched the play of muscle in her buttocks and thighs as she climbed onto the mattress and lay back on the pile of pillows in a centerfold pose. She patted the bed beside her and slanted a flirtatious look at him from beneath her lashes. "So, McMillian, what's your wildest fantasy?"

ଚ

Her hands shook, nerves jumping wildly throughout her entire being.

Jessica jammed her arms into her light jacket. Her ballet flats skidded on the foyer's polished tile and she grabbed for the wall to steady herself. Her keys clattered at her feet and she sucked in a long breath. She needed to calm down. Panicking would get her nowhere. For all she knew, he didn't even know yet, hadn't seen what she'd done.

Everything was going to be just fine. She'd see Tom, tell him about the baby, give him her version of events.

Considering who and what she was handing him on a goddamn silver platter, she damn well expected him to be generous with an offer of immunity too.

She lowered to an awkward squat to grab her keys. She took another long breath, calming the apprehension twisting her gut. Trying to laugh off her worries, she smoothed her hair and swung the door open.

Oh God. The oxygen whooshed from her lungs in a muffled moan.

He stood on her doorstep, a malevolent smile curling his hard mouth. "Hello, Jessie."

She took a step back. The keys bit into her palm and bile pushed into her throat. "You—"

"Going somewhere?" He stepped inside, and when she caught sight of the two men behind him, her stomach revolted.

She spun. Her shoes slid on the floor again and a sinewy hand grabbed her arm, shoved her into the wall. The skin split on her cheekbone. Pain shot through her face. Her hand instinctively went to her belly, but he held her too forcefully, keeping her from covering the unborn child.

He pushed her harder against the wall, his mouth close to her ear. Warm breath washed over her neck, a twisted echo of other times she'd been this close to him. She struggled for air, the baby kicking in protest of the tight compression of her womb. He chuckled and nausea churned in her gut.

"Did you really think I'd let you screw me over, Jessie?" He coiled her arm up behind her back, darts of agony shooting along her nerves. She whimpered, his hips pressed against her buttocks, the solid wall of his chest preventing her from moving, from fighting, from escaping. He pushed her arm higher. She felt a tearing at her shoulder, and pain flooded her. He shoved harder. "Did you?"

"P-please," she said, her voice a harsh whisper. Panic sizzled in her, dots dancing at the edges of her vision. Her lungs clawed for oxygen. "The baby—"

"Oh, don't you worry your pretty little head about the baby, Jessie," he murmured, dragging his tongue down her neck in a mockery of former caresses. "What do you think we came for?"

𐆜

"Oh, I think this ranks right up there."

McMillian's raspy voice filtered through the rush of blood in Celia's ears. Maybe he hadn't been able to tell her legs shook from anxiety, that she'd had to push the outrageous words through trembling lips.

The burn of his gaze on her set off a different tremor within her body, a vibrating expectancy that bubbled and fizzed along her veins.

Make them come to you.

She lifted her arms and spread her hair over his pillows, aware the movement thrust her hardened nipples higher. His harsh indrawn breath tickled her ears, heightened the excitement pulsing low in her belly. Every nerve throbbed with increased sensitivity—the soft sheets an unbearable abrasion along her skin, the air a chilly kiss where her damp suit had been, the sound of his ragged breathing a rough caress over her whole body.

She ached for him, for his touch, for the hardness of him inside her.

If she was this aroused already, one touch of those strong hands and she'd come apart.

He rested a forearm along the doorjamb, his posture relaxed and negligent. "Close your eyes."

She levered up on her elbows. Her hair, damp at the ends, danced over her shoulders. "What?"

"Close your eyes." He pushed away from the door and tugged the white polo over his head. It hit the floor in a soft rustle. He settled into the chair sitting at an angle to the bed and folded his arms behind his head. Muscles tautened in his upper arms. The shark smile appeared once more. "You asked me what my wildest fantasy was. I want to watch you, Cee."

The words kicked her in the abdomen, driving the air from her lungs. A thrill traveled through her, the pulsating ache between her thighs growing stronger. The tip of her tongue darted out to moisten dry lips. "McMillian—"

"Close your eyes. Pretend I'm not here. Show me what happened when you were fantasizing about me."

Her lids fluttered down, and she drew in a deep breath. She'd never felt like this with anyone before—exposed, vulnerable, titillated.

Aware of his soft breathing, she rubbed her hands over her arms, smoothing away a rash of chill bumps. Pretend he wasn't there. Build a fantasy. She smiled, conjuring up images on the back of her eyelids. *His office and that big mahogany desk. His tall frame dressed for court, the impeccable dark suit, the blue tie that brightened his gaze to cerulean. She paused in his doorway, watching him.*

God, she wanted him. Wanted his hands and mouth on her. Wanted him filling her emptiness, over and over. Wanted him to take her, to claim her, to make her scream.

Her palms drifted up her arms to her shoulders, across her clavicle in a feathery caress. Heaviness grew in her breasts, the nipples tightening further, and liquid pressure pooled in her belly.

He looked up, catching her gaze on him. His eyes darkened and he beckoned her inside. She closed the door.

Her fingers spread over her throat, stroking the skin, savoring the heavy thud at her pulse point.

No words passed between them. She slid off her jacket, unbuttoned her blouse as she approached him. He rose, his features rigid with sudden lust. She left the blouse on, merely pushed it open, her breasts pressing against the soft lace bra, straining against the confinement. She rested her ass against the desk; he leaned over her, a hand on either side.

The excitement pulsed, throbbed, threatened. She smoothed her hands down to her breasts, imagining *his* palms cupping the sides, hefting, shaping, stroking. *Pulling the cups down so he could thumb the hardened tips.*

Sensation arced from her nipples straight to her core as she rolled and pinched the stiff flesh, imagining his mouth, his teeth closing over them. A smothered moan slipped past her lips. She arched, seeking the moist touch of her fantasy lover.

She let one hand drift lower, over the tremulous muscles of her abdomen, and pictured a large hand stroking up her thigh, edging beneath her skirt. Her legs shook and she spread them wider, air rushing over her aching flesh.

Her fingers delved through silky curls, anticipation hovering. She smoothed the skin of her thigh, her other hand pressing harder at her breasts, scraping a thumbnail over a nipple, circling an aureole.

She envisioned leaning back on his desk, neat files hitting the floor, voices passing in the hall, the threat of discovery heightening her passion. *Strong fingers burned into her thighs, a hot, wet mouth tugged at her breast.*

Head thrown back on a groan, she cupped the heat between her legs. She was wet, open, ready for him, only him. The first touch shot sensation through her, a minitremor of what was to come.

With his fingers moving over her, pressing in exactly the right places, circling, stroking, pushing, she reached for his belt, unzipped his fly. He was hard and heavy in her hand, and thrills zinged through her. On the desk, she opened wider for him, leaned back on her hands. He loomed over her, stroked her once more before driving into her. His mouth took her startled moan.

Rustling cloth, the crinkle of cellophane and a harsh hiss tried to penetrate the buzz of stimulation holding her prisoner. Her fingers pressed harder into her slippery folds, the first contractions setting off in her belly, radiating out in an intense pressure. She moaned, embracing the initial flutter of her orgasm.

The bed dipped, strong hands circled her wrists and brought them above her head, a knee nudged her thighs wider. Her lashes flew up and she glimpsed his face, flushed with male excitement, eyes glittering. The reality meshed with her fantasy, the orgasm barreling through her body, her chest heaving beneath him.

"Close them," he muttered. She complied, unable to resist, and he entered her with a hard thrust. She screamed, the sensation too much as he drove high inside her, pushing her up toward a second climax.

He filled her, hips pressing hers into the bed, fingers biting into her wrists. She arched, wanting more of the pistoning hardness, breasts rubbing the stone wall of his chest.

His teeth grazed her throat, his harsh breathing rushing over her ear. The soft slap of their bodies together filled the air and she lifted her hips to meet his pounding thrusts. Electricity arced from the contact, pressure building in her womb.

"My God," he groaned, the words tense and gritty. "You're so fucking tight, Cee."

She flexed her wrists within his grasp, pushing into him. Her body stretched around him, the sensation of fullness exquisite, but not enough. "Harder. I want you harder."

He slammed into her, the base of his erection pushing against her sensitized clit. "Is that what you want, Cee?"

"Yes." Her head tossed on the pillow, her body seeking release from the incredible weight within her. Their bodies slid together, slick with sweat, his chest rubbing over her breasts. He bit her shoulder and she gasped. "Oh, yes."

He drove into her harder, higher, his torso heavy against her. "Open your eyes."

Her lashes lifted, and she stared into his face, the skin tight over his high cheekbones. His eyes shone with a predatory triumph and the aching flutters began deep inside her. "McMillian—"

"Come for me, Cee. Now."

She arched into him, the climax slamming through her. Her eyes slid closed, the pleasure so intense it bordered on pain. Above her, he stiffened, thrusting deeper, a guttural groan falling on her ears.

Slowly, she came back to herself, lying limp and boneless beneath his weight. Aftershocks of continued pleasure thrummed through her body. Collapsed against her, he gasped for breath and finally released her wrists. She lifted a heavy hand and smoothed her palm down his damp back.

He laughed and buried his face against her throat. "I'm too old to be doing this. Too much of that and you'll kill me."

She smiled, threading her fingers through his crisp hair, tracing the edge of his slightly receded hairline. "What a way to go, huh?"

Lifting his head, he planted his elbows on either side of her, rubbing a thumb over her cheekbone. "Hot damn, Celia, what the hell was that fantasy about?"

She laughed and wrapped her arms around him, pressing her body along his, loving the feel of his hot skin. "I'll show you sometime."

Nuzzling her jaw, he blew out a long breath and relaxed. "Sounds good to me."

Her hand drifted down his back, following the dimpled line of his spine, lingering at the indention above his buttocks. She sighed and let her eyes drift shut on a wave of lazy contentment. When was the last time she'd felt this attracted to a man? There'd been none of the usual awkwardness between first-time lovers. She fit with him, in a way she hadn't experienced before.

He ran his palms down her arms. "I may not ever get enough of this."

Some of her well-being dissipated. She stilled beneath him, his weight a burden now rather than a pleasure. Of course, this wasn't going to last. They'd agreed to explore the attraction. Once it wore off, they'd go their separate ways.

Shifting, she gently pushed him to one side. He rolled to his back, closing his eyes on a humming exhalation. The picture of pure male satisfaction. A chill washed over her with the rush of cool air on her bare skin.

She tunneled a hand through her tousled hair. "I should get dressed and head home."

His eyes jerked open and his head came off the pillow. "What?"

Stupidly aware of her nudity now, after the way she'd displayed herself for him earlier, she slid from the bed and gathered her bikini. "You have meetings tomorrow, right?"

"Yes." He sat up, seeming unconcerned with his own naked state as he dispensed with the condom. She glanced away and stepped into the skimpy bikini bottoms. Her stomach tightened, a shadow of coldness working its way down her spine. "But it's early. You don't have to go yet."

She fastened her top and adjusted it over her breasts. "I still have some research to do."

"Celia, wait." Cloth moved behind her. She reached for her shorts and warm hands settled on her waist. With gentle pressure, he turned her to face him. A scowl slashed between his brows. "What's going on?"

She shook her hair away from her face. "Nothing. I have a ton of records to finish going through. Is that a problem?"

"No." His mouth drew into a taut line. "I just thought...never mind."

"Dinner was wonderful." She forced a smile, hiding the emptiness coiling around her heart. What had she expected? That something special would bloom from what was basically meaningless agreed-upon sex? Please. That was the furthest thing from either of their minds and she had no reason to feel shortchanged. "And dessert was fantastic."

"That it was." His face relaxed and he leaned in, brushing his mouth over hers. Her traitorous body insisted on leaning into him too. Her nose prickled; she could smell her scent on his skin, mingled with his male sweat and lingering chlorine. She blinked and shot a look at the bed. This was the first kiss they'd shared since the passionate interlude in his pool. What had taken place in his bed had involved only their bodies. She shivered.

He ran a hand down her arm. "When can I see you again?"

She stepped away. "Nine o'clock tomorrow morning."

"Funny. That's not exactly what I had in mind."

Make them come to you. She needed to keep this on her terms. If he held too much control, she'd end up hurting— badly. She reached up and patted his jaw. "You made the first move, McMillian. Second one's mine."

Tom poured a couple fingers of Scotch and carried it to the glass wall at the back of the house. Lights from other homes glimmered on the lake and a boat trawled a lazy route through the water. The view defined peace and contentment.

Exactly what he should be feeling after that mind-blowing interlude with Celia.

Instead, a vague dissatisfaction skulked in his gut and he really wanted to punch something. He lifted the glass, the alcohol burning a trail to his stomach. The sex had been incredible.

And that's all it had been: sex. All he'd expected, a fulfillment of the attraction between them. Watching her, feeling her close about him at the height of her climax, had been a living fantasy.

Why wasn't it enough? He wanted more from her, but he wasn't sure what.

Maybe not being in such a hurry to get dressed and leave

his bed? He hadn't expected her to stay the night, wasn't sure he'd have wanted that, but she'd certainly hit the floor running. She'd left him with the distinct impression it had been a case of wham-bam-thank-you-Tom.

He felt used, probably like Cook's one-night stands did the morning after. She'd been every guy's dream, and instead of being suffused with male satisfaction, he was pissed as hell.

So she thought the next move was hers? Eyes narrowed, he tossed off the remainder of his Scotch.

Hardly.

Celia St. John had a lot to learn about him.

Chapter Six

Pain filled Tom's senses, the metallic tang of blood hanging heavy around him. Darkness closed in, his lungs clawing for oxygen. Stabbing agony tore through his abdomen.

He wakened, a harsh groan strangling in his throat. He sat up and tossed the twisted sheets aside. A lingering trace of Celia's scent drifted up and he dragged in a deep breath, letting the lush memory of her body's pleasures soothe away the remnants of his nightmare. Rubbing a hand over his hair, he pushed up from the bed. A couple of miles on the treadmill would erase the persistent anxiety from his mind.

Maybe it would help him lose the memory of Celia rushing from his bed.

He tugged on shorts and a T-shirt, added his running shoes and grabbed the cordless phone on his way to the spare bedroom. Setting the treadmill for a brisk pace, he punched in the code to access his voice mail. He deleted the first message, a telemarketing pitch from his credit-card company. The second was a hang-up. Unease traveled over his spine, images from his dream flashing in his mind. Shaking his head, he tucked the phone into a nook on the treadmill display. Nightmares, shivers over a damn wrong number. Obviously, he'd been working too hard. Maybe he should arrange for some time off, take a minivacation.

Maybe he could convince Celia to tag along.

One of those three-day cruises out of Mobile to Mexico could be nice. Warm sand, blue ocean, Celia in that black bikini.

Celia in his stateroom, naked, sunlight spilling over her smooth skin and shining hair.

A different shiver moved over him, arousal firing to life low in his gut. He smiled. Somehow he needed to persuade her to go ahead and make that second move she was so determined to have.

"So how was it?"

Celia groaned and buried her head under her arms. "Cis, it's too early."

"It's after six." The bed dipped under her sister's weight. Celia curled into a tighter ball. Maybe if she just ignored Cicely, she'd take a hint. Cicely patted her shoulder. "Come on. I brought coffee."

Aware she couldn't avoid the interrogation, Celia flopped over and stared at her ceiling. A pleasurable lethargy gripped her body and a feminine ache lingered between her thighs. She closed her eyes and rubbed a hand over them. All the symptoms of a woman who'd been well-made-love-to.

No. That hadn't been lovemaking. Everything that had happened between her and McMillian could be defined as pure sex.

"Cee?" Cicely nudged her knee. "You didn't answer the question."

With a heavy exhalation, Celia pushed up against the pillows and reached for the coffee mug. "It was fantastic."

Her face troubled, Cicely pleated the comforter between her

fingers. "You don't sound happy about that."

"What's not to be happy about?" Celia buried her nose in the mug, inhaling the strong aroma and taking a long sip. Her stomach compressed into a quivering knot of anxiety. Was she making a mistake, indulging in this affair?

"I don't want to see you hurt."

"I'm a big girl. I know what I'm doing."

"Do you really?" Sadness flickered in Cicely's pale green eyes. "Don't you think Mama told herself that every time?"

Anger churned in Celia and she set the mug aside. "I'm not Mama."

"I didn't say you were."

"This isn't the same thing. I'm not looking for promises of love or forever. McMillian's not that kind of guy." How could he be? She'd seen the way he'd looked at Kathleen. He still had issues there. Expecting anything from him was a sure ticket to heartbreak. Expecting anything from any man was. She'd learned that priceless little tidbit the hard way. "And I'm not that kind of girl."

Definitely not after Brian Turello had damn near ruined her career.

Not to mention her life.

"Cee, I wish you'd—"

"I need to shower." Celia pushed the comforter aside and slid from the bed. "Thanks for the coffee."

"Cee?"

Cicely's tentative voice stopped her at the bathroom door. Celia glanced at her sister over her shoulder. Uncertainty lingered in the sea green of Cicely's eyes; concern tightened the line of her mouth.

"Please be careful."

Celia smiled, her face aching with the stiff expression. "Of course. Don't worry about me."

She showered and dressed, ate a quick breakfast and arrived at the office an hour before it opened. McMillian's Mercedes already sat in its spot, and combined unease and anticipation rolled over already sensitized nerves. Alone in the office with him. That could definitely be a blessing or a curse.

No way could she go in his office, not after that fantasy last night. She'd be ready to carry it out. God, her learning curve must be huge—she wanted him as much this morning as she had last night, despite the potential for hurt. She'd act like it was any other morning, bypass his office, go directly to her own, finish going through the database of birth records.

His office door stood closed. She eased down the hall, feeling like a teenager trying to sneak past vigilant parents. Ridiculous. They'd agreed to leave the affair outside the office. She could do that.

With a deep breath, she immersed herself in the paper trail.

Minutes later, her office door closed with a soft click. She glanced up, her stomach flip-flopping. McMillian leaned against the door—wearing his dark suit and that damned blue tie. The man must be able to read her mind.

She tapped her pen on the blotter. "Good morning."

He nodded, tilted his head and studied her. She stared back. How many times had she seen him use that particular trick on a recalcitrant witness? Laughter bubbled in her throat. She'd faced down a drugged-out thug with a knife, without backup. Did he really think his prosecutor's stare would get to her?

With a shrug, she dropped her gaze to the records. She heard him move, the whisper of his suit as he came to stand behind her. The subtle scent of his aftershave, something clean and woodsy, enveloped her. A strong hand appeared on either side of her, flat on the desk. Excitement fluttered in her belly and a sweet ache throbbed lower in the secret places he'd delved into the night before.

"What are you doing?" The warm rush of his breath, a blend of mint and coffee, stirred the hair beside her ear.

"Going through birth records." At least her voice remained steady. She kept her hands in her lap.

He chuckled, a deep, throaty sound. "Last night was incredible."

"I thought we were keeping this out of the office."

"We are." His mouth moved closer to her ear. "I'm not touching you."

She laughed. Twisting, she looked into his eyes. A devilish gleam lurked in the blue depths and her breath caught. Relaxed, playful, he was amazingly handsome. Amazingly sexy. "I think that's a technicality."

His gaze dipped to her mouth. "I'm a lawyer. I live for technicalities."

A smile curved her lips. "Of course. How silly of me."

He crooked a finger at her. "If you moved just an inch or so this way, we could call that the second move you're so determined to have."

Oh, he was smooth. She leaned forward, paused and pulled back. "Don't think so, Counselor. I had something a little different in mind."

"Really?" A slanted smile quirked at his mouth. "And I suppose I have to wait for tonight to find out what that is?"

She couldn't resist a teasing jab. "Patience, McMillian. Didn't we establish that good things came to those who—"

"Make them happen." He pressed in, feathering his mouth

over hers. Their lips met, clung. He pulled back, rubbing his thumb over the corner of her mouth. "Now it's a good morning."

Her skin jumping with the passion he'd wakened with one simple kiss, she flattened a hand against his chest. "You must get out of here. I have work to do and you're a major distraction."

With an easy laugh, he straightened and walked to the door. "I'll leave you to it, then."

"Great. I'll just sit here and keep running into dead ends." She looked up at his wide shoulders. "McMillian?"

At the door, he stopped. "Yes?"

She swallowed. "I can't promise you closure on this case. There are too many unknowns and too few leads, and if those fingerprints don't kick something back to us, I'm afraid it's going to go cold."

The corner of his mouth turned up, his face softening. "Celia, there's no doubt in my mind you can do this."

The door closed behind him. She stared at it. She was glad one of them was so confident.

"I have something."

Celia's excited voice pulled Tom from the disclosure statement he was drafting. He glanced up, pinching the bridge of his nose. Nagging pain sat between his eyes, a holdover from a restless night, his attempts at sleep disturbed by those weird and violent dreams. The best part of his day had been that swift kiss between them, blocking out the tension and pain for a few seconds.

"What?"

She waved a paper at him. A flush highlighted her cheekbones and her eyes shone with enthusiasm. "A couple

117

from Cader County applied for a homebirth certificate at the beginning of the week. They didn't have the witness affidavit and when the clerk followed up, they told her they wouldn't need the certificate after all."

He lifted his brows. "Any reason why?"

"No." She shrugged. "Anyway, I'm going to run over and interview them. I might take Cook with me—"

"I'll go with you."

She gestured at the papers spread across his desk. "You're busy."

"It can wait." He slid on his jacket. "As long as I'm back by one to make the county-commission meeting."

"If you're sure."

He resisted the urge to roll his eyes. "I'm sure. I want to hear what they have to say and having the local prosecutor with you might be helpful. Let's go."

She folded her arms. "Did anyone ever point out that you're a bossy son of a bitch?"

A laugh rumbled up from his chest. "A tough one, too. Come on."

His hand at the small of her back, he ushered her from the room. While she retrieved her bag from her office, he left instructions with his assistant.

Outside, Celia jingled her keys at him. "I'm driving."

His stomach dropped into the pit of his belly. A tremor worked down his spine, a montage of images flashing in his head—a screech of tires and metal, broken glass, blood marring Celia's face. His footing fumbled on the last step and she put out a hand to steady him.

"McMillian?" Concern coated her voice.

He shook his head, heat flooding his face and neck. Icy

beads of sweat popped out on his upper lip. "I'm fine. Let's take my car. I'll drive."

"But I—"

"I said I'll drive."

She stared at him and his skin crawled. Slowly, she tucked her keys away. "Okay. Whatever you want."

Feeling foolish, he followed her to his car. Without speaking, she slid into the passenger seat and fastened her belt.

He flexed his hands on the wheel. "I'm sorry. I shouldn't have snapped at you."

She shot him a glance, a wistful expression darkening her eyes. "You're a hard man to figure out, McMillian."

Shifting gears, he backed out. "You can call me Tom, you know."

Especially after last night.

She blinked and reached down to adjust her skirt. "I don't think of you as Tom."

He slanted a sardonic smile in her direction. "Don't you think you should?"

Under her suit jacket, her shoulders moved in a careless shrug. "I never really considered it. I mean, we agreed this wouldn't last and we'll go back to our professional relationship. Why change the way I address you?"

One night and she was already looking for the end. The realization caused irritation to flow through him. "That doesn't mean you can't call me by name."

"I do call you by name." She looked his way and he caught a glimpse of confusion in her eyes. "What's the difference?"

He braked for the traffic light at Highway 19. "How would you feel if I called you St. John all the time?"

She laughed. "In case you hadn't noticed, most people I know do."

Because they were all damn cops. Why was he making such a big deal of this? It didn't matter what she called him. Except her addressing him by his last name didn't set him apart from the other men she knew, and when she did it, he couldn't forget what she was.

A cop.

He'd sworn, never again. Maybe it was stupid, but it was the way he felt. He couldn't live with another woman who turned her emotions on and off like a tap.

But that excuse was a load of bullshit, because he wouldn't be living with Celia. This wasn't a long-term arrangement. Hell, it didn't even qualify as a relationship. He was tying himself in knots for nothing.

They left town behind, farmland opening up around them. His car hugged the road, zipping around curves and snapping along the straightaways. Celia remained silent, staring out the window, her fingers stroking over the silver chain at her neck.

He darted a glance at her, his gaze dropping to her waist. What was she wearing beneath the gray suit? The belly chain? Silk or lace?

The heavy, putrid odor of chicken barns came in through the air vents, permeating the interior. Celia wrinkled her nose. "I hate that smell."

"Doesn't everyone?" Tom downshifted as the minivan in front of him slowed to take the hairpin "S" curves before Stocks Dairy Road.

She rubbed at the end of her nose. "I wonder if the chicken farmers get used to it?"

The ping of her cell phone forestalled his reply. She pulled it from her waist. "St. John."

A long pause, and she darted a glance at him. "On my way to Cader County with McMillian. Sure. I can do that. Do me a favor, would you? Call over to Moultrie and check on our fingerprints again. Remind Whitlock that he owes me. Thanks."

She folded the phone. Tom gripped the wheel tighter. "Let me guess who that was."

"Why do you dislike him so much?"

He hadn't, not until this case. Thinking about the motive behind his sudden aversion to Mark Cook wasn't something he really wanted to do. He rolled tense shoulders. "Maybe I don't like the way he looks at you."

She laughed. "How would that be?"

"The guy's a sleaze."

"He's a damn good cop."

"And that makes everything okay? What he does personally doesn't matter, as long as he's good on the job? God, I hate the way you compartmentalize your lives."

She fixed a cool look on him. "Kathleen Harding really did a number on you, didn't she?"

His stomach folded as if she'd punched him. "We are not talking about my ex-wife."

"Oh, that's right." She tapped a slender finger against her temple, her tone sharp. "We're not going to have that kind of relationship. Talking about our pasts is unimportant."

"Cut it out, Celia." The minivan drifted across the centerline. The driver, just visible through tinted windows, glanced over her shoulder, perhaps seeking something on the back seat. "Anything that happened with me and Kathleen has nothing to do with us."

"That's right. Because we're all about the sex. That means

there is no 'us'." She narrowed her eyes at him. "Did you hate her career that much?"

"I don't give a good damn about her career." He lifted his foot from the gas as the minivan slowed once more, approaching the crossroads ahead. "Can we drop this?"

Celia lifted a hand. "Consider it gone."

He blew out a long breath. "Damn it, I should have stayed in the office."

Her eyes narrowed further, thinning to glittering slits. "It's not too late to turn around."

He didn't miss her double meaning. Frustrated, he jerked his gaze back to the road. From the right, an unloaded chicken truck rumbled toward the crossroads. Tom frowned. The guy was taking his sweet time about slowing for the stop sign.

"McMillian." Celia's hand fluttered over his biceps. His gut tensed.

"Shit." He grabbed for the gearshift, hit the brakes.

"Oh God." Her panicked voice filled his ears.

The truck blew by the stop sign, barreled into the intersection.

Celia screamed.

Adrenaline pulsed under Celia's skin, an uncomfortable wave that quickened her pulse and shortened her breath.

"Oh my God," she whispered, fumbling with her seatbelt, her gaze trained on the crumpled minivan, its front end crushed against a small stand of trees. Finally free of the restraint, she pushed the door open, barely waiting for McMillian to get the Mercedes to a complete stop on the shoulder. "Call 911."

He unfolded from the driver's seat, already punching in numbers on his cell. She paused at the edge of the blacktop, assessing the scene, letting her training settle the tension and lingering sense of panic. The trailer lay across the road, bent cages scattered in every direction. Steam and smoke drifted lazily from the metal accordion of the van. Gas and diesel fumes mixed with the acrid smell of electrical circuits shorting.

She glanced over her shoulder at McMillian, phone at his ear. "If you have hazard cones, put them out. And stay here. I'm going to check the victims."

"Celia, wait." He caught her arm, his gaze sweeping over the van and the thickening smoke. "It's dangerous. Wait for the police."

"Don't you get it, McMillian? I am the police."

His hand dropped away and he spoke quickly into the phone, relaying details. She turned to the carnage, but not before catching the expression tightening his face. She jogged across the road and picked her way down the steep incline to the ditch where the van and semi lay.

Coughing from the fumes hanging in the air, she crouched by the van first and peered through the shattered windshield. Blood spattered the interior, and although she didn't have to touch the female driver to know she was dead, she shifted to check the woman's pulse anyway. An infant car seat was wedged behind the front seat, but no cries rose from the wreckage.

She closed her eyes. *No. Please.*

Dark tint and trees kept her from seeing clearly inside the rear of the van. Unable to reach into the backseat, she rose. She had no way of knowing if the van was stable and having it roll over on her, posing a further risk to any child in the car, wasn't an option. The distant cry of sirens filled the air and relief pulsed in her. She stepped over pieces of metal and fiberglass, shattered glass sparkling among the weeds in the ditch. The sirens grew closer, louder.

She looked through the windshield of the semi. The driver, blood trickling from a cut at his temple, slumped over the wheel, but she could see his shoulders moved with regular breaths. Vehicles stopped above her on the road, doors slamming, voices calling instructions and questions.

"Hey, St. John, you okay?" Cook skidded down the incline, a swarm of emergency personnel—firefighters, EMTs, fellow deputies—with him.

"I'm fine." She swiped a loose hank of hair away from her face. Her nerves jumped, a trembling setting into her limbs. She stiffened her spine, rubbed her clammy palms down her hips. "Busted down to traffic detail?"

He shrugged, his gaze moving toward the van. "I was just a couple miles away, en route from Albany."

A pair of EMTs half-jogged, half-slid down the embankment. "What have we got?"

"The van's driver has no pulse. There's an infant seat in the backseat, but I couldn't tell if there was a child. The truck's driver is unconscious, but breathing."

Firefighters assessed the scene, tied the van off with rope secured to nearby trees and opened the semi so an EMT could reach the driver. Another man draped a tarp over the van, hollering that they'd have to cut the driver out.

"What happened?"

Celia dragged her gaze away from the scene. "The semi blew off the stop sign."

His eyes narrowed as he studied the semi. "That's Nate Holton's truck. Son of a bitch was probably drunk. You've got blood on your face."

She swiped at her chin, a tinge of red on her fingers. Pain

stung her skin. "I must have cut myself."

"Come on. They're gonna have to pull a wrecker in here and Parker has this under control." Cook held out a hand as they neared the top of the incline. Her gaze immediately tracked to McMillian, despite the chaos. He stood by the Mercedes, talking to a young deputy who scribbled in a notebook. McMillian looked up, his glacial gaze clashing with hers. He focused on her chin, his posture tightening, and she brushed at the trickle of blood there once more.

Hooking his thumbs in his belt loops as they approached the Mercedes, Cook jerked his chin toward McMillian. "I know you were taking him to Cader County, but I'd like to be there."

She glanced at him, not wanting to deal with the tension between the two men. "McMillian and I can handle it."

"It *is* my case, St. John."

She looked at McMillian once more. He pointed toward the intersection, his face taut. Her stomach flipped. Right now, the last thing she needed was to get back in that car with him and wrangle with more of the mess they'd managed to create between them.

Between them?

Oh hell, who was she kidding? The only thing between them was one sexual interlude and an asinine agreement to explore their attraction. Hadn't their argument before the accident proved that? Sleeping with him hadn't given her entrance into his life on any level.

She'd lost her ever-loving mind. It didn't matter how good it had been or how much she'd enjoyed dinner, seeing him away from the office, the glimpses of the real man she'd gotten. None of it mattered, because it wasn't *real.* It meant nothing. She meant nothing.

Her throat aching, she met Cook's sharp gray eyes. "You're

right," she said. "It's your case. I'll tell McMillian you and I will handle the interview."

Cook nodded. "Sounds good. I think Troy Lee and Parker can deal with this and we can head out for Cader County."

Ignoring the shakiness in her legs, she walked away from him and crossed the road to where McMillian and the deputy stood. Her skin crawled with the aftereffects of adrenaline and she wrapped her arms over her midriff, avoiding catching McMillian's gaze. She didn't want him to see how shaky she felt, how badly the scene in the van had gotten under her skin. She waited until he'd finished his statement before giving her own. Finally, the young officer strode over to talk with the state patrol's accident-reconstruction specialist, who'd just arrived.

McMillian shot a glance at the ditch, where firefighters were using the Jaws of Life to cut away the top of the van. "How are they?"

"Not good." She looked over her shoulder, following his line of sight. Her stomach pitched, images of blood on a shattered windshield stark in her memory. "The driver of the van didn't have a pulse. The truck driver was breathing, but out cold. Cook thinks it's Nate Holton."

His mouth drew into a grim line. "Son of a bitch. Alton Baker should have pulled his license when he got that last DUI instead of slapping his wrist with community service."

She ran her thumb over her necklace. "Cook wants to handle the Cader County interview. I'm going with him, so you're free to head back to town."

If anything, his expression tightened further, into a glower. "I want to see you when you return."

Fury burned her. She was tired of his habit of giving orders and expecting them to be obeyed without question. Fine, he was her boss, but she wasn't a rookie who needed to constantly be told what to do. Hell, right now, she was tired of his ass completely.

Except her throat hurt from a sudden press of tears, and if she relaxed at all, she'd be a shaking mess. A ridiculous urge to throw herself into his arms and hold on to his solid frame, the strength of which she'd experienced the night before, wound through her. The weakness pissed her off even more. He wasn't someone she could depend on. That wasn't part of their deal.

Arms crossed, she tilted her chin. "You have a county-commission meeting and I don't know how long this will take. I'll fill you in tomorrow."

"I have some things to finish up in the office." His voice hardened. "I'll wait for you."

So he could suck her back into a meaningless sexual tryst? So she could toss her self-respect away again? Jesus above, and she'd agreed to it, agreed to his crazy idea of a no-strings affair. Clearly, she'd tossed away her good sense as well.

At least Turello had put a diamond on her finger, prettied up what they were doing with words of love. At least he'd pretended she was worth something to him, even if it had been nothing but lies.

Where McMillian was concerned, she was a warm body, an easy lay, a quick fuck.

A conquest.

Her stomach turned. She glared at him, determined not to show the tears scratching at her eyes. "Don't bother."

She spun and walked away from him.

Damn. Tom took a step forward, anger spurting through him, mixing with the wreck-inspired tension, leaving him jittery and off-kilter. The bright smear of blood on her face had jolted him, made him want to tug her close, run his hands over her, make sure she was all right.

Considering her current mood, good thing he hadn't.

She was pissed at him, but hell if he could figure out why. Because he wouldn't talk about Kathleen with her? She needn't hold her breath, waiting for that. He didn't discuss that particular failure with anyone. Celia's withdrawal, the way she just walked off instead of letting him have it, made him angrier. He wanted to go after her, have her look at him, make her tell him just what the problem was.

He opened his mouth, her name at the tip of his tongue, and closed it with a snap. He'd been here before. *Kathleen, baby, talk to me. Let me hold you. Kathleen, damn it, don't shut me out. Kath, don't go. Don't leave like this. Kathleen, come back to me. Give me another chance. Give us another chance.*

The litany rolled through his brain. He'd opened himself to Kathleen, pleaded with her, begged her, and none of it had made a difference in the end. She'd left him long before she'd divorced him, had basically disappeared from his life the day their son died. The eight years she'd slept in his bed, lived in his house, kept him at arm's length afterwards had meant shit. She'd been his wife and opening himself up, trying to maintain their connection after Everett's death, hadn't been worth anything in the long run.

Doing the same thing with Celia to keep a sexual fling going was insane. As good, as incredible as the sex had been, it wasn't worth this crap.

"Hey, Cookie!" The youngest deputy yelled across the road and Cook glanced around at the nickname. "No kid in the van. Just the driver."

Relief swamped Tom, weakening his legs. *Thank God.* He lowered his head, trying to clear the roar of blood in his ears. He felt used up, worn out. Blowing out a harsh breath, he straightened and glanced around for Celia. Other than that blood-curdling scream when the truck had struck the van, she'd been remarkably composed.

Cold. Removed. The perfect cop.

He watched her talk to Cook across the roof of the unmarked patrol car, her fine features tense and closed. She shook her head at something Cook said, her gaze tangling with his own for a brief moment before she turned away deliberately.

He stiffened his stance. Hell, no, she wasn't worth it. No woman was. His belly, still jumping with stress and anger, tightened to match the weird constriction in his chest. When he saw her again, he'd tell her it was over. He chuckled, a harsh and rusty sound, and turned away to his car as she climbed into the patrol unit with Cook. Like she'd care. It had never meant anything to her anyway.

He'd never meant anything.

Chapter Seven

"My wife is not well." Wesley Campbell didn't step back to allow Celia and Cook entrance into the foyer. "I have no intention of disturbing her."

"I'm sure you can answer our questions." Celia narrowed her eyes at the man framed by the wide oak doorway. At his feet, sunlight glinted off white Italian marble. To match his Italian loafers, she supposed. If the house, his clothes and the expensive import sedan in the driveway were anything to judge by, money wasn't a problem for Mr. and Mrs. Wesley Porter Campbell.

Wesley frowned. "What is this about anyway?"

Beside her, Cook popped his gum. "Earlier in the week, you applied for a certificate for a home birth. Is that why your wife isn't feeling well?"

"Oh, God." Wesley passed a hand over his eyes.

Celia, sensing weakness, pounced. "However, the clerk of court tells us you claimed later you didn't need it. Would you like to explain that?"

He stepped back then. "Maybe you should come inside."

With Cook, she entered the high-ceilinged foyer. Light from a sparkling chandelier dappled the floor. Wesley led the way into a formal living room off the foyer, furnished in rich shades of gold and cream. He crossed to stand at the fireplace, staring at the photos lining the mantel in polished platinum frames.

"So what happened to the baby, Mr. Campbell?" Celia asked, keeping her voice quiet and even.

"We tried for years to get pregnant." Wesley turned, the lines around his mouth and eyes suddenly deeper. "All Ashley wants is a child. She...she has had health issues that kept us from pursuing adoption through a state agency. My father has a rather large farming interest here and he employs a number of migrant workers. One of the girls...she said she didn't want the baby, and Ashley was so desperate. I paid for her medical care, paid *her...*"

His voice trailed away and Celia glanced at Cook, his sharp gaze trained on the other man. "And?"

A shuddering sigh shook Wesley's frame. "She changed her mind. Took the baby and ran off to north Florida, where her mother lives, her roommate says. So we didn't need the birth certificate after all. Ashley...Ashley hasn't gotten out of bed since Wednesday."

Cook folded his arms over his chest, department polo straining against his biceps. "You can't buy a baby, Mr. Campbell. It's against the law."

Wesley's entire face went taut, an ugly light entering his eyes. "We'd have given that baby everything. What kind of life can she offer her?"

Shaking his head, Cook pulled his notebook from his pocket. "We'll need the roommate's name and address."

He scribbled as Wesley rattled off the information. When he was finished, he lifted his head. "Just out of curiosity, what's the going rate for a healthy infant these days?"

A flush spread over Wesley's cheekbones. "I've told you what you wanted to know. I'd like you both to leave now."

Outside, Celia glanced back at the imposing brick façade of the Georgian design. "Did you believe him?"

Cook snorted. "Not enough that I'm not going to check out every aspect of his story. Did you hear him? He actually believes there's nothing wrong with what he did."

She pulled open the passenger door. "What do you do when the kid gets older? How do you tell her she was bought and paid for?"

Cook shook his head. "He said 'her'. The baby they were going to purchase was a girl."

"So was our Baby Doe."

He fired the engine. "He'd better hope his story checks out."

She'd had blood on her face.

Tom leaned against the wall outside the conference room in the chamber of commerce building. He couldn't shake that vision—Celia, cold, composed, blood trickling from a small cut on her chin. If they'd been a few seconds sooner, if they'd been ahead of the van, it could have been so much worse.

If they hadn't had that stupid argument over who was driving.

A disagreement he'd instigated because of another vision—pictures of blood and Celia's face, crumpled metal—tumbling through his head as they left the office.

He shuddered. A coincidence. It didn't mean anything. None of it did—the flashes of foreboding, the images, the dreams, the fantasies. If it meant anything at all, it was the fact he was working too hard again.

The impulse he'd had to take control, to drive, was just that, a weird urge that had ultimately worked in his favor. In Celia's favor. He stiffened, tension creeping up his neck. No more thinking about her. No more thinking about the odd flickers of awareness and compulsions that had been part of him forever.

He stared at the new carpet under his shoes, tracing the golden curlicues in the hunter green background. His vision blurred and he blinked, fighting off the questions and guilt he knew were coming. The what-ifs that had damned his entire adult life.

What if he hadn't let Kathleen sleep that morning?

What if he'd turned back at the door to check on Everett?

What if he'd blown off the fact he was running late for class?

What if he'd given in to the sense of foreboding and walked back to the nursery, lifted his sleeping son, woken him?

Irritated, he ran a hand over his eyes, pinched the bridge of his nose. He couldn't change any of that. If-onlys didn't do anything but make a man crazy. They weren't good enough for a judge or jury. He dealt in facts and the facts were easy. His son was dead. He hadn't been enough for Kathleen. She was out of his life forever. He was alone.

The absolute rightness of having Celia wrapped around him filtered through him and he straightened with a muttered oath. Having sex with Celia St. John didn't change his reality and had probably been his most asinine decision to date. She hadn't been able to get away from him fast enough, last night or this morning.

Hell, he wasn't enough for her either.

"Tom." Rhett's voice cut through his reverie and he looked up. Rhett watched him, his ebony gaze inquisitive. A wave of heat flushed Tom's neck. How many times had the ADA called him, anyway?

Tom cleared his throat. "Yes?"

Rhett jerked a thumb over his shoulder. "Meeting's cancelled. Bob Harrell's daughter-in-law was killed in that accident this morning. He's gone to be with his son."

"Damn." The ache between his eyes pulsed, and Tom pinched his nose again. Harrell, the county-commission chairman, was a good man, who'd recently celebrated the birth of his first grandchild. Tom hated that the morning's carnage affected his family. Or any family.

He lifted his head to focus on Rhett. "We're going to make sure Nate Holton is prosecuted to the fullest extent of the law. We need to put a bug in Judge Baker's ear about not letting him off with that 'time served' bullshit again too."

With his usual wolfish smile, Rhett tilted his head toward the end of the hallway. "Here he comes. Tell him yourself."

Tom turned. Alton Baker strode toward them, his fat county-commission folder under his arm. "A word, Your Honor?"

Baker stopped, his eyes keen in his gaunt features. "Of course, Mr. McMillian."

"You heard about Amanda Harrell?"

"I did." Baker lifted his chin.

"If you'd followed the sentencing guidelines the last two times Nate Holton was in your courtroom, maybe she'd still be alive."

Baker's mouth tightened. "I hardly think how I run my court is any of your concern."

"Somehow, I think your constituents would disagree."

"Be careful, Mr. McMillian. Remember you have to stand before my bench on a regular basis."

"Is that a threat, Your Honor?"

A feral smile spread over Baker's mouth. "It's whatever you want it to be, Mr. McMillian. Let's just call it a friendly reminder. Good day, gentlemen."

"The sheriff's in the squad room. He said to go on back."

Tom pushed aside the swinging half-door and strode down the hall until it opened into the department's day room. He stopped short at the doorway. Sheriff Stanton Reed leaned against the counter running along one wall, a coffee mug cradled in one hand. With him was Jason Harding, sheriff of neighboring Haynes County.

Not to mention Kathleen's new husband, father of the baby she carried.

Ignoring the burning tightness in his chest, Tom nodded at both men but focused on Reed. "Sheriff."

"Hey, McMillian, take a look." Reed waved his free hand at the small television taking up one corner of the counter. "Your girl made the news."

His girl? What the hell? Tom advanced to stand beside Reed. The television displayed the midafternoon news break. On the screen, Celia, in her gray suit and with a small bandage on her chin, answered a blond reporter's questions about their Baby Girl Doe.

Reed clapped him on the shoulder. "Gotta love that even though it's our investigation, they're interviewing your investigator."

Tom shook his head as Celia offered a sincere smile and noncommittal answers as the reporter continued probing. "She's not my anything. She merely works for my office."

Merely. He ran a hand along his jaw. Who was he kidding? She was the best damn investigator he'd ever seen—cool, thorough, professional. She was a beautiful, intelligent woman. And as a lover...hot damn. He couldn't begin to describe her.

He narrowed his eyes. It wasn't enough. He wanted more than her body. All the interlude had done was whet his appetite. He wanted to separate the woman from the cop, to figure out who she really was. He wanted to know what caused the flashes of sadness he saw in her eyes sometimes, what lay at the end of that silver chain and why she so rarely took it off. He wanted to know why law enforcement and why his office. Above all, he wanted to know why some lucky guy hadn't snapped her up a long time ago.

Oh hell, he was in deep shit.

"I'm trying my best to steal her away from you, McMillian."

At Harding's amused drawl, his head snapped up. He glared at the younger man, the one wearing Kathleen's wide band on his finger. "What the hell are you talking about?"

Harding motioned between himself and Reed. "Actually we're both trying to snag her to fill investigative openings. She's not biting, though."

Tom's gaze drifted back to the television, but the story had shifted to the state lottery's record-breaking worth. He relaxed his jaw. "Give it your best shot, Harding. I don't own her."

Instead of replying, Harding glanced at his watch. "Shoot, I've got to get moving. Kathleen's appointment is in ten minutes. She'll kill me if I'm late."

Tom blew out a long breath and let Reed's teasing rejoinder wash over him. He had to let go of all this damn resentment. He wanted Kathleen to be happy, didn't he? Even if he'd always expected her to come back, to be happy with him.

"So what did you want, Counselor?" Reed lifted the coffee carafe and Tom waved the offer away. He'd made the mistake of accepting once.

"I was checking in on Nate Holton's arrest status." Tom briefly outlined his conversation with Alton Baker.

Reed grimaced. "Son of a bitch needs to do some time. It's not like anything else has changed his behavior. His daddy's not around anymore to bail him out and I can tell you his sister's damn sure not going to."

"Good." Tom nodded. "Make sure I get a copy of the accident-reconstruction team's report and Holton's blood test results from the hospital."

"Will do."

Outside, Tom exchanged greetings with a couple of deputies entering the department. He paused at the foot of the steps, his gaze caught by a familiar flash of coppery hair. Down the street, Kathleen stood, her arm linked with Harding's, gesturing as she talked to a brunette in a somber suit. As he watched, his ex-wife squeezed Harding's arm and smiled up at him before laughing.

Tom wrapped a hand around the railing, his knuckles aching. He'd never made her smile like that, not even in the early days of their marriage. He swallowed. She was happy, happier than he'd ever seen her. She'd moved on, completely. Somehow, that left him free in a way he couldn't quite understand.

He turned away, pulling his keys from his pocket. In his car, he tapped a thumb against the steering wheel as the air conditioner chilled the warm air around him. He needed to let go. With a harsh curse, he dragged a hand down his face, then reached for his cell.

"St. John." Celia picked up on the third ring, her lush voice smoothing over him.

"Where are you?" He winced at the harshness of his own voice. Eyes closed, he rested his forehead on his fist, elbow on the door.

"We're checking out Wesley Campbell's story," she said, her tone cool. In the background, Cook muttered something over the squawk of a police radio. "Hang on a second."

He caught a snatch of her conversation with Cook as she asked him for a private moment and the investigator grumbled about being thrown out of his own damn car. A door closed with a thud.

"What did you want?" Celia asked.

"I want to see you later."

"I think we established that earlier, McMillian."

Call me Tom, damn it. He swallowed the words. "Not like that. I meant have dinner with me again tonight."

A pause vibrated between them. "I don't think that's such a good idea."

He blew out a breath. "Why not?"

"Because." Irritation hovered in the word. "Do we have to talk about this now?"

"Have dinner with me tonight, Celia. Just dinner. I swear."

"Like that's going to happen."

He picked up the self-deprecating humor in her voice and smiled. Remembered sensations tumbled through him—her skin soft under his hands, the silky wetness of her body around his, her head thrown back on a moan. He shifted. "Say yes, Celia. I want to see you."

"Why?" Uncertainty trembled between them.

He pressed his fingers against his temples. "Because I meant what I said. I want to get to know you as a woman. Last night was fantastic, but it wasn't enough. I want...listen, we'll have dinner. We'll talk. That's all I'm asking."

"I don't know."

"Think about it." He swallowed hard. "Please. I'll call you later."

"Don't bother." At her words, his gut plummeted. A hesitation stretched. "My place. Seven o'clock."

Flipping the phone closed, he killed the connection. His ears roared and he sucked in air to lessen the sudden tightness of his chest.

What the hell was he doing?

ॐ

He was late.

The back door stood open and Tom mounted the steps to Celia's porch, a knot of tension sitting at the base of his neck. How had being with her gotten to be so important so fast? Slow music wafted from inside and he knocked once on the doorframe. "Cee?"

"Come on in."

He followed the music and her voice through a small, neat laundry room and into the vintage kitchen he'd glimpsed from her living room two days before. He paused in the squared-off doorway to her dining area. A pizza box waited with a couple of plates. "Hello."

"Hey." From the other side of the table, she watched him. Snug jeans hugged her hips and thighs and a shimmery pink haltertop skimmed her curves, leaving her shoulders bare. She lifted her chin and tucked her hands in her back pockets, the gesture emphasizing the swell of her breasts. "I hope pizza and a beer is okay. I was running late."

"It's fine." He was with her and she was worried about what

139

they were going to eat? He swallowed a strangled laugh. Food was the last thing on his mind, despite the way his empty stomach gnawed away at him. He stepped forward, wrapped his hands around the back of a dining chair. "You look great."

"Thanks." Her smile didn't quite reach her eyes. She tilted her head toward the kitchen. "Do you want a beer?"

"Yeah. A Sam Adams if you have one."

She laughed and the sweet trill actually sounded genuine. "Somehow I figured you wouldn't be a cheap date. You have your choice, Counselor, of a Bud Light or a Corona."

"Corona's fine."

She slipped by him into the kitchen, fluttering a hand across his arm as she went. His skin tingled under the easy contact. "Your other choice is pizza off a plate or out of the box."

"The box is fine." He leaned against the doorjamb to watch her pull a pair of beers from the fridge and pop off the tops. When she reached him and held out one of the bottles, he took it, holding her gaze. "I'm just glad to be here with you."

She didn't look away, but bit her bottom lip. "We changed everything last night, didn't we?"

He nodded. "I'm not sorry about that, Cee. Are you?"

Sadness invaded her eyes and she dropped her gaze. She walked to the table and flipped open the box. Savory aromas of tomato and cheese rose. "I can be sorry later, can't I?"

Something in her voice pulled at him. He crossed to stand beside her and set his beer aside. Cupping her shoulders, he turned her to face him. "Celia?"

Eyes closed, she shook her head. "This wasn't very smart, McMillian. We can't go back now. We have to work together. Hell, you're my *boss*—"

"Not here." He slid his hands over the smoothness of her

shoulders and upper arms, soothing the palpable tension there. "Not tonight. Here, now, I'm just the man who wants to be with you."

She opened her eyes then. "What are we doing?"

Fingering the silk of her hair, he tucked it behind her ear. "We're moving on."

"What does that mean?" She tugged away from his easy hold. "You said it wasn't enough, McMillian, and you're right. I thought I could be your lover, let it be all about the sex, but I can't. It's not...it's not me."

He trailed a finger down the side of her throat, brushing the fine links of the silver chain about her neck. "We don't have to set all the parameters now, Cee. Why don't we just let things be, see where they go?"

She gave him a look. "Oh, I don't know, McMillian. Probably because if they implode, we still have to work together—"

His kiss stopped the words. "Enough. For tonight, it's just you and me. No office, no cases, just the two of us. Okay?"

With a sigh, she nodded. "All right."

"Good." He kissed her again. "Because right now, all I want to do is look at you and listen to your voice and forget about how close Nate Holton came to taking us both out."

A shudder traveled over her and he felt it under his hands. She pulled away. "I heard you already had a run-in with Judge Baker about him."

"That was real productive." He accepted the warm slice of pizza she proffered and sank onto one of her dining chairs. She curled into another, feet tucked under her. "Although I swear if Baker lets him off with a reduced sentence this time, I'll file a complaint."

A grin flirted with her mouth. "You're a tough son of a bitch, McMillian. I like that."

He swallowed the urge to ask her what else she liked, along with a bite of pizza. Savoring the spicy blend of cheese and pepperoni, he cast about for something to say. She left him tongue-tied in a way he couldn't remember another woman ever had.

All right, hot shot, you said you wanted to get to know her. Keep up your end of the conversation.

A look around the room didn't offer any clues to her life outside the job. He washed the pizza down with a swig of Corona. "So tell me about Celia St. John away from the office."

She lifted her bottle and sipped, her gaze shuttered. "There's not much to tell."

He leaned back, spinning the bottle on the table. "No pleading the Fifth, Ms. St. John. What are you doing while I'm swimming, watching the Braves and collecting baseball cards?"

"Don't forget the golf." She picked a piece of bacon off her slice. "Everyone knows you're obsessed with improving your handicap."

"Celia. Stop evading."

"I don't know." She shrugged, an uncomfortable roll of her shoulders. "I go to the range and work on my aim. Cicely and I do this movie-and-dinner thing every couple of weeks. I run several times a week. I used to play tennis, but my doubles partner moved to Macon, so it's been awhile."

"I play, although my backhand's not as strong as my handicap." He let the bottle rest and reached to pick up her hand, rubbing his thumb over her knuckles. A grin tugged at his mouth. "We could play one Saturday. You can wipe up the court with me."

Her fingers tightened around his briefly, warming him. "Sounds like false modesty, McMillian."

They finished eating, washing down slices of pizza with sips of beer and small talk. Tom felt the tension gripping his neck and shoulders slip away. Afterwards, he carried the empty pizza box out to her trashcan and returned to the kitchen to find her stowing empty bottles in a recycling container under the sink. He paused in the doorway, struck by the ordinariness of the evening. When was the last time he'd found such satisfaction in such simplicity?

He honest to God couldn't remember.

She straightened, and catching his gaze on her, smiled. This time, the expression lit her eyes, turning them to shining crystal. Arms crossed over her midriff, she leaned against the counter, her gaze traveling over him like a touch.

Under her scrutiny, he altered his stance. "What?"

Still smiling, she lifted her chin and crossed the distance between them. Heat kicked off in his gut, arousal buzzing to life in his groin. She rubbed a finger down his tie. "I love this tie on you."

A surprised laugh tore from his throat. "Yeah?"

She tilted her head back to meet his gaze, her hand wrapping around the blue silk. "Oh, yeah. But I think I might like it better off."

Fumbling with the knot, she pulled him into her. He dipped his head, taking her mouth, and she laughed against his lips, tugging him toward the dining room.

"I thought this was all about dinner," he said, rubbing his hands over her bare back. Even as he uttered the words, he knew they were a token protest. No way he would turn down the opportunity to make love to her again. He hardened, excitement sizzling through him.

"You talk too much, McMillian." Hands flat on his chest, she pushed him into a dining chair. She straddled him, resting on his thighs. He shifted, unbearably aroused, and she leaned in to stroke the tip of her tongue over his lips. "Maybe you should put that talented mouth to better use."

He gripped her waist and pulled her tighter against him. With a harsh chuckle, he nuzzled the curve of her jaw. "Like this?"

"Like that." She slid his tie free and tossed it aside. He slid his mouth to her ear, grazing the lobe with his teeth, and she shuddered. "Just like that."

She pulled his shirt open, hauled his undershirt free and ran her hands over his abdomen. At her urgent touch, his muscles contracted, a flush of excitement tingling into his belly and lower. She ground into him, an exquisite pressure. He groaned. "Damn, Cee."

Her head fell back and he trailed his mouth along her throat, pulling the tie of her halter loose at the same time. He slipped his hands up to cup the warmth of her breasts, his gaze tracing the line of her necklace. A silver uniform button rested against her cleavage. With his mouth, he caressed the spot just above the "V" of the chain. She made a tiny sound in her throat, a cross between a moan and a sigh.

Opening her eyes, she caught his gaze, her eyes dark with need. She pushed up. "I want you inside me. *Now.*"

She snapped open the button-fly on her jeans and skimmed them down, taking a scrap of white satin with them. His eyes on her, Tom lifted one hip to free his wallet. He laid the plastic-encased condom on one thigh and fumbled with his own fly. She gave him a wicked smile and brushed his hands away. "Let me."

In moments, she dispatched his button and lowered his

zipper. She wrapped a hand around his erection and he closed his eyes, a smothered growl escaping him as she stroked him, up, down, up again.

"Celia." He forced her name out and opened his eyes, need burning. "Come here."

With a sultry laugh, she rolled the thin latex over his hard dick and sank onto him, thighs flexing against his, the silky wetness of her body enfolding him. He thrust upward, seeking, needing to be deeper inside her. Her husky laughter turned to a slow, guttural moan that punched him in the gut.

Shaking back her tousled hair, she settled her hands on his shoulders, lifting and rising over him. Her teeth caught her lower lip, face flushed with passion. He stroked the sides of her breasts, cradling them, flicking at the hardened tips with his thumbs. He pushed harder inside her, lost to everything but her and the sensations sparking between them.

"You're beautiful," he whispered.

"McMillian." His name left her lips on a torn murmur and jolted him with an urge to taste it. He cradled her head in one hand and pulled her mouth to his for a series of nipping kisses, matching the rhythm of his upward thrusts.

Damn, this felt right, being with her, losing himself in her.

His thumb brushed the tiny bandage on her chin, covering the small cut there, and a visceral shudder worked through him, images of Holton's truck barreling through the intersection alive in his head again. He could have lost her, in an instant. The idea hurt more than it should.

"Don't," she murmured against his jaw, her voice broken and raw. "Don't think about it. Not now."

The warmth of her pushed the chill from his skin. Urgency built in him, something not quite satisfied by the movements of her body on his. He wanted more, *needed* more.

He needed something to set him apart, something that gave him a unique spot in her life. He refused to examine the why of that, but he accepted it.

"Say it," he whispered near her ear.

"Say what?" She arched into him, her voice breathless. Her nails bit into his shoulders.

"My name. Let me hear you say it, Cee."

Her eyes slid closed and she bit her lip again. "McMillian—"

"No, not—"

Her breathy moan warmed his skin, her body contracting around him. His body reacted, the sudden climax slamming into him, stealing his ability to think, to breathe.

She collapsed against him, panting, laughter shaking her.

He rubbed a hand down her damp back, shaking off the cold emptiness trying to take up residence in his chest. He didn't want that here with her. "What's funny?"

Pushing her hair away from her face, she lifted her head, sultry amusement glinting in her eyes. "Your tie is all I got off."

It sank in then, the erotic picture they must make—him still fully clothed in the straight chair, a naked, satiated woman sprawled over his lap. A satisfied exhale rumbled from his chest and he hugged her close, smoothing both palms down her back. He closed his eyes, even as her sweet laughter wrapped around him, filling the gaping hole he'd carried around with him forever.

Celia sighed against his throat. "Hmmm, that was nice."

"Nice?" He laughed, inhaling the warmth of her scent mingled with his own. "That was fucking fantastic."

"It was, wasn't it?" She looped her arms around his neck, her cheek against his shoulder. With a gentle finger, she traced the edge of his collar. "McMillian, I don't...it's been a while since

I've done this, the whole getting-to-know-you thing. I'm not...I haven't had time for it."

He hadn't made time for it, hadn't wanted to get to know any other woman the way he did this one. He molded the line of her spine, her skin smooth under his questing fingers. Warm tendrils of acceptance and contentment unfurled within him. This was good, simply being with her this way. With her hair tickling his cheek, he nuzzled her ear. "I'm glad you found time for me."

"So am I." She lifted her head and slid her hands forward to grip his collar. She kissed him, mouth clinging to his, nipping lightly at his lower lip. He held her closer, soaking in the peace and the way being with her felt totally right. Her fingers made short work of the remaining buttons on his shirt and she pushed the fabric aside, a whimsical smile curving her lush mouth. "Why don't we carve out a little more?"

Chapter Eight

"Glad I dropped by for breakfast?" McMillian's deep voice purred near her ear.

Celia laughed, her hands shaking a little as she tried to measure coffee into the filter. The heat of him along her back, the pleasure of his hands cupping her breasts, his touch warm through her short gown, made it difficult to concentrate. "I don't think breakfast is what you came for."

"I don't know what you're talking about." He nipped at the side of her neck and rubbed his thumbs over her aching nipples in slow, teasing circles. "Ms. St. John, surely you're not implying I had other motives?"

"Not motives, plural," she sighed, abandoning the coffee to lean into his strong form. Her eyes slid closed, reawakened desire stirring in her. Amazing she could still want him this much, after everything they'd done the night before. "More like motive, singular."

"Oh, I've definitely got one thing on my mind." He rolled a hardened nipple between his thumb and forefinger, sending pleasure through her, wringing a gasp from her lips. "You."

She settled her hands on his thighs, muscles taut beneath her touch. She pushed back into his evident erection. "The famous McMillian focus?"

He chuckled, a hand easing down her waist to her hip,

along her thigh to the hem of her gown. Hot fingers slid beneath, moving the fabric upward, slowly, inexorably.

"Something like that." He turned her in his arms and she caught a glimpse of smoldering blue eyes before he lifted her to sit on the counter. A hand planted on either side of her, he loomed over her. "Tell me about that fantasy from the other night."

She shook her head. "You first. Tell me one of yours."

He fingered the thin straps of her chemise. "Let me show you. Old prosecutor's trick...one demonstration's worth a thousand explanations."

He lowered his head, mouth brushing the skin exposed as the bodice slipped. With a soft push, the satin pooled at her waist. He captured her mouth and slid his hands along the inside of her thighs. Celia arched into him, burning up, very glad he'd stopped by for breakfast mere hours after he'd finally left her bed.

She sighed, sinking into the memory of the night before, of his rough husky groan as he entered her, the rumble of his laughter while they talked afterwards in her dim room. She liked him, the man inside, more than she should, liked being with him. His thumbs traced the edges of her panties. He lifted his mouth, face taut and hungry with need. "Where are the toys?"

Excitement speared through her. She was *very* glad he'd dropped by for breakfast, even gladder it was Saturday and they had the entire day before them, hours upon hours to spend discovering one another. "Upstairs in—"

The ping of her cell phone stopped the words, and she sighed as McMillian groaned. "Damn it."

"Keep your focus, McMillian." She slipped from the counter and spun to grab the offending object, still pinging imperiously.

As she lifted it to her ear, McMillian tugged her against him, rubbing a hand across her bare midriff and up to her breasts. She struggled to keep her voice even, swallowing the moan building in her throat. "St. John."

"I've got something you might want to see." Cook's voice vibrated with tension.

"Wh-what's that?" Celia placed a hand over McMillian's marauding fingers and he stilled behind her. His hot, humid breath trembled along her nape.

"Got a 10-43 call this morning," Cook replied, the murder ten-code drawing her attention completely away from the man behind her. "You know Jessica Grady, the divorce lawyer?"

"I do." Celia swallowed, her mouth dry. How often during those early weeks at the DA's office had she seen Jessica Grady with McMillian? They'd been involved in one of his notorious affairs of "limited duration". She closed her eyes. Jesus above, what was coming next? "Why do you think I need to see the scene?"

"Because according to the ME, Ms. Grady was pregnant when she died. If not full-term, damn close to it."

"C'mon, Cook, get to the point." She shrugged irritable shoulders and slipped away from the wall of McMillian's body, tugging her gown back into place. She didn't look at him.

"Cause of death looks like massive blood loss. Someone *cut* the baby out of her."

"You're kidding."

"Would I joke about something like that?"

Her thoughts winged to their deceased infant. "Estimated time of death?"

"Twenty-four hours. Or longer."

She tugged at her chain, the links rasping against her skin.

"Okay. Are you still on scene?"

"Yeah. Probably be here most of the day. ME's not even ready for us to move the body."

"I can be there in fifteen minutes." She flipped the phone closed, not giving him time to reply. Foreboding snaked through her.

"What?"

She dragged in a deep breath and turned to face McMillian. "That was Cook. He's on a murder scene."

McMillian lifted a hand in silent inquiry.

Another deep breath didn't relieve the nerves twisting through her belly. "The victim is Jessica Grady."

Shock bloomed in his eyes, dulling the blue gaze. He recovered quickly, features morphing to his impassive prosecutor's mask. "Why call you?"

She didn't want to go here with him, and suddenly, she wished he hadn't come by for breakfast. She'd already done the math—if Jessica had been pregnant with a full-term baby, it was very likely the man standing before Celia could be the father.

"Because she was pregnant." She rubbed her thumb over her necklace. "It looks like she may have been killed for the baby."

His lips parted, a stunned expression clouding his face. Celia swallowed again, aching. He looked like she'd delivered a roundhouse to his groin. Mouth tightening, he straightened and picked up his keys from her counter. "Get dressed and let's go."

She frowned. "McMillian—"

"I said let's go."

She wanted to reach for him, but the boss-employee gulf was definitely back in place. "I guess you're driving again."

One hand on the wheel, Tom pinched the bridge of his nose, trying to stop the thoughts, the images trickling through his mind. Jessica, struggling, fighting, hurting.

Dying.

He blew out a ragged breath, thankful for Celia's silent presence. In the passenger seat, she stared ahead. His brain clicked through the numbers, counting off months. If Jessica had a baby...

He could be the father.

His stomach cramped. God, no. He couldn't face that again.

"You didn't know, did you?" Celia's soft voice washed over him, pulling him back from the abyss. "That she was pregnant."

"No. We hadn't talked in weeks, months." He clutched the steering wheel with enough force that his knuckles ached. He cleared his tight throat. "That baby could be mine."

"I figured as much." She dropped her hand from her neck, brushed his wrist atop the gearshift with her fingers. The soothing comfort of her touch pierced the fear wrapped around him. He wanted to grab her and hold on.

He turned left, the Mercedes purring along the road fronting the emerald golf course, then slowed to pull into Jessica's long asphalt driveway.

Her luxury Toyota sat in the drive, flanked by the GBI's crime scene van, a bevy of cars from the Chandler County's Sheriff's Department and the coroner's wagon. Yellow crime scene tape cordoned off the immaculate yard and a Chandler County deputy stood guard at the open oak door. Tom killed the engine and stared at the front of the fashionable brick home.

"Ready?" Celia touched his hand again, a brief smile curving her mouth, although her eyes remained serious.

He swallowed a rough laugh. Ready for what? To see Jessica's body? To find out whether or not he'd fathered her missing baby? He nodded. "Come on."

She walked a little ahead of him as they approached the house and he sensed her withdrawal. Despite the strain twisting his gut, a half-hearted smile twisted his mouth. Moving in cop mode already. She exchanged a quick greeting with the deputy guarding the door and waited for Tom to join her. Together, they entered the house.

Cook stood inside the door, watching a GBI crime scene technician photograph the scene. Tom's stomach rolled. Jessica lay on the floor of the foyer, a white tunic pushed above her breasts and twisted about her torso. Black slacks tangled about her ankles. Her eyes stared upward, the irises cloudy, the pupils fixed. The rancid smell of death hung heavy in the air— blood, body fluids, early decay. Blood had pooled beneath her body, staining the cream-colored carpet, congealing into a stinking mess. A trail of dried blood led from a crusted-over cut on her cheekbone to her ear.

Her abdomen gaped like an obscene mouth.

"Christ."

"Fancy seeing you this morning, Counselor." Cook frowned at him before focusing on Celia.

She shrugged and glanced quickly at Tom. "Early meeting."

Cook's eyebrows winged upward. "On a Saturday?"

She narrowed her eyes. "What do you have so far?"

"Friend dropped by early this morning after Grady missed a dinner party last night. When Grady didn't answer her phone or her cell or open the door, the friend called us. That was about seven. Ford figures we're looking at probably thirty-six to forty-eight hours dead."

Celia slanted a sharp look at the investigator. "What about last known contact?"

Cook jerked his head toward the door. "Tick's out in the car, trying to run that down now."

The minutiae of their investigative talk washed over Tom, his gaze drifting back to Jessica's body. Pain throbbed at the base of his neck. Damn it, she hadn't deserved to die like that. No one did. She'd been a damn good lawyer. A friend and sounding board. Fun in bed and a great date for those infernal political events. Neither of them had wanted anything further, and when it was over, it was over, no hard feelings, no regrets. He'd liked her; everyone had.

His gaze skittered away from the wound spanning from her sternum to her pelvis. Who the hell would do something like that to her?

"...do a walk-through." Cook's voice infiltrated his thoughts. "Her office is a holy mess. Not sure yet if it's a staged burglary or if someone was looking for something. We need to pull her phone records, start talking to her friends."

"I can help with the scene." Celia glanced up at Tom. "This is going to take hours and there's nothing you can do now. Why don't you go home?"

He stiffened. Leave? Without knowing anything? "I'd rather—"

"McMillian, there's no reason for you to be here. I'll call you as soon we know something."

Oh yeah, the cop was back and he was on the outside, all over again. Jaw clenched until it ached, he nodded. "You do that, Ms. St. John."

He spun on his heel and stalked back to his car.

"God, why couldn't she have a smaller house?" Celia straightened from her hunched position by the bed and rotated her neck. Jesus above, the prints on the furniture. Didn't the woman ever dust? As she'd assured McMillian, the painstaking work of processing the scene had taken hours and they remained far from finished. They'd settled on an easy routine— Celia dusting and lifting prints, Cook collecting and bagging physical evidence, while Tick Calvert, Chandler County's lead investigator, interviewed Jessica's friends and clients.

"Because she's a lawyer. Ever seen one who wasn't pretentious?" Cook stepped over a broken lamp lying amid a jumble of clothing from the closet. He eased open the armoire door and whistled, long and low.

She labeled and logged yet another print before glancing up at him. "What?"

He indicated a stack of DVDs, seemingly undisturbed. "Home videos."

Celia rolled her eyes. "Everyone has those."

"I don't think these are birthday parties or family dinners. Not the way they're labeled." Cook tilted his head, gaze trained on the armoire. "Underwood. Swanson. Campbell. Burns. Oh, and lookee here."

Unease prickled over her. She didn't even have to ask.

Cook lifted a DVD. "McMillian."

She caught the evil glint in his incisive eyes as he glanced from the DVD to the player. "Cook, no."

"Oh, come on, St. John. Aren't you a little bit curious?"

"No, I'm not." She had no desire to watch McMillian making love to the woman the coroner had removed not an hour ago. She wanted any images she had of him naked to involve only her.

However, Cook was either stubborn or freaking deaf.

The DVD slid into the player with a series of whirs and clicks.

The television flashed blue. Images blurred, cleared on the screen. The bedroom behind them. Jessica Grady, very much alive, on the bed, naked and moaning. Tom McMillian between her thighs, muscles in his back and buttocks flexing.

Celia's stomach dropped and bile flooded her throat. She glanced away, curling her shaking fingers until her knuckles ached. Just because Cook was an ass didn't mean she had to watch the damn thing. The pictures didn't go away, still flashing on the surface of her mind, joined by the sounds coming from the television. They merged with her own memories, tainting the private time she and McMillian had carved out in her dining room, in her bed, the night before.

Her gaze pulled to the screen again. God, she didn't need this, didn't need the emotions seeing him with another woman aroused—anger, jealousy, disappointment.

"Are you finished getting your jollies over there, Cook?" She made sure her voice was damn level. Showing anything now would be completely untenable. Anger flashed in her. McMillian deserved better than this.

Cook stepped back, frowning, his gaze trained on the screen. "I don't think he knows he's being taped."

"What do you mean?" She flicked a look at the television and away. Heaven help her, how would she be able to look at McMillian again without seeing this?

"Look at her." With a gloved finger, Cook pointed at Jessica's face. "What do you see?"

What did she see? Her lover thrusting inside someone else, red nails clutching at his ass, pulling him deeper.

"St. John. Look." Exasperation filtered into Cook's voice. "She's acting. And she keeps glancing at the camera. The angle's wrong for a tripod. It's more like..."

Squinting, he walked to the bed and looked along the adjacent wall. "There. See? She could hide it in the plant shelf."

"Sure, but..." Compelled, Celia looked at the television again. "What makes you think he doesn't know?"

Cook shrugged. "She's watching the camera. He's focused on her. Well, on what they're doing anyway."

On screen, McMillian tensed, his body stiffening, his guttural groan filling Celia's ears. She swallowed. "So she kept a video diary of her sexual conquests. Big deal."

Cook punched the eject button and shot her an amused glance. "You're smarter than that, St. John. Think."

"Blackmail?" Celia shook her head. "She has a thriving practice."

"Maybe she got greedy. Could be one of them decided to cut off the gravy train, permanently. Maybe he decided to take care of the problem her baby represented at the same time." He snapped a new inventory sheet on his clipboard and shook out an evidence bag. "And maybe we have a veritable library of suspects here."

Her gaze darted to the DVD case in his hand. *McMillian* had been scrawled on the clear plastic in bold, black marker. "But that means..."

"Yeah." Cook glanced up, his eyes gleaming. "Your boss is a suspect."

"Well, I've talked to everyone local in her address book." Investigator Tick Calvert dropped into the chair facing the empty desk adjacent to Cook's. He scattered a handful of peppermints across the desktop and offered one in Celia's direction. Brows lifted, he eyed the television Cook had set up on the counter running along one wall. "So that's the movie?"

Trying to ignore the ache pulsing at her temples, Celia reached for a mint. "One of them."

Thank God Cook had taken a break from analyzing the films. He'd paused the DVD, so she had a few minutes' reprieve from listening to Jessica's theatrical moaning. She was beginning to agree with Cook—Jessica had been quite the actress and none of the men involved seemed to realize they were being taped. Celia glanced over her shoulder. On the screen, Jessica straddled a state representative, frozen in time.

At least it wasn't the film of her and McMillian.

Celia bit down on her peppermint, breaking it into tiny pieces. "So what did you get from your interviews?"

Tick flipped open his notebook. "Not much. The weirdest and probably most important thing? No one knew she was pregnant."

"Nobody?" Cook strolled in, paging through a fax. He picked up the remote and settled in his desk chair.

"Not even her OB/GYN." Tick ran a finger down the page. "Hadn't seen him since her annual physical early in May; she wasn't due for another until next month. Couple of friends and neighbors noticed she'd put on some weight, but knew nothing about a pregnancy."

"Get this." Cook held the fax aloft. "It's our preliminary autopsy report and some early fingerprint results."

Celia stared at him. "You're kidding. It's barely been six hours since they removed the body."

"Guess screwing the DA gets you moved to the top of the line. McMillian called Botine as soon as he left Grady's place this morning, asked them to 'expedite' anything we needed." Cynicism coated Cook's voice. "Wonder if he'd have done that if he'd known his prints were going to turn up in her bedroom. On the back of the headboard."

Her stomach dropped. "Big surprise. They'd been lovers."

Cook handed off the autopsy report to Tick. "You don't think he did it."

Shrugging, she tried for a smooth expression. "No, I don't."

"Why not?"

With Cook leaning back in his chair, studying her, she tapped her pen on her notebook. "Why would he?"

Surprise flickered in Cook's eyes and he exchanged a look with Tick. "Oh, I don't know. Maybe because she was trying to shake him down? That movie, her baby. That kind of shit kills political careers and it's no secret he wants to be more than the local DA."

"Fine." She crossed her arms over her midriff. "Then why did we find the movie? Why not take it with him, if that's why he killed her?"

Cook's broad shoulders moved in a casual shrug. "He had the baby to deal with. Could be he panicked and forgot the DVD."

A disbelieving laugh bubbled from her throat. "Have you met him? I don't think panic is in his vocabulary."

Shaking his head, Cook tossed his pen down. "Oh, shit."

Celia tensed.

"What?" Tick glanced up from the report, his dark gaze alert.

Ignoring his partner, Cook fixed Celia with a disgusted look. "You do have a thing for him."

She tilted her chin. "That's ridiculous—"

159

"And you're approaching this the wrong way because of it."

Heat flooded her face, her stomach turning. How had they ended up here? Maybe the floor would open and swallow her. "What is that supposed to mean?"

He settled deeper into the seat. "It means you're looking for reasons why it's *not* him, rather than approaching the case objectively. You don't want it to be him, so you're going to prove it's not."

Anger, at him, at herself, trembled in her. "And you're objective? How many other directions have you considered?"

"At least eight." He flipped open a folder and slid a sheet of paper across the desk. "Those are the men on the other videos."

She lifted the sheet, scanning the list. All political figures. The state representative. A municipal judge, a mayor, three district attorneys, a police chief, a county administrator.

And McMillian.

"St. John."

At Cook's grim voice, she looked up. "What?"

"I can handle the fact you don't want it to be McMillian. I can even understand it." His dour expression matched his tone. "But if we're going to work together, I need you to be honest with me. I can't be worried you'd hold something back to protect the son of a bitch."

Her anger returned, flaring hotter. "I wouldn't do that."

"I'd hate to think so, but you've got to promise me that whatever the hell is going on with you two isn't going to cloud your judgment here."

"There's..." She couldn't force the denial out. They'd gone beyond sex and claiming there was nothing between them would be a flat-out lie. "If it's him, it's him."

Tick examined her, openly assessing. "And you could take

him down if you had to?"

"Of course."

He held her gaze for a long moment, his chocolate eyes serious. "That's all we need to know."

Cook harrumphed, pulling a stack of Jessica's financial records forward. "Just remember, you believed Turello too."

Celia tugged hard at her necklace. He had to bring that up. "That was different. I was younger; he had me snowed."

Gray gaze gleaming, Cook gave her a curt nod and reached for his pen. "Good. Then don't let McMillian turn into a blizzard."

She shook back her hair, meeting Cook's gaze straight on. "Trust me. He won't."

"This is interesting." Tick's voice broke the tension. He tapped the report. "Ford checked Grady's blood type against your deceased baby, on the chance it was hers."

Celia leaned forward. "And?"

"Could be. Your baby's blood type was AB positive. Grady was A negative. From the pieces of placenta left in Grady's uterus, Ford knows Grady's baby was AB positive. She'll have to run DNA tests to know for sure." He laid the paper aside and pointed at the television with the small stack of DVDs beside it. "That blood type info can help us rule out the men on those tapes."

Cook nodded. "Because the father has to be AB or B positive."

"Exactly." Tick shrugged. "But."

"But what?"

"Time of death is off for Grady to be the mother. Your baby was discovered Tuesday night, right? Ford thinks Grady was killed sometime Thursday evening, which fits with what I heard

161

in those interviews. People saw Grady Wednesday and Thursday."

Thursday evening. Celia rubbed a hand over her eyes. She'd been with McMillian Thursday evening...dinner by the pool, the interlude in his bed. She was his alibi.

The cop in her knew she was only a partial alibi. She'd left his home once she'd left his bed. There'd been the rest of the night to kill Jessica Grady. He'd had plenty of opportunity. Just like Turello.

Except he was nothing like Bryan had been. Bryan Turello had smooth-talked and charmed her into believing him, believing he was innocent of the accusations lodged against him.

McMillian didn't have to say a word. She couldn't believe him capable of what she'd seen at Jessica's home. That level of belief frightened her beyond words.

"I thought I'd find you here." Celia, standing at his office doorway, dragged Tom's attention away from the motion he was drafting.

Or more like, attempting to draft. Although he'd spent the day closeted in his office, he couldn't keep his mind away from the images of Jessica's body, the idea that he might have fathered her baby.

He tossed his pen on the legal pad and leaned back, happier to see Celia than he had a right to be. "Anything new?"

She eschewed the chairs before his desk and leaned against the windowsill. Late evening sunlight glinted on her hair. She clutched the sill's edge, tapping her short nails on the wall. "Preliminary autopsy report is in. Some fingerprint results."

He hated the way she avoided his gaze. "I suppose some of the prints are mine."

Nodding, she darted a glance at him, her eyes shuttered. "Yes. In the bedroom. What blood type are you?"

He frowned. "B positive."

A visible tremor ran through her. Foreboding crashed through him.

"What aren't you telling me, Celia?"

Her chest lifted with a deep breath. "Jessica's baby had AB positive blood. She was A negative. Even without DNA, we know the father had to be AB positive as well or—"

"B positive." He jerked a hand over his hair. "Damn it all."

"You really don't want to be this baby's father, do you?"

He glanced at her. How to explain he didn't want to be any baby's father, ever again? He couldn't do it, couldn't live wondering every day if he'd have to bury another child. He cleared his throat. "What I want doesn't matter now, does it? There's a very good chance I am."

"Did you know about the video?"

The odd note in her voice sent a shiver over his spine. "What video?"

Arms crossed, she lifted an eyebrow, her expression bordering on mocking. "Oh, come on, McMillian, no need to be coy. I've seen it."

She was doing the cop thing with him. Angry disbelief shuddered to life in him. She stood there, after everything, working her interrogation techniques on him. Like hell.

He crossed to stand before her, close enough he could feel the warmth of her body, and glared. "What video?"

For a long moment, she stared at him, her blue eyes cool and measuring. "In her bedroom, we found a stack of DVDs.

163

Homemade movies."

"Homemade..." He gazed down at her. Surely she didn't mean what he thought she meant. "Sex tapes?"

She nodded.

He rubbed a hand over his eyes, pinched the bridge of his nose before looking at her once more. "I'm on one?"

Another nod. "Yes."

"Shit." He spun away to pace the office. "Fuck." His stomach roiled. "Son of a bitch."

"The others are also men who are well-connected politically."

"The others?" He stopped, staring at her. "How many others?"

"Eight." Her shoulders moved in a tight, uncomfortable shrug. "One is a municipal court judge from Bryant County."

"Hell." He dragged a hand over his face again. "I don't believe this."

"You didn't know, did you?" Celia's soft voice washed over him, oddly comforting, its earlier edge gone. "That she was taping you."

He shot her a look. "Of course I didn't know."

"Cook's theory is that she may have been blackmailing the men on the films. And that one is the baby's father."

"And one of them killed her?" He narrowed his eyes. "Like me?"

A low laugh trembled from her lips, completely lacking in humor. "Of course I don't think it's you."

"But Cook does, right?" He turned away, rested his hands flat on the desk, his head falling between his shoulders.

"McMillian?"

He straightened, looked over his shoulder to find Celia eyeing him, her expression strained. "You watched the tape."

She bit her lip. "Yes."

And it had hurt her. He could see the remnants of that pain in her eyes. He dropped his head. Damn it. The idea of her watching him screw Jessica turned his stomach. Shit, everything was going to hell.

That wasn't his baby, missing and possibly endangered.

Jessica hadn't taped him fucking her.

And Celia hadn't watched it.

Damn it, what if it was all true? How was he going to handle this?

First, he'd offer Celia an out. No reason for her career to go down with his. If she was as smart as he knew she was, she'd take it and run. The level of sorrow that ricocheted through him with the thought startled him. He couldn't have gotten in that deep that fast with her.

He cleared his throat. "Keep me informed. I want to know about anything you turn up, immediately."

Eyes closed, he waited for the soft click of the door closing behind her.

The soft touch of her fingers fluttered over his back. She smoothed the hair at his nape, and surprised, he lifted his head to look at her. She gazed back at him with solemn eyes.

"All the way over here, I kept thinking the easiest thing to do was walk away from you now." A slight smile trembled around her lips and disappeared. "I can't do it."

Relief rushed through him and he released the breath he hadn't even known he was holding.

"God, Cee." He tugged her into his arms, burying his face against the tousled silk of her hair. She wrapped her arms

165

around him, rubbing soft circles at the small of his back. For the first time that day, he let go of some of the tension, soaking in the comfort of having her in his arms.

"Yeah, St. John, I'd say your judgment is completely cloud-free."

At Cook's cynical tone, Celia jerked in his arms and tensed. Tom let her go and turned toward the door, where Cook stood waiting with Tick Calvert. Cook leaned an arm on the doorjamb and smiled, a predatory expression.

"Counselor, we'd like to ask you a few questions."

Chapter Nine

Ankle crossed over his knee, Tom drummed his fingers on the table while Tick Calvert set up the video camera in the sheriff's department interview room. Impatient irritation thrummed along his nerves. They were wasting their time questioning him, losing precious investigative time. He blew out a long breath. At least this would be out of the way and they could shift their focus elsewhere.

Like finding the person who'd really killed Jessie.

And finding the baby.

"Mr. McMillian, although you're not under arrest at this time, I need to advise you of your rights." Cook scratched the date and time across the top of a Miranda waiver form. "You have the right to remain silent. Anything you say can and will be used against you in a court of law. You have the right to talk to an attorney and have him present with you while you are being questioned. If you cannot afford to hire a lawyer, one will be appointed to represent you before any questioning, if you wish. You can decide at any time to exercise these rights and not answer any questions or make any statements. Do you understand each of these rights I have explained to you?"

Tom narrowed his eyes at the investigator and resisted the overwhelming urge to call him an idiot. "Yes."

Unperturbed, Cook checked off an affirmative box. "Having

these rights in mind, do you wish to talk to us now?"

He clenched his teeth. "Yes."

Cook slid the form across the table. "Sign here, please."

Tick pulled a chair away from the wall, glanced at Celia, standing near the door, and indicated the seat. Her posture tight and uncomfortable, she shook her head. "I'm fine."

Tom lifted his eyes, met her gaze briefly before turning his attention to the two Chandler County investigators. Tick turned the chair around and straddled it, arms folded along the back. "Tom, I know you're pissed because we pulled you in here. I can understand that, but you have to look at it from our point of view. You had a relationship with Ms. Grady. Your prints are in her bedroom. Her phone records show your number as the last one she called the night she was killed. There's that video and the baby. If you were me, who would you be looking at?"

"Me." Tom laughed, a short, wry sound. "Only one problem with your line of thought, Tick. I didn't kill her."

Cook looked up. "Oh man, that's a new one. Hell, Tick, he didn't do it. Let's turn him loose right now."

Celia shot a deadly glare at the back of his head. "Cook, stop."

Tick gave them both a quelling look and sighed. "Tom, why don't you start by telling us where you were Thursday night."

Again, Tom's gaze shifted to Celia. Her face was pale and the line of her throat moved with a swallow. His mouth thinned. "I—"

"We were together." Celia tilted her chin, her gaze focused on Tom's. "We had dinner at his place."

Tick glanced around at her. "What time did you leave? Or did you spend the night?"

"Ah hell, I need some air." Cook jerked a pack of gum from

his pocket and shoved back from the table. He glared at Celia as he pulled the door open. "It's Turello all over again, isn't it, St. John?"

Her face reddened, temper snapping in her eyes. She looked at Tom. "Excuse me."

She walked out, the door swishing closed behind her, and Tom frowned. What had that been all about?

Tick tugged a hand through his hair. "What time did she leave, Tom?"

He pulled his attention back to the other man. "A little after nine."

Tick nodded. "Did you go anywhere after that? Anyone else come over?"

"No. My mother called from Rome, around ten. We talked for fifteen, maybe twenty minutes. I worked until eleven-thirty or so and went to bed, alone."

Another nod. "Ms. Grady's call to your number was very short. What did you talk about?"

"We didn't." That had to have been the hang-up on his voice mail, the call he had let go because he hadn't wanted to be pulled away from Celia. A frisson ran up his spine. What if he'd answered? Would Jessie still be alive?

Tick shrugged. "Why not?"

Tom met his gaze straight on. "Ms. St. John and I were having dinner. I didn't take the call because I didn't want us to be disturbed."

"So you didn't know Ms. Grady was pregnant?"

Frustration burned his throat. "Not until this morning, when Ms. St. John informed me of that."

"Would you be willing to give us a DNA sample?" Tick glanced up, his gaze assessing.

Tom settled back in his chair. "Bring it on, Investigator."

"What the hell?" Celia caught up to Cook on the department steps. Anger pulsed under her skin, seeking an outlet. "Where do you get off, Cook, bringing up Turello like that? I thought you were my friend."

"Yeah." Cook popped a piece of gum in his mouth, chewing hard. "So did I."

"What does that mean?" She wrapped a hand around the rough iron railing. "Just say it."

He turned on her. "You fucking lied to me."

A harsh laugh bubbled in her throat. "What?"

"You lied, St. John. 'If it's him, it's him.' Isn't that what you said, when you were giving me that line of bullshit about not hiding anything to protect him?"

"I'm not hiding anything."

"Like hell." Shaking his head, he fixed her with a condemning stare. "Why didn't you tell me this morning you'd been with him Thursday? Why not just say you were screwing him?"

"Because I knew what you'd think."

"What? That you've lost your damn mind? Hell, St. John, he's your boss. And now he's a suspect in a murder investigation I let you in on. You should have said something then." He looked away. "I trusted you and you fucking lied."

"Cook—"

"You're off the case. Both of them—Grady and the baby."

"You can't—"

"Like hell I can't. Maybe you're not seeing clearly, but I sure am. I refuse to let your infatuation with McMillian get in the way." He spun and stalked back into the building.

Celia gripped the railing until the uneven paint scraped her palms. Jesus above, what was she doing? Trusting McMillian, believing in him. Making the same mistake she'd made with Turello? She shook her head, blinking away a sudden burning rush of tears. No. He was different, nowhere near the lying bastard Turello had been. She knew McMillian in a way she hadn't known Turello.

Turello had dazzled her from the beginning, with his good looks and flattery. She'd never really known him, not until she'd finally realized the ugliness beneath his handsome façade.

She'd known McMillian as a professional first, had seen his dedication to the law, to making sure those who broke it paid the consequences. Hell, that was the very thing that had drawn her to him from the start.

He was a stand-up guy, gray areas and all.

"Celia?"

She dragged in a deep breath before turning to face McMillian. He stood at the top of the steps, watching her, his face expressionless. She lifted her chin. "Ready to go?"

A frown tugged his brows down. "I thought you'd want to talk to Cook and Calvert."

"I'm off the case." The words hurt her throat. She started down the steps.

"What?" Icy tension coated the word. His loafers scuffed on the concrete and he caught her arm as she reached the sidewalk.

"You heard me." She couldn't make herself face him, didn't want him to see how badly her pride was hurt. She'd never been removed from an investigation. Ever since Turello, her record had been impeccable. "Cook kicked me off the case. He's worried about my objectivity."

"I'll talk to Reed."

"No." She shook her head, staring across the parking lot, nearly deserted in the dusk of late evening. "I don't want you fighting this battle for me."

"Why not? Aren't you fighting for me?"

She stilled. "I don't know what I'm doing."

Tugging away from his easy hold, she continued down the sidewalk. Three steps away, she stopped, a humorless smile twisting her mouth. Of course, he'd insisted on driving. She had nowhere else to go. Shaking her head, she faced him, still standing where she'd left him.

She was in with him for the long haul, obviously.

She tapped the center of her chest, where her father's uniform button lay at the end of her chain, over her heart. "In here, I feel like I know you and I know you couldn't have done this."

A wry half-smile lifted the corner of his mouth. "Thanks."

Ire flashed over her. He didn't get it. How could he? She really didn't get it herself. She just knew how she felt. "Stop it, McMillian. Just...stop."

He closed the distance between them and tapped a gentle finger against her forehead. "The cop in here wants to side with Cook and Calvert, doesn't she?"

"Yes." She shrugged, not sure how to explain her torn loyalties. "But I can't."

"You don't know how glad I am to hear that." One of his rare grins appeared, banishing the strain of the day from his features. He cupped her chin, staring into her eyes for a long moment. Emotion glimmered in his blue eyes and then was gone. "Come on. Let's get out of here."

In the car, she glanced sideways at him as she fastened her seatbelt. "So how did it go?"

He started the engine. A grim smile played about his mouth. "I answered Calvert's questions and made him happy. Agreed to a DNA test."

She nodded. She'd expected as much—he'd want those DNA results as much as Cook would.

He pulled onto Durham Street and braked for the stoplight. A couple of pickup trucks rumbled through the intersection. "I want you to continue the investigation on your own."

Startled, she glanced at him. "McMillian, it's not my case."

"I want to know what happened to Jessie. I need to know if the baby..." He cleared his throat, thumping a finger on the steering wheel. "I trust you, Celia."

"You realize we'd be stepping all over Chandler County's toes."

His mouth twisted. "I can handle the heat if you can."

She swallowed a sigh. If Cook had been pissed with her before, he really wouldn't be happy when he learned she was poaching his case.

"I'll need copies of the lab and autopsy reports," she said. "And you're going to have to assist me with the victimology. I'll need you to help me get into Jessica's life."

"Why?" The light turned green and he accelerated. He looked at her quickly, and from his expression, she knew he was discomfited by the idea of them delving into Jessica's life together.

"Because that's where the answers will be. More than likely, we'll find them in the twenty-four hours before she died."

"I found a company in north Georgia who can do a twenty-four-hour turnaround on DNA testing. I talked them into doing a test on Sunday, if we send this out by courier tonight."

Celia's voice washed over him and Tom glanced up from Jessica's banking records. The office lay quiet and deserted around them. He pulled off his reading glasses and laid them aside. "That was fast."

She held aloft a plastic evidence bag. "I need to swab you."

He nodded and pushed out of the chair. "What do you need me to do?"

Pulling on a pair of latex gloves, she smiled, the expression holding little humor. "Just open up and say 'ah'."

Hands clenching the edge of the desk, thighs spread, he leaned against the end and opened his mouth. She stepped between his legs, a long swab in hand.

"This will only take a second." Her gaze flitted up to his and away. With her this close, he could smell her—faint traces of soap and shampoo, the warmth of her skin. Despite the day's stressful events, arousal tugged at him, a low, hot pooling below his belt. Her eyes trained on his mouth, she scraped the cotton swab down the inside of his cheek. "That's it."

She stepped away and dropped the swab in the bag. He straightened, watching her graceful hands as she sealed the bag and labeled it.

"Who's Turello?"

"Who's Turello?" A visible tremor shook her fingers as she recapped her pen. When she finally looked at him, her eyes were bleak, although a wry smile flitted around her lips. "I guess Bryan Turello is my Kathleen Harding."

Her name didn't send all the old pain and frustration crashing through him. Thinking of her, even for a second, did nothing. All of his attention, his being, was focused on Celia.

"God, I was so *stupid*." A harsh laugh burst from her lips.

"Stupid?" He reached for her, pulled her back into the cradle of his thighs. Right now, he wanted nothing more than to smooth away the tension the old memories brought her. He brushed her hair away from her face. "I doubt that."

"Naïve, then." She didn't look at him, her gaze fixed on his throat. "I was a rookie with the DCPD. Turello was my training officer. He was a decorated road cop, very smart, very good looking." She swept a finger over his collar, her face pensive. "Very, very charming. I fell hard. I was sleeping with him within my first two weeks on the force. That was a really intelligent decision, let me tell you."

She'd been beating herself up for it ever since. One more thing they had in common—an inability to forgive themselves for past failures. He rubbed his thumb along her jaw. "What happened?"

"By the end of the first month, I'd moved in with him. He did put an engagement ring on my finger, I'll give him that much. Whether or not he really intended to marry me? Who knows. A few weeks later, a college girl from Americus filed a complaint against him, said he'd let her out of a speeding ticket in return for oral sex. The media got a hold of that and the other girls started coming out of the woodwork. He'd been using the badge for a while, to get whatever he wanted from them.

"When the GBI came around, asking questions about one particular incident..." Her lashes fell. "I lied for him, because he asked me to and I believed in him."

Tom swallowed an oath.

She opened her eyes, meeting his gaze, her own filled with self-recrimination. "A grand jury indicted him. The night before he was to surrender to the GBI, he called me from a payphone outside that little dive bar in Putney. He'd been drinking and he was crying. Confessed to all of it and then he shot himself with his service revolver."

"With you listening." Tom cupped the back of her head, massaging the tension lying along her nape.

She nodded. "Everyone knew I'd lied. It's a wonder I didn't lose my certification and my career, all three months of it."

None of this had come up when he'd checked her references—everything he'd been told was glowingly positive. Obviously, she'd moved beyond it, at least professionally. "Why didn't you?"

Her eyes lifted to his again. "Because Cook fought for me. He was convinced I'd make a good cop, that I'd simply made an error in personal judgment. He went to bat for me with the chief, the GBI, the review board. I owe him everything."

That explained a lot, including Cook's extreme reaction to learning about their relationship. "He thinks you're making the same mistake with me."

A sad smile touched her mouth. "Yes."

Tom frowned. "You don't agree."

"I never questioned Turello's culpability. I simply accepted on blind faith what he told me. If I'd thought about it...well, maybe I'd have seen what he was capable of." She shrugged, a soft roll of her shoulders. "I've considered what I know about you, McMillian. I've questioned your culpability."

He sifted his hands through the soft fall of her hair. "And?"

"And I know you're not capable of what I saw at Jessica Grady's home this morning." She glanced away. "I know if you'd known about that baby, that it might be yours, that you'd never have done anything to put it at risk."

Peace spread through him at her words. Exerting tender

pressure, he pulled her toward him.

"What happened with Turello was a long time ago. You're not the same person you were. Just like I'm not the same man who married Kathleen, who lost Everett. Turello doesn't matter anymore. Neither does Kathleen." He lowered his voice to a whisper, his mouth brushing hers. "This is what matters."

He kissed her, soft caresses that were more about connection than desire. She wound her arms around him, pressing nearer, so he felt the slight trembling of her body. He tugged her closer. He drew her bottom lip between his and her fingers shaped the line of his jaw.

She pulled back, tracing his mouth with her shaking index finger. "We have a lot of work to do."

She was right. The emotions developing between them mattered, but Jessica's case, her baby, had to take priority.

They had plenty of time for them later. A vista of new opportunities opened before him.

Opportunities that would be well worth waiting for.

He leaned in, brushed his mouth across hers once more. "Let's get to it, then."

Celia frowned at the bank records in front of her. "McMillian, does this look normal to you?"

Setting his chopsticks and carton of fried rice aside, he moved to look over her shoulder. The lingering clean scent of his faded aftershave tickled her senses. "What?"

"She was moving a lot of money through her account." Celia highlighted a line of deposits and withdrawals. "A *lot* of money."

"Let me see that." He picked up the paper and settled into

177

his chair. "Which account is this?"

Celia consulted the list. "The law firm. There's some activity in the one for the real estate company she's invested in, but not nearly as much."

"These are cash deposits." He blew out a breath and rubbed at his chin. "It looks like normal money laundering."

"I thought so too. See?" She pointed out another sheet. "She was transferring part of each deposit to the real estate company and part to an offshore account."

"Which we don't have records for."

"Right."

"What the hell was she doing?"

"I don't know, but look...for the last few months, she'd been making regular deposits to the account, deposits which *weren't* withdrawn or transferred. More cash deposits. They're smaller, but if you add them up, it's over fifty thousand dollars."

"Since July." McMillian rubbed a hand over his mouth. "Around the time she got pregnant."

Celia looked at him. "Someone paying her for the baby?"

"Maybe. Fifty thousand for an infant." McMillian shook his head. "Damn. Who's that desperate?"

"Probably lots of people. I wonder..." She frowned, pawing through the files laid across the table in McMillian's office. She picked up the preliminary autopsy report and flipped through it. "I thought I read that."

"What?"

"Ford won't know until she's done the complete autopsy, but she doesn't think this was Jessica's first pregnancy."

McMillian blinked, then laughed. "That can't be right."

Celia glanced up from the report. "Why?"

He shook his head. "You'd have to know Jessie. She was very vocal about never having children. Said it ruined a woman's body."

Cynicism trickled through Celia. "Amazing how enough money can change someone's mind, isn't it? So if this isn't the first baby, how many times has she done this?"

"You two look busy." Rhett High's deep voice at the door drew their attention away from the files. Celia smiled, instinctively easing away from McMillian by sitting up straighter in her chair. Casually dressed in jeans and a thin sweater, Rhett moved farther into the office and glanced at the paperwork on the table. "Which case?"

McMillian leaned back in his chair, arms folded behind his head. "Jessica Grady."

An apologetic grimace twisted Rhett's face. "I heard about that while I was over at the clubhouse. I'm sorry, Tom. I know you two were close."

"Thanks."

Rhett waved a hand at the paperwork littering the table. "So are you assisting the sheriff's department?"

"Something like that." Celia and McMillian exchanged a look. McMillian straightened, exhaling hard. "Cook would love to pin this one on me."

"You?" Rhett laughed. When no one smiled, he sobered. "You're kidding."

"I wish. And if it were anyone but me, I'd think he was onto something."

Rhett lifted his eyebrows. "What's he got?"

"My prints in the bedroom." McMillian glanced at Celia again. "A fucking sex tape of the two of us last summer. The fact she tried to call me the night she was killed."

"Man."

Celia looked between the two men. McMillian hadn't mentioned the baby. It wasn't a secret; the local news had been running an Amber Alert for the missing child every thirty minutes. He and Rhett were close friends, and he discussed his feelings about fathering the baby with her rather than bring it up with Rhett. That had to mean something, didn't it?

Rhett jerked his chin at the table. "So what angle are you working?"

"Right now?" McMillian rubbed at the back of his neck. "We're taking a look at her finances."

Mild interest flared in Rhett's dark gaze. "Finding anything?"

McMillian shrugged. "What might be some money laundering. Other than that? Not much."

Rhett shook his head. "Maybe it was random. Burglary gone wrong, you know?"

Celia's phone pinged and she pulled it from her waistband. The screen read "private caller" and she sighed. "I'm going to step outside and take this."

Tom watched her disappear into the hall, disquiet creeping down his spine. His nerves had started jumping as soon as her phone rang. Sensations of darkness and cold flashed in his head, an overall impression of looming threat. He tossed his reading glasses aside and pinched his nose, fighting the ache at his temples and the pictures in his head.

Damn it all, not this. Not now. He needed his focus.

"Tom?" Rhett's quiet voice brought him back to reality.

He shook himself free of the images and directed his attention to Rhett. "Does Mariah know about Jessie?"

"Yeah." Regret flashed over Rhett's expression. "She was

upset."

Tom could imagine. The two women had been long-time friends, and Rhett's wife had been the one to introduce him to Jessie in the first place.

Eyes narrowed, Rhett regarded him with friendly concern. "You okay?"

"I'm fine." Tom rubbed his hands down his thighs. The movement didn't ease the unpleasant sensations prickling over him. "Just tired."

"And a little stressed." Rhett chuckled and dropped into Celia's vacated chair.

"The cops turned up a fucking sex video of me. Yeah, I'm a little tense." He tried to breathe through heavier flashes of foreboding. "And then there's the baby."

"The baby?"

"Jessie was pregnant. It looks like she was killed for the baby." He sucked in a harsh inhale. "It's possible I might be the father."

"Shit. Like you needed that." He paused and looked toward the door. "You and Celia here together...it's about more than just this case, isn't it?"

The idea of lying crossed Tom's mind. If Rhett had noticed something, what sense was there in denying it? Rhett knew him too well and respected Celia enough not to gossip outside the office. Finally, he nodded. "Yes, it is. A lot more."

Rhett frowned. "Do you know what you're doing?"

Living. He was actually fucking living for the first time in...for the first time since he'd buried his son. The memories were still there, but their painful power to hold him prisoner had weakened. He had Celia to thank for that.

And damn if he would let her go. Damn if he would let

anything screw this up.

He laughed, despite the lingering stress of the day. "Yeah, I do, Rhett. I honest to God do."

"All right, man, if you're sure. Because the DA getting involved with a subordinate? That's some major shit to hit the fan. Might even be bigger than that tape you're worried about."

"It's not like that, Rhett. It's different." Hell, he didn't know how to explain it to his friend. How to explain the way Celia was freeing him from the past? He cleared his throat. "What are you doing here on a Saturday night, anyway? I thought it was your date night with Mariah."

"She's packing." Rhett passed a hand over his bald head. "I came by to pick up some files. We're taking Amarie up to Emory in the morning and I'm going to work from there for a few days."

Apprehension made its way over Tom again. Local doctors had been treating Rhett's daughter for aplastic anemia for nearly a year, with little success. A trip to Emory Hospital couldn't be a good thing. "What's going on?"

A wide grin split Rhett's face. "We have a possible bone-marrow donor. A distant cousin of Mariah's. The docs are going to do the preliminary blood work tomorrow."

"That's great." Laughter rumbled in his chest and Tom pounded the other man's shoulder. As Amarie was adopted, they'd struggled with locating a suitable donor. This was good news. "That's really great, Rhett."

"Yeah, we're really excited. We've still got a long road—chemo, antibiotics, all that jazz—but this is what we've prayed for, man." He pushed out of his chair. "I'd better get going. Mariah wants to leave out before daylight."

"Drive safely." Tom rose to offer a hand. They shook and Tom pulled him into a quick hug, slapping his back. Rhett returned the slap and both men laughed. "Listen, anything you need, you call, okay?"

"You got it, my man. I'll be in touch." He passed by Celia at the door as he exited. "Take care of him, Celia. Keep him out of trouble."

"Will do." Her smile died as Rhett walked away.

Tom frowned, watching her fidget with her chain. "What's up?"

She held up her cell phone. "That was Sheriff Reed. He'd like to meet with us, first thing Monday morning. And he didn't sound happy."

Tom nodded. "You know my philosophy on that, right, Cee?"

She smiled, although her eyes remained serious. "Always make them come to you."

Chapter Ten

Bright moonlight flitted through the oak trees framing the back of Celia's home. Leaning against the railing, she flipped through her keys and glanced up at McMillian. All the weariness and stress of the day dragged at his features, and suddenly letting him go home to his big, empty house was the last thing she wanted.

She ran a finger over her house key. "Do you want to come in?"

A half-smile quirked at his mouth. "If I come in, I'm not going to want to leave."

Pushing away from the railing, she stepped close to him. A slight wind rustled through the trees, casting moving shadows on his face. Even in the dimness of the porch, his eyes gleamed down at her. She curled a finger into the open placket of his shirt. "Maybe I won't want you to leave."

She lifted her face and he closed the distance, mouth covering hers. She drank him in, the kiss going on and on, soothing away the awful tension of the day, leaving healing warmth in its wake. The wanting remained, lurking beneath the surface, but the need, the growing emotional connection, was stronger.

When he finally lifted his head, she touched the strong jut of his chin, stubbled under her fingertip. "Stay with me,

McMillian."

In silent answer he took the keys from her and unlocked the door. She wrapped her fingers around his and drew him through the downstairs rooms and up to her bedroom. Once there, she turned into his arms, accepting the soft ravishment of his kiss with avaricious eagerness. His tie had disappeared earlier in the day, the top two buttons on his dress shirt undone.

Mouth open, tongue twirling around his, she rubbed his arms, biceps hard and hot under her palms. Excited desire speared through her, setting off a low ache in her belly, between her thighs, but blended with the sexual need was a different emotion, something deeper, truer. Not a need for his body, the pleasure he could bring her, but a need for this man, for the fledgling connection unfolding between them and slowly drawing her to him with thin threads of steel.

"You don't know what it meant," he murmured, pressing damp kisses down her neck, to her collarbone, to her sternum. His lips brushed against her necklace. "This evening, to have you stay with me."

She smoothed her fingers over his short hair. "I couldn't leave you alone with that."

"I'm glad." He spread his hand over her back, supporting her while his lips moved even lower, to where her blouse gaped at the curve of her cleavage. She let her eyes slide closed, hot breath and the warm wet glide of his tongue heating her skin, sending more liquid desire pooling deep within her.

Urgency driving her, she stepped back and unbuttoned her blouse, letting it fall away under his hungry gaze. She stepped out of her slacks and kicked them aside, watching as he peeled away his own shirt and reached for his belt. She caught his hands, easing them aside, dispatching buckle, button and zipper herself. She slipped the gray pants and navy boxers off together, freeing his erection to her greedy touch.

She folded her fingers around the hard length of him, his skin smooth and soft. Eyes closing on hissed inhale, he fumbled with her bra, letting it hang on her arms while his hands covered each breast, stroking, squeezing, stoking the flames licking between her thighs. He caught her mouth again and she mimicked the rhythm of his tongue with the slide of her hand on him.

"I want you, Cee," he muttered into her mouth, his voice rough and raw with passion and something deeper, something she was afraid to define.

"I think you have me, McMillian." She pushed him toward the bed. "So take me."

His eyes flared and he spun, pinning her beneath him with an agile pounce. He hooked two fingers in her panties and yanked, tossing them away while she did the same with her lacy bra. With one hand tangled in her hair, holding her gaze beneath his, he dipped a hand between her thighs, sliding two fingers inside her, thumb rubbing across her clit. The combined sensation sent her arching off the bed with a raw moan. God, how could it be so powerful, so good with him, with just the simplest of caresses?

"You're wet for me," he rasped, tightening his hold on her hair. His hand pulsed between her legs, a steady rhythm that still wasn't enough. She bit her lip and opened further to him.

"Yes, for you." She wrapped a hand around him again, slipping her palm up and down, passing her thumb over the head until he groaned. "Take me. Make me yours."

He pulled his fingers from her body and left her long enough to extract a condom from his wallet. He sank between her thighs and slid inside, withdrew, thrust deeper. She arched into him, taking him further, harder. Reality narrowed to the joining of their bodies, the wet skate of skin and tongues and moans. Nothing existed but him, the pleasure he created within her, growing, billowing, burning until an intense climax stabbed through her, until he braced against her with two deep thrusts, a groan seeming to rip from his throat.

He slumped in her arms and she wrapped them about him, his skin damp and hot beneath her fingertips. She buried her face against his throat, blinking back a rush of tears she couldn't explain.

With an audible exhale, McMillian rolled to his back, taking her with him. Celia ran a finger down his stomach, tracing the line of his abs. Muscles jumped beneath her touch and she smiled against his ribcage.

"What are you doing?" His voice, lazy and drowsy, rumbled at her ear.

She pressed a kiss to the small scar below his nipple. "You'll laugh."

His hand ran up her back, sifting through her hair. "What?"

"Nothing important." Satiated and flushed with contentment, she levered up on an elbow to study him. Eyes closed, he rested against her pillows, her decidedly feminine floral sheets making him appear even more masculine, more virile. She was happy, here with him like this, and she squashed the tiny tremor of fear the realization aroused.

Being happy frightened her, because it never lasted.

He opened his eyes and smiled. The dark depths of his blue eyes were clear and warm, and the flutter kicked off in her chest by that expression took her breath. She swallowed and averted her gaze, her heart thudding a heavy beat. This was scary. This felt *real*, because she could see a line of nights like these—filled with laughter and lovemaking, sharing secrets and kisses—stretching into the future.

She gnawed at her bottom lip. He'd said he wanted to get to know her, that he wanted more. They weren't all about the sex any longer.

And she found herself wanting all those things too.

He smoothed a finger up her cheek, tucked her hair behind her ear. "That's a contemplative expression if I ever saw one."

She smiled, smothering the doubts, not wanting them to intrude on this interlude with him. She trailed a finger along the line of his ribs. "Just making a memory."

"About?" He stroked her throat, danced a fingertip along her clavicle.

"You. This." She lifted her eyes to meet his. "Us."

A hand at her nape, he pulled her down, feathering his lips across hers. She curved a hand along his jaw and kissed him back. Afterward, she subsided onto her pillow, staring at the ceiling, hugging the warmth of their connection to her.

He rolled to his side, resting his weight on an elbow. Above the sheet, he traced the length of her chain, rolled the button onto the pad of his finger. She closed her eyes, knowing what he saw—a button from an Air Force dress uniform, the silver surface worn from being constantly touched for more than thirty years, traces of tarnish along the design. A sigh worked through her.

"It was my father's," she said, her voice quiet in the still room. "He went to Vietnam before I was born. He was killed when I was four months old."

"I'm sorry." Sincerity colored his tone.

When she opened her eyes, she found him watching her with that same intensely clear gaze. She shook her head, ignoring the sudden tightness of her throat. "Don't be. I never knew him."

"Bullshit, Cee." He replaced the button carefully against her skin. "Or this wouldn't be around your neck every day."

She shifted to rest against the headboard. His hair brushed her shoulder, and she threaded her fingers in her lap. "When I was little, I used to pretend it was all a mistake, that he'd come home, and I'd have a real daddy, you know? We'd be a real family—not that we weren't, Mama and Cis and I—but we'd be more of a family. There were a lot of men in Mama's life, men who didn't stay."

"Like your sister's father?"

"Yeah." Her attempt at a smile hurt. "Like him. He wasn't around long enough for Mama to tell him she was pregnant. I was older before I figured out she wanted it that way. She pushed them away before they had a chance to hurt her."

His thumb rubbed her upper arm. "You don't have to push me away, Cee."

"I don't want to. That's what scares the hell out of me, McMillian."

He moved, leaning over her, his face close to hers, the warm strength of his hands holding her shoulders. "If it's any consolation, I'm scared shitless too."

Shaky laughter bubbled to her lips. She wrapped her arms around his waist and tugged him down, their mouths meeting, clinging, meshing.

She traced her hands up his spine and whispered against his mouth. "I really like being with you, McMillian."

He chuckled and rolled to lie against the pillows, keeping her against his side. "It's mutual, baby."

Her eyes burning from weariness, but still feeling too keyed up to sleep, she curved a hand around his rib cage. "What will you do? If you are the father?"

Tension tightened the line of his body, but he slowly relaxed under her touch. "I don't know. Deal with it, the best I can."

Sliding her hand down his arms, she tangled her fingers with his. "I'll be there, if you want me to."

"I want you to." Turning his head, he brushed his mouth across her forehead. She settled more firmly into his side and let the steady thrum of his heartbeat soothe her into an uneasy sleep.

ℬ

Tom woke, lying on his stomach, surrounded by soft sheets and Celia's clean scent. Residual pleasure and contentment lingered in him and he smiled into the pillow.

I'll be there, if you want me to.

The intensity with which he craved that support, craved her, speared through him all over again. However, she wasn't here now. He was alone in the bed. He shifted to his back, the sunlight streaming in at the window indicating it was well after dawn.

The rushing of the shower filtered through the bathroom door. He rolled from the bed and followed the sounds of water and Celia's quiet humming. In the bath, steam rose in lazy curlicues and the frosted glass door blurred the lines of Celia's nude body. An eagerness beyond mere sexual wanting settled in him.

He slid the shower door aside. Water streamed over Celia's body in a shimmering fall. Her gaze met his, a smile curving her lips. Sultry passion flared in her eyes.

"Good morning." She slicked dripping hair away from her face.

Resting a hand on either side of her head, he leaned in and kissed her. "Now it's a good morning, even if I did wake up without you."

"I went for a run." She laid her palms flat against his pecs. "You looked so peaceful I didn't want to wake you. The last couple of days have been rough."

"You make it better." Zings of pleasure shot out from the soft caress of her fingers on his damp skin. He leaned in again to take her mouth in a wet, open kiss. On a quiet moan, she slid her hands up, winding her arms around his neck and pressing into him, the slick globes of her breasts gliding against his chest. Parting her lips further, she gently sucked his tongue deeper into her mouth. Renewed desire slammed into him. With a low growl, he backed her into the wall.

She moaned again, a low sound of approval. He caught her chin in one hand, holding her under his kiss until he lifted his mouth from hers long enough to whisper, "Mine."

"Yours." She murmured the affirmation into his mouth, arching into him. He slipped his other hand between them, down the wet surface of her stomach, sifting his fingers through the curls between her thighs and skimmed two fingers along the damp cleft of her sex. She gasped and he caught the sweet intake of breath with his lips.

"Open to me."

She complied, thighs falling apart, allowing him greater access. Water fell about them, sheeting on heated skin, caressing. He stroked her, circling her clit, delving a pair of fingers into her clenching wetness. Another muffled moan rewarded him. She sagged against the wall, holding onto him

191

with fingers that dug into his muscles.

"I love the way you kiss me," she breathed. He trailed his mouth down her neck, suckling, nipping. She bit her lip, a raw groan slipping free. "Love the way you touch me."

He twisted his fingers inside her, driving higher, sweeping his thumb across her clit in tiny circles. "I love how you respond to me."

"Because it's you." She threw her head back, offering him more of her throat. "God, McMillian, I want you inside me."

"Not this time, baby." He deepened his thrusts, keeping up the rhythm between her thighs. Being with her kept the uncertainties surrounding Jessie's death, his possible paternity at bay, but even more, the need to pleasure her, to return in this small way the simple peace she'd brought to his life, consumed him. In this one moment, isolated from the world, she was his. And he was hers. "Let me."

A ragged sigh puffed from between her lips. Letting his other hand slip to caress and tease at her breast, he closed his teeth on her neck in a light, scraping pressure. She grabbed for his shoulders. "McMillian..."

Muscles contracted around his fingers, heat spreading along his nerves as the orgasm took her body. She cried out, nails abrading his skin, and he continued touching, thrusting, kissing, tweaking, until the small tremors died away and she slumped into his embrace, face pressed to his throat. A warm tightness took his chest, squeezing his heart and lungs in a weird pleasure-pain. Smoothing wet, tangled hair from her face, he cupped her jaw and lifted. Her lashes rose, eyes filled with lazy satiation and a reaffirmation of her promise from the previous night. He dipped his head to take her mouth once more, but in a softer kiss permeated with tenderness.

He could do this, could face the unthinkable, as long as he

had her.

Breaking the kiss, eyes clenched against a wave of hot emotion and cold fear, he wrapped her close. Against his chest, her still-thundering heart thudded in a heavy, reassuring rhythm. He clung to that pulse like a lifeline in deadly seas.

Twenty-four hours. By this time tomorrow, he'd know if he faced his greatest nightmare all over again.

By this time tomorrow, he'd know whether or not he'd fathered a child he could do nothing to protect.

捱

"Gentlemen, thank you for coming." Ignoring Cook's icy look, Tom closed the conference room door and indicated the chairs around the polished table. Beyond the room, activity stirred in the offices: phones ringing, low conversations, the muted buzz from the television playing the local station's midmorning newsbreak. "Ms. St. John will join us shortly."

"I won't lie, Tom." Sheriff Stanton Reed pulled out a chair. "I'm not happy about your hijacking this case."

Tom shrugged, not deigning to sit. Cook remained standing also, his shoulders set in a tight line. "What hijacking? I merely had Ms. St. John explore another line of thought than your investigators."

Relaxed in a chair, Tick Calvert rested his chin on his hand. "Word games. You're poaching and you know it."

"Considering I'll be prosecuting Jessica's killer, I wouldn't call it poaching."

"Prosecuting yourself. Interesting concept." Cook folded his arms over his chest. "Kind of like being told to go fu—"

"All right." Reed held up a quelling hand and shot a hard

look at Cook. "That's enough. I'm all for cooperation, Tom, and I'm open to what you have to share with us. I'm also not opposed Celia's rejoining the investigation."

"And what are you planning to offer in the way of sharing?"

Reed and Calvert exchanged a look. "We have some interesting DNA results."

"So do we." Celia spoke from the doorway. Tom glanced around at her. She looked calm and cool, her hair twisted into a sleek chignon, a navy pinstriped suit hugging her body. He remembered their hands tangling the night before and his palm tingled as a rush of well-being spread through him. "Who wants to go first?"

"The deceased baby from Tuesday?" Cook tugged a chair away from the table with a tight, frustrated movement. "Jessica Grady wasn't the mother."

"I sense a 'but' there." Celia crossed the room and took the chair across from him. She lifted her chin, a challenging expression on her face.

"But there are similarities in DNA between the baby and the placental remains in Ms. Grady's uterus."

Tom frowned. "Similarities?"

"The babies share some of the same genetic material," Cook explained. "Ford believes they're related in some way. Siblings, with the same father, or cousins, maybe."

"Well." Celia tapped the faxed report in front of her. "That father is definitely *not* Mr. McMillian."

She met Tom's gaze and he saw his own relief reflected in her eyes. Finally able to completely relax, he pulled a chair away from the table and sat before his suddenly weak knees put him on the floor.

"We got a hit from the national database on our John Doe

suspect's prints." Cook's steady, icy voice pulled Tom's attention back.

Celia leaned forward, excitement spiking on her face. "Who is he?"

"His name is Danny Blanton." Tick pulled a folder from the small stack he'd brought. "He's from Hamilton County, Florida. Has a list of priors a mile long, mostly small-time stuff."

"So, what are we saying?" Celia frowned. "He escalated to kidnapping?"

Tick smiled and shook his head. "He's associated with a bunch down there out of Taylor County that I remember from my days with the bureau's Organized Crime section. His main function seemed to be as a courier or a runner for them."

"Are we talking the mob here?" Tom asked.

Tick shook his head. "Dixie Mafia. These boys in Florida had loose ties to the Reeses and Hollowell up here. You can't tell me there aren't still people they're associated with around here. And you know they'd be into anything with money attached."

Celia arched an eyebrow. "Like money laundering?"

Tick laughed. "Definitely. Prostitution, drugs, gambling. You name it, they've done it. Less organized than the traditional mob, but they're definitely still around."

Her eyes narrowed in calculation, Celia looked at Tom once again. "We need to look deeper into Jessica's life. There'll be a connection somewhere. We just have to find it."

Cook waved a hand in an annoyed gesture. "Would you mind sharing, or are you two going to continue talking in secret code over there?"

"In going through Jessica's banking records, we discovered some evidence of possibly money laundering—large cash deposits, withdrawals, transfers."

"And we think someone may have been paying her for carrying this baby."

Eagerness dawning on his face, Cook tapped a finger on the table. "Grady specialized in family and divorce law, didn't she?"

Tom frowned. "Yes."

"Does that include adoptions?"

"I don't know."

"Yes, it does." Tick cleared his throat. "Cait and I talked to her about what was involved in a private adoption earlier in the year. She said she had people who helped her find birth mothers. We, well, something about the way she said that made it seem like it was something we didn't want to be involved with."

"Oh God." Celia stared at Tom. "You don't think...?"

"A baby ring." Disgust colored Cook's voice. "You said it, Tick. Anything with money attached. Wonder what a healthy white infant goes for these days?"

"Obviously more than fifty grand."

"You know who I want to talk to again? That couple from Cader County."

Celia nodded. "Both of them."

"We want to make them come to us." Tom rubbed a hand over his jaw. "I think we also want to take a look at any adoptions she's put together in the last year as well, especially any she had in the works when she was killed."

"Couple's name was Campbell." Cook looked up from his notebook and focused on Celia. "Now where have we heard that name before?"

Awareness dawned on Celia's features. "The DVDs. One of them was labeled Campbell. But I don't remember seeing the

196

husband on any of the ones we watched."

"Because he's not. The husband is Wesley Campbell. The Campbell we have on the DVD is Jameson Campbell, the county administrator from over in Cader County."

"They're brothers," Tick offered. "I've met Jameson once or twice and my brother bought some farm equipment from Wesley."

"Coincidental, isn't it?" Cook lifted an eyebrow. "Wesley and the wife wanting a kid so bad, and Jameson has an affair with a woman who turns up dead with her baby cut out of her belly?"

Tom chuckled. "Coincidental enough that I think we want to invite both the Campbell brothers and the wife over to the sheriff's department for a little talk."

Cook cleared his throat. "Well, St. John, feel like going for a little drive?"

"I made a couple of calls to agents I knew from the OCB." Tick handed Tom a cup of coffee. "According to them, neither of the Campbell boys is on the bureau's radar."

Tom sipped the hot brew, grimaced at the strong taste, and studied the white board set up in the department's small conference room. Celia's neat handwriting filled in areas not covered by Cook's slashing script. They'd spent thirty minutes or so writing up leads and theories on the board before heading out to Cader County. In the corner of the board, Celia had written *Jessica, second pregnancy?* The notation niggled at him as much as it seemed to bother Celia.

He slanted a look at Tick. "You said Jessie told you she had ways to find birth mothers?"

"Yeah. And something about the way she said it? Made my

skin crawl."

His attention drifted back to Celia's notes. Jessica had said the same thing once about the idea of being pregnant. If she'd had access to birth mothers, why carry a baby herself? The money?

What made that particular baby worth so much?

"I started looking through the records we pulled from her law offices." Tick indicated a banker's box on the table, a stack of manila folders beside it. "Her laptop is gone, so I'm afraid some of what we wanted to look at was on it. All her files at home were personal stuff."

"Find anything?"

"You're the lawyer." Tick handed him the topmost file. "They look okay to me. They're 'open' adoptions. Records of contact between the birth mother and the adoptive parents before the baby was born, questionnaires on the adoptive parents, home studies, that kind of stuff. The waiver of parental rights from the biological parents, the adoption orders."

Tom frowned. "Let me see the others."

With a shrug, Tick slid them across the table. "Be my guest."

"I don't believe this." Tom flipped through them quickly. A disbelieving laugh rumbled through him. "All of these orders are signed by the same judge."

"That's not kosher?"

Tom shook his head. "Adoption orders should be filed in the county in which the couple resides. Somehow, I doubt all of these people live in Chandler County."

"Who's the judge?"

Tom dropped the files back on the scarred tabletop. "The Honorable Alton Baker."

"That's...interesting."

"Do me a favor." Tom pulled a legal pad in front of him and began a list of the adoptive parents and birth mothers. "Run these. See if we can get current addresses and phone numbers on any of them."

Tick reached for the paper. "Will do."

"I don't fucking believe it." Tom stared at the names before him.

Interest flared in Tick's dark eyes. "What?"

Tom turned the paper so the investigator could see it. "Look at this."

Tick whistled. "Holy hell."

"So, was offering to take me along an olive branch, Cook?" In a low murmur, Celia tossed the question at him as they followed the unhappy Campbells up the department steps.

He shrugged. "Something like that."

"Still pissed at me?"

With a quick glance at her, he caught the door behind Wesley Campbell and held it for her. "I worry about my friends, St. John. I don't want to see you hurt."

Touched by his gruff concern, she grinned. "I'm a big girl this time around, Cook. I know what I'm doing."

"I sure as hell hope so," he muttered. "Come on, let's see where your boss is."

He ushered the Campbells into the squad room and she smiled at the careful, almost undetectable way he separated the three. Watching the woman and two men in the squad room, she and Cook stepped to the doorway of the conference room. Surprised, Celia stared.

McMillian and Tick had flipped the white board to use the opposite side. His jacket and tie gone and sleeves rolled up, McMillian stood at the board, writing a list. "All right. I've got four Stephanie Nichols, three Jennifer Skylars, and what looks like two Natalie Bradleys."

Tick nodded, looking up from a legal pad balanced on his knee. "That's what I've got."

"What's going on?" Celia asked and Tom glanced around at her, excitement glinting in his sharp blue gaze. He waved her into the room.

"Come look at this."

She stopped at his shoulder and looked at the list—repeated names with dates beside them. "It's a list of names."

His mouth twisted. "Funny. Look, Celia. These are the birth mothers Jessica listed on the adoption papers."

"Rather prolific, aren't they?" She frowned. "Those are not nine-month spans between babies."

"Oh, it gets better." Tick tossed a small stack of Internet articles on the table. "Stephanie Nichols died of leukemia when she was three. Jennifer Skylar? Car accident before she was a year old. Natalie Bradley drowned at age four."

"My God." Celia shook her head. "That's nine babies. Where did they come from?"

"Good question," Cook said. He jerked a thumb over his shoulder. "Maybe the Campbells can help us find an answer."

"I don't know what you're talking about." Jameson Campbell laid his hands atop the table, obviously preparing to leverage up from the chair. "I damn sure don't know anything about a baby, either."

"You want to know what I think?" Celia tilted her head to

one side and leaned forward, lowering her voice. "I think you had an affair with Jessica and she got pregnant. I think she told you about the video and the baby and tried to shake you down. And then? Then I think you killed her."

"You're crazy."

"Where's the baby, Mr. Campbell?" Cook scraped his thumbnail along his teeth, appearing bored by the whole proceedings. Bored like a big, edgy lion waiting to pounce.

"I don't have to stay here and listen to this bullshit."

"No, you don't. You're free to go at any time." Cook dropped his feet from the corner of the table and sat up straight. "Hey, St. John, you still got that friend at the TV station, right?"

He fixed Celia with an inquiring look and she swallowed a laugh. "Yeah, I do."

Campbell's gaze swung between them in a wild arc. "What are you talking about?"

Cook spared him a pithy glance and shrugged. "You don't want to tell us where the baby is and we have to find it. Figure when our friends over at the NBC affiliate run the next Amber Alert, they can show your video with it. Someone's bound to put two and two together for us."

Celia smiled. "Of course, they'll have to blur parts of the film."

Cook nodded. "But it's about to be sweeps month. Hell, Mr. Campbell, you might make *Dateline*."

Panic flickering in his eyes, Campbell shook his head. "You can't do that."

"Sure we can." Cook shrugged. "Whether or not we have to is up to you."

Celia pitched her voice to a gentler tone. "Where's the baby, Mr. Campbell?"

"She's dead!" Campbell slumped in the chair. Celia looked at Cook, her heart clenching in her chest. Campbell rubbed a hand over his face. "She's dead, all right?"

"I told the other detectives everything." In Tick Calvert's office, Wesley Campbell kept a tight grip on his wife's hand. "Our adoption fell through and the birth mother went to Florida. There is no baby for us. End of story."

"There's only one problem with that, Mr. Campbell." Tom leaned against the windowsill, arms crossed over his chest. "We don't believe you."

Anger flashed over the man's face. "What do you want from me? I can't tell you what you want to hear because I don't know anything."

Tick folded his hands atop his desk. He smiled at Ashley Campbell, who huddled into the chair next to her husband. Beneath her tidy dark hair, her thin face was pale. "You wanted this baby very much, didn't you, Mrs. Campbell?"

She darted a look at her husband. Her tongue slipped out to moisten her lips. "Yes."

"I'm sorry it didn't work out. I understand how hard this is for you."

Campbell made a disgusted sound in his throat. "You understand jack shit."

Tick ignored him, his attention focused on Ashley. "My wife has had two miscarriages in the last six months. We lost another baby farther along in a pregnancy the year before that. The doctors keep telling us it may never happen for us, because of damage to her uterus, but she's having a hard time accepting that."

For the first time, a spark of life appeared in Ashley's hazel eyes. She twisted her hands together in her lap. "It's so hard. She probably blames herself."

Naked pain flickered across Tick's face. "I know she does. It tears her up inside, even though she tries to hide that from me."

"You can help her. There are other ways." Ashley leaned forward. "There are people who would help you. Like Ms. Grady helped us—"

"Ashley, shut up!" Campbell recovered himself quickly, covering her hands with his as she cowered away. He glared at Tick. "That's enough."

Tom unfolded his arms and tucked his hands in his pockets. "Actually, I'm interested in what your wife has to say. How did Ms. Grady help you, Mrs. Campbell?"

"We're leaving." Campbell rose, pulling his wife to her feet. She glanced at Tom helplessly, then away, her expression lost and filled with a devouring pain.

"Mrs. Campbell?" At Tick's gentle prompting, she turned her bruised gaze his way. "You don't have to have your husband's permission to talk to us. Someone murdered Ms. Grady. They cut out her baby and we have no idea where that baby is—"

"I said that's enough." Campbell dragged her toward the door.

"No!" She pulled away, tears spilling from her wild eyes. "You have to tell them, Wes. God knows where that baby is and she tried to help us. We have to help her now. You have to tell them everything."

"What do you mean, she's dead?" Celia eased into a chair at the table. "Just slow down and tell us everything, Mr.

Campbell."

Jameson rubbed his hands down his face and dropped back into his chair. "All Wes and Ashley wanted was a baby. They'd tried for years and...nothing. The doctors said Ashley would never be able to conceive. Jessica said she could help."

"By giving them her baby?" Cook asked, his voice quiet.

Poison saturated the glare Jameson cast in Cook's direction. "No. She told me she could find a girl who wanted to give up her baby. A private adoption, but perfectly legal. I had no reason to doubt her."

With a sinking sensation, Celia glanced at Cook. Mouth twisted, he returned her look. They had no doubt which baby Jameson had told them was dead. Jesus above, they'd never be able to sort through this mess.

Cook rubbed a hand over his face. "When did she tell you the baby died?"

Jameson blew out a long breath. "I called her after I saw the news report about that dead baby found in the roadblock. It seemed too coincidental not to be Ashley and Wes's baby after she'd phoned to tell us the baby had been born."

Celia shook her head. "Why didn't you come forward then?"

"Why?" A rough laugh vibrated Jameson's frame. "And have her release that damn movie of us? Have Wes and Ashley's pain splashed all over the news? Do you know what that would do to Ashley?"

Celia exchanged a look with Cook, then turned to Jameson again. "You love her too, don't you?"

"Does it show?" Jameson buried his face in his hands. "God. All I wanted was for Ashley to be happy, to have that baby she wanted so damn much. Look at this mess."

"Did you know Jessica was pregnant?"

Jameson lifted his head, surprise registering on his features. "No. Jessica didn't like children personally. She was adamant that she'd never get pregnant. She said it ruined a woman."

"Tell them, Wes." Ashley's voice broke, pitching higher with each word.

"Yeah, Wes." Tom rocked back on his heels. "Tell us."

Wesley dropped his head and drew in a deep breath. "She said she could help us. That for the right amount of money, she'd find us a baby."

"How much money?"

"Fifty thousand." Wesley's mouth twisted. "Twenty-five grand up front, another fifteen a few weeks later, and ten when the baby was born."

"So what happened? Did she renege, so you decided to take the baby from her?"

"No." Wesley shook his head. "The baby died before she got to us. Hell, y'all found her during that roadblock the other night."

"That was the baby you were supposed to get?" Tick asked, his voice quiet.

"Yes." Ashley blinked rapidly. "That was our baby."

"Did you ever meet the birth mother?"

"No, I wanted to meet her, but Ms. Grady said...she said it was better if we didn't. She sent us updates, sonograms, that kind of thing."

"Do you still have those?"

Ashley nodded.

"We'd like to see them. It might help us."

Tom waved a hand at Wesley. "How did this work? Did you ever meet with anyone except Ms. Grady?"

Wesley shook his head again. "No. We actually only met her once or twice. Jameson handled most of it for us. That's really all we can tell you, all right? We're leaving now."

"I don't think Jameson Campbell is our guy, even if he did know about the video." Cook popped a fresh piece of gum in his mouth. He tapped a thick finger on the stack of adoption files. "Maybe one of these couples can tell us something more."

Celia leaned against the table, staring at the white board. Nine babies. Fifty thousand dollars per baby. Almost a half a million dollars.

Maybe one more baby, worth so much someone would kill for it?

McMillian jerked his chin at Cook. "Why don't you and Tick start those interviews?"

Cook waved a finger in the air. "And what, pray tell, Counselor, are you and St. John going to do?"

A feral grin crossed McMillian's face. "Ms. St. John and I are going to have a little conversation with the Honorable Alton Baker."

Chapter Eleven

"Mr. McMillian. Ms. St. John." A bright, false smile curved Judge Alton Baker's mouth as he rose from his plush leather chair. The discreet maid who'd shown them in faded into the hallway. "To what do I owe the pleasure?"

"We'd like to ask you a few questions," Celia said. Standing behind her, Tom shook off a frisson of uneasiness. Ridiculous when Baker wasn't a threat to them in his own home, when Celia could more than take care of herself.

"May I offer you a drink?" Baker crossed to the bar and lifted a decanter, amber liquid glowing in the lights from a large crystal chandelier.

"No, thank you." Before he could fight the protective instinct, Tom took a step closer to Celia. She glanced at him over her shoulder, blue eyes cool and shuttered.

A grin quirked at his lips. She was in full cop mode. Funny how he was beginning to like that on her. Maybe because when they were alone together, that cop was nowhere to be found. Then it was all-woman mode. His woman.

Baker splashed liquid in a tumbler and came around the bar to settle back in his leather armchair. He waved a hand at a luxurious couch. "Please, sit."

Celia's chin tilted higher. "We'll stand, thank you."

"Suit yourself." Baker sipped at his drink and fixed them with an inquiring look. "Now, what can I help you with?"

"You finalized several private adoptions for Jessica Grady over the last year or so."

Nodding, Baker set his drink aside. The glass clicked against the polished rosewood table. He steepled his fingers together. "Yes, I did. Why?"

Tom narrowed his eyes, the uneasiness bouncing along his nerves again. "We have reason to believe some of those adoptions may have been fraudulent."

Baker didn't appear worried. "Really?"

"Yes."

Tom folded his arms over his chest. "What exactly was your relationship with Ms. Grady?"

Baker laughed. "Not quite what yours with her was, I assure you, Mr. District Attorney. I've known Jessica for years, God rest her soul. She clerked for me her first year out of law school. If she asked me for a few favors in expediting mutually agreed-upon private adoptions, I don't see the harm. Everyone was happy."

"Except many of the adoptions had the same birth mothers' names on them." Celia's tone was cold, firm. "Names belonging to girls who died years ago. And now not only is Jessica Grady dead, but her own baby is missing. And you don't see the harm?"

The judge's face hardened, but he waved away the question with another laugh. "I'm afraid I can't help you. Yes, I signed off on the adoptions, but that's all. Jessica arranged them alone."

"I'm sure the state judicial council will be interested in hearing about how you 'helped' her."

"Is that a threat, Mr. McMillian?"

"No." Tom smiled. Everyone who knew him knew he didn't make idle threats. He made set-in-stone promises.

Baker's gaze narrowed to burning slits and he pushed up from the chair. "If you'll excuse me, I have a dinner engagement. I trust you can show yourselves out."

Tom gave him one last hard look before ushering Celia outside. Humid air washed over them, doing little to alleviate the heat of anger buzzing under Tom's skin.

"You know he's lying." Squinting against the setting sun, Celia looked at Tom across the roof of the Mercedes.

He jerked the door open. "Of course he's lying."

Celia slid into the passenger seat. "Did she ever mention clerking for him?"

"No." He fired the engine. Discussing Jessica with Celia made him edgy. He didn't want Celia thinking what they were doing meant as little as his involvement with Jessica. Even if he couldn't find a way to articulate, even to himself, how deeply Celia had worked her way into his life in a few short days.

Wait. Who was he kidding? She'd been working her way into his life since the day he'd interviewed her, since she'd started working in his office.

"How long ago did she graduate law school?"

"Ten, eleven years, I guess." He shrugged. "Why?"

Celia rested her head on her hand, her gaze trained on the large house as Tom wheeled around the circular drive. "He's smooth. Charming. Just wondered what the extent of their relationship was."

"I'm not sure charming is the word I'd choose to describe him, Celia." His humorless laugh hovered between them. "Jessica was a very sexual woman. Does that answer your question?"

"It helps explain why y'all never got around to talking about your past legal experience."

Tom slanted a quelling look in her direction. "Not funny, Cee."

"All right, I'm sorry, I'll stop." She sighed. "I keep thinking about that previous pregnancy of hers. Did she put that child up for adoption? And this baby. Why is *this* baby so important?"

"I don't know." He swung out of the driveway onto the quiet country highway. His own frustration matched what he heard in Celia's voice. He didn't like unanswered questions.

"We need to find out about that first baby, McMillian. I'm telling you, it's important."

As arranged, they met Cook and Tick back at the sheriff's department. In the conference room, with their notes and questions still on the whiteboard and files on the table, tension seemed tangible in the air as she and McMillian entered.

His face tight with irritation, Cook tapped his pen atop his notebook. Celia caught his gaze. "What's going on?"

"None of these people want to talk to us." He tossed the pen down with a sharp, frustrated movement. "Not that I'm surprised. If I bought a kid, I probably wouldn't want to admit that either."

McMillian tugged out a chair, offered it to Celia, then pulled another for himself. "You got nothing?"

"Nada." Chair tilted back to a dangerous angle, Tick shook his head. He didn't open his eyes. "All right, we know Blanton was Grady's courier for the Campbell baby. We know he has links to the Dixie Mafia, such as it is. We suspect Grady was laundering money for someone. She told Cait and me she had access to birth mothers."

Cook huffed. "Are you going somewhere with this?"

Tick opened his eyes and the chair's front legs hit the floor with a soft bang. "What else is the Dixie Mafia known for?"

"Hmm, let's see." Celia tilted her head to one side, mentally running through the list Tick had given them earlier. "Gambling. Bootlegging. Prostitution—"

"Exactly." Tick nodded. "Can you think of a better source for their baby ring?"

The cold-blooded reality slithered through Celia's mind. She shuddered. "Oh my God."

"The problem," Cook said, "is making the link between Grady or Blanton and whoever's really heading this up."

McMillian rested his chin on his hand, rubbing a finger against his lips. "And none of the adoptive couples were willing to talk?"

"Not a single one."

"Maybe a subpoena to appear before the grand jury will change that." He slanted a look at Celia. "We'll make sure Judge Baker receives one as well."

Tom slumped on his couch, a tumbler holding two fingers of Scotch balanced on his leg. The house was quiet, save for the quiet rustling of Celia going through more files from Jessica's office. Something about having her close did more to settle his jangling nerves than anything else. A weary smile tugged at his mouth. He could get addicted to her calm presence.

Papers crackled. Gentle fingers removed the tumbler from his hand and glass clinked on wood. Celia straddled his lap, her massaging touch soft at his temples.

"What are you over here smiling about?" she whispered. Her clean scent surrounded him.

"You," he murmured, giving in to the temptation to allow her to take care of him. He relaxed deeper into the sofa. She was definitely becoming his favorite addiction.

Her fingers eased down his neck and over his shoulders in firm strokes, pushing away all of the tension. He swallowed a groan and let his hands settle at her hips, the faded denim of her jeans supple under his palms. There was nothing sexual in her touch, no desire rising in him, except the need to keep her here with him, close like this, touching him, for as long as she liked.

"You're relieved, aren't you?" She rubbed down his arms to his hands, working the strain away. "That the baby isn't yours."

He lifted heavy lids, not even the powder keg of the topic disturbing the magic she was working on him. She watched him, her face open, caring, concerned.

Nonjudgmental.

"Yes, I'm relieved." He stroked down her hip. "I can't face that again."

Some of the tightness invaded him once more. He waited for her to withdraw, to pull away. This was why he'd chosen to hide behind his feelings for Kathleen all those years, why he'd gone for brief affairs with women so far removed from maternal instincts they might as well be in another universe. For those women, he'd been what they wanted. He'd been enough.

But Celia was different—caring, tender, giving.

The kind of woman who'd make some child a fantastic mother.

A subdued shudder moved over him.

"I can understand that." With her thumb and index finger,

she exerted gentle pressure at the base of his thumb. He did groan then, relaxed pleasure radiating through his entire body. She laughed, a low, husky sound that sent shivers up his spine. Sliding off his lap, she tugged at him. "Come on. Bring your drink upstairs and I'll give you the full-body version."

"God, where did you learn to do that?" He retrieved his glass and let her pull him toward the stairs.

She laughed again. "Cis. She's a certified masseuse too. It's her sideline from the store. She does the whole package thing, with private yoga classes and massages."

He wrapped an arm around her waist, nuzzled her shoulder, contentment curling through him.

At the foot of the stairs, she shot him a glance beneath her lashes. "You know it doesn't matter, don't you, McMillian?"

He didn't have to ask what *it* was.

She curved a hand along his jaw and his heart jerked at the soft emotion glowing in her blue eyes. "In case you haven't noticed, with me, it's all about you."

Before his stunned mind could formulate an answer, her cell phone pinged from the living area. Her head fell back. "I have to get that."

He let her go, still trying to take in the reality of her words. She leaned down to retrieve her phone from her bag, the silvery strands of her hair shielding her face. "St. John. Oh, hey, I was just talking about you."

She straightened and looked at Tom, mouthing "my sister". He smiled, watching the way her face lit up as they chatted. Damn, she was even more gorgeous when she let down the walls, when the real Celia shone through.

He wanted her around more and more. She made his life seem less empty, less cold.

Upstairs, the phone rang in his office. He sighed, images of his full-body massage scattering away. Catching Celia's eye, he pointed upstairs and she nodded, waving him on.

"Um, I don't think so. Not tonight." Her voice followed him. "*How* much to fix your transmission? Of course I don't mind if you use it. You know where the keys are..."

He jogged up the stairs and grabbed the phone from its charging cradle. "Hello."

"Tom, it's Rhett." The cellular connection rattled and hissed. "I wanted to check in, let you know we made it up here okay."

"Good to hear from you." Tom dropped into his desk chair. "How's it going?"

"Okay so far." Weariness slid into Rhett's deep voice. "The initial blood tests look good, according to the doctors. The donor seems to be a match, so Amarie starts the chemo tomorrow."

"That's great. I'm glad, Rhett. How's Amarie? And Mariah?"

"They're both pretty tired. Excited. A little anxious, I think." Rhett's voice faded, came back stronger. "So what's going on down there? Turn up anything today on Jessica's case?"

Tom filled him in quickly on the day's events. The line continued to hiss between them, so he wasn't sure how much the other man caught. Finally, Tom gave up. "I'll call you tomorrow, Rhett. Focus on your family. Don't worry about what's happening here."

"I'm focused, but I want to be in the loop." Another crackling took the line, Rhett's voice rising and falling again. "If you get a lead, call me. Doesn't matter what time. I've got my cell with me constantly."

"Will do. Give Mariah and Amarie my best." He replaced the phone in the cradle. Traces of his former tension seized his shoulders. He could empathize with Rhett's situation. He lifted his glass and tossed off the Scotch.

Celia's soft footsteps sounded on the stairs and she appeared in the doorway. "Hey."

He smiled. "Hey."

"That was Cis, wanting to take my Xterra tonight. Her car is still in the shop at Lawson's." She tilted her head toward his bedroom. "Still want that massage?"

"Are you kidding?" He levered out of the chair. A stack of the slick plastic sheets holding his baseball-card collection slid to the floor.

She laughed and moved forward to help him gather them. They rose together and he took them from her, replacing them on the stack of notebooks. Celia stilled and he followed her gaze, knowing what he'd see.

A framed photo of Everett.

He leaned forward and picked it up, holding it where they could both see it. In the photograph taken when he was three months old, a big toothless grin graced Everett's mouth, his brown eyes wide. Thin swirls of russet hair covered his head. He wore a miniature baseball uniform bearing the Yankees logo.

"What a beautiful boy." Celia traced a finger along the edge of the frame. She smiled up at him. "He has Kathleen's coloring but he looks like you, his chin, around the eyes."

"I wonder all the time, you know." He rubbed a thumb over the glass, the old grief as new and raw as that day at Mercer, when the law-school dean had pulled him from class to tell him he was needed elsewhere, that his beloved son was dead. "What he'd be like now, what he'd grow up to be. God, I loved him. I looked forward to all the things we'd do together."

His eyes burned and he blinked and cleared his throat

roughly. She wouldn't want to hear this. Hell, Kathleen hadn't wanted to, hadn't allowed him to talk about the baby in her presence, and she'd been Everett's mother. Tom set the frame back in its space.

"McMillian." Celia took his hand, pulled him into her loose embrace, her arms about his waist as she looked up at him. "You don't have to put him away. He was your son. Of course you wonder. If you want to talk about him, I want to listen."

He frowned, sifting his fingers through her hair. She couldn't be real. She couldn't be.

"Stop looking at me like that, McMillian," she said, a hint of testiness entering her voice. "And stop using her to measure all women. It's not fair."

"I'm not—" He swallowed the words. Of course he was. He'd let his marriage, everything it had been, everything it hadn't been, color his life. If Celia could look beyond the ghost of Bryan Turello to see the man he really was, he had to do the same for her. He rubbed her hair between his fingers, wrapped the shining strands around his hand. "You're right."

An impish smile lit her face. "Oh, McMillian, somehow I like the sound of those words on your lips."

He laughed and hugged her close. She pulled away and took his hand. "Come on. I owe you a massage."

No air.

Darkness pulsed.

Pain, searing, biting, burning.

Blood, staining soft floral sheets.

Tangled hair, silvery blonde, spilling over the side of the bed.

He was awake, heart pounding, chest heaving, a muffled groan ripped from his throat.

"McMillian?" Celia's hands curved into his biceps and he knew she'd called him more than once, shaken him awake, shaken him free from the clutches of the nightmare.

He shuddered, the images heavy and real in his head. Dragging in a deep breath, he pulled up his knees and rested his elbows on them, letting his head fall forward and down. "God."

"McMillian, are you all right?" Her voice shook.

He lifted his head and tried to focus on her. The lights blazed around them and dimly he remembered falling asleep with her sprawled over his chest after her massage had led to much, much more. Celia frowned at him, eyes dark with concern. Wearing his discarded shirt, she knelt by him on the bed.

He moistened dry lips. "I—"

The impressions seared through him once more, burning flashes of sensation and vision, sending pain crashing through the back of his skull. He leaned forward, yet another groan pulled from him.

"Jesus above, McMillian, you're scaring me." The bed shifted as she wrapped her arms around him. Some of the cold fear dissipated under her touch. She brushed her lips across his temple. "What's wrong?"

He opened his eyes, the edges of her hair swinging at his peripheral vision.

Tangled hair, silvery blonde, spilling over the side of the bed.

Fighting the sensory overload, he shook his head and looked at her. "It's you."

Hurt flashed in her eyes and she recoiled. "What?"

"No, don't." He reached for her, trying to make sense of it all. He wouldn't fail this time. Memories rolled through him—not turning back to wake Everett, the unease when Jessica had died, the phone call unanswered.

Nate Holton's truck barreling through an intersection, moments before them, because he'd insisted on driving. A flash of Celia with blood on her face.

Breathing hard in uneven gasps, he rubbed a thumb over the tiny cut, still apparent on her chin. "My God, it's you."

He wouldn't let it happen.

"What are you talking about?" She stared at him, eyes wide. "What did you see, McMillian?"

He could stop it this time...he wouldn't let it happen to her...

"McMillian!" She gripped his chin and forced him to look at her. "What did you see?"

"I saw you." He swallowed, his throat raw. "Your bedroom. You...there was blood, your hair falling over the side of the bed." He closed his eyes. "You were dead."

"You saw me dead?" Her voice trembled.

He opened his eyes, holding her gaze. "I won't let it happen, Cee. I swear to God, not this time—"

"This time? What do you mean?" She stroked the side of his face, ran her fingers over his temple, gentling, soothing.

Listening. Looking at him with a soothing blend of concern and openness. She'd already given him the gift of talking about his son. Maybe with her he could release the door he kept slammed on the images and dreams, the flashes that had haunted and tormented him longer than he cared to remember.

"I didn't go back for Everett. I turned back at the door, but I talked myself out of it." The words tumbled over themselves in his desperation to explain. "I didn't go back and he died. And Jessica...I didn't answer the phone, but I felt it. I had a dream that night, the night she was killed. The only thing, the *only* thing, I've done right is keep us out of Nate Holton's way. And I am not letting this, whatever it is I saw, happen to you."

"It's okay." She smoothed the hair at his nape. "Nothing's going to happen to me."

Sweat chilled on his body. He rubbed a hand down his damp face. "You're damn right it's not."

She rested her cheek on his shoulder, stroking his back. "So this happens before an incident?"

Finally getting his breathing under control, he glanced sideways at her. "I don't even know what *this* is."

Her lips feathered his shoulder. "My mother would have called it your Gift."

"My Gift?" A harsh laugh wrung free of him. "More like a curse. You believe in this stuff?"

"Don't you?"

He didn't want to believe in it, didn't want it in his life, period. He met her steady gaze again. "I don't know."

She picked up his hand, rubbed her thumb across his knuckles. "I'll be careful, McMillian. And I'll be fine. I promise."

Damn straight she would. He intended to ensure it. He wouldn't lose her now, wouldn't lose her too.

"It's not necessary for you to walk me in, McMillian." Her low heels clicking on the steps to her back door, Celia smiled over her shoulder at Tom.

He lifted his eyebrows at her. Maybe she didn't think it was necessary, but he didn't plan to let her out of his sight. The

219

images from his nightmare were still too fresh in his mind.

Trying to shake off the lingering uneasiness, he watched as she unlocked the door. "When are you going to actually call me Tom?"

She tossed a teasing glance at him. "Is it that important—"

Her voice stopped suddenly as she stepped inside and he went on the alert, vibrating with renewed tension. The fight-or-flight instinct poured adrenaline into his bloodstream. "What is it?"

"Shhh."

He looked beyond her shoulder, through the dining room door. Nothing seemed out of place. The rooms smelled the same, still carried the relaxed air he associated with Celia's home.

Celia reached for her sidearm.

The hair on his arms prickled, lifted on a wave of gooseflesh. "What?"

She shook her head. "I don't know. Something's just...off."

With him at her side, she eased into the dining room and into the living room. Tom looked around. "Is anything out of place?"

"No." She gave a rueful laugh. "It's just not right in here."

Foreboding trickled down his spine. "Let's call the police."

She shot him a look. He sighed. "Fine. I forget sometimes." He waved a hand toward the hall and its stairs. "Lead the way, Investigator."

Shadows hovered on the stairs, thanks to the shade at the landing's window.

A foot on the bottom step, Tom paused and reached for Celia's arm. "Wait."

She looked back at him, inquiry in her eyes. He stared up the stairwell, flashes of his dream stabbing into him. Waves of ice flowed over him. He tightened his hold on her arm. "Just wait."

They stood still and Tom strained his ears. Nothing moved overhead. The clock on the small table at the landing ticked in the silence.

"Come on," she whispered.

He tugged her back. "I'm going first."

"McMillian, I'm the one with the gun. I think I should go first."

With the disquiet sitting like a hard knot in his gut and the nightmarish images lingering in his brain, he wasn't going to argue. He would be the first one up those stairs. He stepped past her. "Humor me."

With their backs to the wall, they slipped up the stairs. He was aware of Celia's quiet tension behind him. Her bedroom door stood ajar, dim light spilling into the hall.

A vaguely familiar odor wafted over him. Tom tensed, frowning. Where had he...?

"Oh my God." Celia pushed past him and he made a grab for her.

"Celia, wait—"

"Let me go." Urgency invaded her voice. "That smell? That's blood, McMillian."

He put himself between her and the door. "I'll check it out. Stay here."

Not waiting for her answer, he stepped sideways to the door. The cloying scent grew stronger. Flares of the burning pain from his dream seared through him. Without touching the door, he looked inside the room.

The slender body lay across the bed, one wrist bound to the headboard with a tie—*his* tie, the blue silk one Celia had laughingly stripped from him Friday night. Her head was thrown back, silvery blonde hair falling over the side of the bed. Blood trickled from her parted lips.

Tom's stomach clenched, plummeted.

Cicely.

She looked like Celia. If he hadn't known she was behind him, he'd have thought—

Oh, God. *Celia.*

He spun, putting his body between her and the room, trying to stop her from seeing.

She screamed.

"No." He caught her in his arms, felt her body sag as her knees gave. He attempted to turn her face into his shoulder. Waves of incredible pain that wasn't his washed over him, swamping him, and he closed his eyes, holding her. "Don't look, Cee."

"No," she moaned, fighting against his arms, sinking further against him, and he felt her tearing sobs vibrate from her body into his. "No, no, *no...*"

Chapter Twelve

"Do you know her name?"

At the foot of the stairs, Tom tried to focus on the city police department's young detective. He pulled his gaze from Celia, sitting on the edge of the couch, holding her elbows, staring straight ahead. "Cicely St. John. She owns the shop next door and lives in the other half of the house. She's Celia's sister."

A camera flash flared above them.

Deep voices came from the back of the house and Mark Cook strode through from the kitchen. He slanted a concerned glance at Celia, but didn't approach her. Instead, he joined Tom and Detective Phillips. "What happened?"

Tom pitched his voice low. "I brought Celia home this morning and we found her."

Cook looked at Phillips. "What's it look like to you?"

"The scene appears staged." Phillips spoke in a whisper. "Come take a look."

With a glance back at Celia, Tom followed the two men upstairs.

"How is she?" Cook murmured.

"She wants to be left alone." Tom shook his head, remembering the way Celia had smothered her sobs and pulled away from him, refusing further contact while they waited for the police to arrive. Cold worry had settled in him as she rebuffed him and any attempt he made at comfort. "In shock, I think."

In the bedroom, Cicely's nude body remained on Celia's bed. A crime scene photographer continued taking an extensive record of the scene. From the door, Tom looked around as the two police officers studied the body. Cicely's clothing—jeans, camisole, sandals, brief panties—lay scattered on the floor. A couple of unopened condoms graced the nightstand. The bottle of scented oil and unboxed dildo stood beside them.

He directed his attention to Phillips. "You said it looked staged."

Cook and Phillips exchanged a look.

"It doesn't look natural." Phillips waved toward the bed. "The clothing is too arranged than if she'd just stripped it off. The body is posed, probably after she was killed."

"The toys and the condoms?" Cook pointed at the table. "We're supposed to jump to a conclusion from those, that this is all about some kind of kinky sex game gone wrong."

Phillips frowned. "If this isn't her side of the duplex, why is her body here?"

"Because it's not supposed to be her," Tom said slowly, a shudder working through him. "It's supposed to be Celia."

Eyebrows lifted, Phillips looked at him in open inquiry.

"She borrowed Celia's truck last night. Her car is in the shop."

"Someone looking for St. John sees the sister come home, driving St. John's vehicle." Cook sighed and glanced toward the bed. "They favor enough to be twins."

"Mistaken identity," Phillips said. "Wrong place at the

wrong time."

"And if this is supposed to be St. John and we're supposed to think it's a little rough sex that went overboard..." Cook trailed off and fixed Tom with a look. "Then we're supposed to think you did it, Counselor."

Foreboding settled over Tom and he turned toward Cicely's still form. "We have to let him think it's Celia."

"What?" Phillips frowned.

"If he thinks Celia is dead and I'm under suspicion, if he thinks he's gotten away with it..."

"It could buy us some time," Cook finished for him.

Tom met the other man's astute gray eyes. "And it could keep Celia safe until we find the bastard."

She couldn't get the memory out of her head.

Celia gripped her father's uniform button, the chain's links biting into her skin with the pressure.

Cicely's eyes, open, staring, all the life and joy gone from them.

Cicely, dead.

In *her* bed. In *her* place.

She shuddered. This wasn't happening. It couldn't be. It was a dream, a nightmare, had to be. Because if Cicely was gone, she had no one left. She was alone.

"Celia, baby." McMillian knelt before her and reached for her hands. Pain darkened his eyes, and disconnected, she realized he was hurting for her, sharing her agony. He rubbed his thumbs over her knuckles. "Cook is going to take you to my place."

"No." She shook her head, trying to pull her thoughts

together. It was important she stay here, be where Cicely was. If she went, Cicely would be all alone, no one left who loved her. She couldn't do that to her sister. "I can't leave her."

"I need you to, Cee." He turned his head, pressing his lips against the inside of her wrist. "There's nothing you can do here and I need to know you're safe."

"She's dead." The words slipped from her, even as unshed tears remained frozen in her throat. The sobs had shaken her earlier, tearing from her throat, but the tears had refused to come. "In my place. Because of me."

He closed his eyes, brought her palm to his cheek. "Not because of you, baby. You didn't cause this."

Didn't he understand? "It was supposed to be me. If she hadn't been in my truck, if I'd been here—"

"No." A visible spasm shook his shoulders. "Don't say that."

She bit her lip, the coppery taste of blood hitting her tongue. "I wish I had been."

His grip on her hands tightened to a painful level and he turned tortured eyes to hers. "Celia, don't do this. I'm sorry she's dead, I know you're hurting, but I can't be sorry you're alive, baby. I can't."

She pulled her hands free. "You want me to leave her here, alone."

His eyes closed again. "I want you safe."

Her throat ached. "But—"

"We don't have a lot of time, St. John." Cook spoke from the doorway, his voice quiet. He cleared his throat, sympathy and apology plain on his face. "The news people will have already picked up the call on the scanner and they'll be on the way. We need to get you out of here."

She couldn't think, couldn't get her mind straight enough

to make a decision.

"Baby, please." McMillian's voice cracked. "Do this for me."

Tom McMillian, with his composure shaken, sounding anything but confident? Do it for him? She stared at him for a long moment, then nodded.

"Cook, you don't have to stay." Celia wrapped her arms over her midriff and clasped her elbows. She was cold, a deep-down iciness she couldn't shake. Even the sunlight spilling in through the tall windows in McMillian's living room couldn't warm her. Instead, it mocked her with the ordinariness of the weather. Outside, the day was bright, sunny, cheerful. People would be going on with their lives.

She didn't have that luxury today.

"It might be a good idea if I hang around."

She dragged a hand through her hair, nails raking her scalp. "I really don't want you here, okay? I need to be by myself."

He sighed. "I tell you what—I'll go, but just to the car. I'll park down the street. That way I'm here, but I'm not."

She nodded, grateful that he understood how close to falling apart she was, that he wouldn't stay to watch it happen. "I can handle that."

He jerked his head toward the door. "Lock up behind me."

Once the heavy door was closed behind him, she trailed back to the living room. Their files and notes from the night before remained stacked on the coffee table. She sank to the floor and traced a finger over a page filled with McMillian's strong handwriting.

Memories assailed her, McMillian thrashing about in the

throes of his nightmare, swearing he'd keep her safe.

Only his nightmare had been reality.

The danger he'd thought threatened her had taken Cicely instead.

Why?

Her gaze fell on the paperwork once more. The answer lay within this case. She merely had to find it.

For Cicely's sake.

"So the question is, why would someone want Ms. St. John dead?" Phillips crossed his arms over his chest. "And why would they want us to think you did it?"

Tom glanced at Tick Calvert. The three were standing in Celia's kitchen, watching the crime scene technicians come and go from upstairs and the media beginning to mill outside the house. "We got too close, made somebody nervous."

Tick nodded. "Someone who thought that if St. John was out of the way and you were tied up trying to clear yourself, it would take the heat of the Grady case off them."

He remembered Celia's hoarse scream, her sobs, when she'd glimpsed her sister's body, the way she'd folded in on herself, the horror in her eyes. Fury flashed through him, tightening his chest. He wanted to put his fist through something.

Or into Alton Baker's face.

"It's Baker," he said, having to unclench his jaw to force the words out.

Phillips looked surprised. "The judge?"

Tick watched him with a measuring expression. "Why do you think so?"

"He had a connection to Jessica, he was involved in those adoptions and he didn't like us questioning him about it." Tom rubbed a hand over his jaw, trying to still the urge to strike out. The son of a bitch had attempted to take Celia from him, permanently, had planned a horrific death for her. And he'd succeeded in destroying what Celia loved most. "The grand-jury subpoena could have put him over the edge."

Hands curled around the tile facing, Tick leaned against the counter. "Odds are, if he's involved in the baby ring and Grady's murder, that puts him solidly in the middle of the Dixie Mafia organization around here. And, odds are, he didn't carry out the murder himself. He'd have someone else do it, like having Blanton courier that baby. The challenge is making the connection between the killer and Baker."

Tom glared at him. "I'll make your connection."

He'd beat it out of the son of a bitch if he had to. Tear him apart, to make sure he never threatened Celia, in any way, ever again.

A subdued grin quirked at Tick's mouth. "I understand how you feel, Tom, honest to God, I do, but we want to be able to put him away. If you go off the deep end, hell'll freeze over before we get a chance."

Phillips scratched his temple. "We need to move fast on this investigation. We're only going to be able to keep the truth about Ms. St. John a secret for so long."

A Coney PD officer slipped in through the back door, a harassed expression on his face. He waved a hand at the media trucks from two local affiliate stations outside. "Damn vultures. We talked to the neighbors on both sides of the street, Detective. Nobody heard or saw nothing."

Phillips released a long, slow breath. "I sure as hell hope this guy made a mistake and the forensics turn up something."

"They always mess up somewhere, Phillips." Tick clapped a hand on the younger man's shoulder. "Trust me. Sometimes it just takes us longer than others to find the mistake."

"Make it sooner rather than later." Tom shoved his hands in his pockets.

Tick's cell phone rang and he pulled it from his belt. "Calvert. Are you sure?" He glanced at Tom, excitement glinting in his dark brown eyes. "Listen, fax that over to the station, will you? I might need it to get a court order. Thanks."

He returned his phone to its clip, a grin curving his mouth.

Tom threw out his hands in frustration. "What?"

Tick's grin widened. "I'll tell you in the car."

Phillips gestured toward the window and the reporters outside. "What about them?"

"Got it covered." Tick tugged his cuffs free. "Let's make it look good, Counselor."

Once outside, Tom's hands cuffed before him with his suit jacket half-tossed over them and Tick's hand on his arm, the handful of reporters rushed to the flimsy barrier of yellow crime scene tape. A barrage of questions assaulted them.

"Is it true Ms. St. John was murdered?"

"How long had she worked with the district attorney's office?"

"Is Mr. McMillian under arrest?"

"Can you tell us anything, Investigator?"

"Why is Chandler County's sheriff's office assisting with this case?"

Tick's expression didn't change. "No comment."

At the unmarked unit, he pulled the passenger door open and shielded Tom's head as he pushed him down into the seat.

Ignoring the clamoring reporters, he crossed to the driver's side. A city officer waved him into traffic.

Tick pulled onto the quiet side street. "We just put a dent in your professional reputation."

"It doesn't matter." Tom stared forward, his jaw aching from being clenched repeatedly. Rage at Alton Baker continued to pulse along his nerves. "Nothing is more important than Celia and keeping her safe."

He caught the surprise in the glance Tick sent his way. The investigator's reaction didn't matter, either. The truth of what he'd said sank into his consciousness. *Nothing* was more important than Celia. Not his past, not his reputation, not his career.

She was everything.

The emotion had sneaked up on him, disguised as wanting and desire, and somehow in the past few days, maybe even the past weeks and months, she'd wound herself around his soul.

Tick cleared his throat. "There was tissue under one of Jessica Grady's fingernails. Ford pulled a DNA sample from it."

Tom looked at him, trying to make the transition from thinking about his feelings for Celia to focusing on the investigative process. "And?"

"You'll be happy to hear that the DNA didn't match to your sample."

"I knew that."

"It did, however, match to a degraded sample we pulled from her bedroom." Tick swung onto the town's main thoroughfare, in the direction of the sheriff's department. "Ford says there's a ninety-nine point eight percent chance the person with that DNA fathered Jessica's baby."

"The baby's father killed her." Tom narrowed his eyes. "But

the other videos didn't match up the time period for conception, did they?"

Tick shook his head, braking for a red light. "Obviously, she was sleeping with someone other than you last summer. Either she didn't film him or he found his DVD the night he killed her."

"Plus our killer is related to the first baby. Not enough of a match to be the father, but probably a close relative."

"Sounds like you need DNA samples from the men on those DVDs."

"It would be helpful."

"When you apply for your court order, add Alton Baker's name to the list."

As he pulled into the parking lot at the sheriff's department, Tick glanced at him. "Any particular reason?"

"Just call it a hunch."

"Where's Cook?"

McMillian's too-calm voice lifted the hair at her nape. Engrossed in reviewing the files from Jessica's office, she hadn't heard him come in. She glanced around to find him standing in the foyer, watching her, his body tense and tight.

She turned her attention back to the adoption record before her. "Down the street in his unit. I kicked him out."

"He's supposed to be with you." His voice was nearer this time, somewhere just over her shoulder. Thinly veiled anger pulsed in the deep tones. "Watching over you."

Irritation trickled over her. Couldn't he see she was busy? She had to get to the bottom of this case. She needed to, owed it to Cicely. "I don't need a keeper, McMillian."

His hand closed around her arm in a gently firm grip, and he tugged her up to face him. "This isn't a goddamn game, Celia."

"Don't you think I know that?"

His jaw tightened, a muscle ticking in his cheek. "Then why the hell is Cook outside?"

She tried to remove her arm from his hold and failed. The tears she'd been unable to shed all day stung her eyes. "Because I didn't want him here."

He released her arm, sliding his hand up to cup her face, his thumb caressing her jaw. He didn't say anything else, but the silent compassion in that touch broke her.

"I needed...I needed to be alone." Her voice cracked, the frozen sobs welling into her throat, choking her. The tears slipped free and he caught the first one on his thumb as it slid down her cheek. "I didn't want him here."

"I know." He smoothed her hair away from her face, a slow, rhythmic movement. "I know, baby."

She closed her eyes as more tears fell. One of the clawing sobs tore from her throat, turning into a strangled moan. Another followed, and another, huge gulping sounds that hurt and frightened her. Still stroking her hair, he pulled her close. His deep voice murmured soothingly near her ear, although the words were lost to her own crying.

With him, away from the world, she could let go, let the grief have its way. She clutched at his shirtfront and held on, as the sobs and waves of sorrow battered her.

"I just want it to go away." She gasped the words against his throat. "And I know it won't."

"Oh, Celia," he whispered. "Baby, I'm sorry."

"Tighter." She pressed into him, wanting the solid warmth

of him to chase away the memories. "Hold me tighter, Tom. I need you to."

"I'm here, baby." He moved, sliding an arm beneath her knees and lifting her against his chest. He carried her to the couch and settled with her on his lap. With her wrapped close, he rubbed a soothing hand over her back. She wept into the curve of his neck, crying until sleep finally took her into blessed numbness.

His concentration was shot to hell.

Tom lowered the file he'd picked up and glanced over his reading glasses at Celia, asleep on the couch. He'd covered her with a soft throw and turned the downstairs phone off. After she'd given in to her grief in his arms, he'd not wanted her relief from the consuming emotion disturbed. She'd clung to him, claimed to need him.

She'd called him Tom.

Even now, the rush of warmth the simple sound of his name on her lips created lingered, although he'd have rather had that blessing prompted under far different circumstances. However, the tenderness couldn't quite displace the pervading sense of disquiet he'd carried with him since early that morning.

Beyond the tall glass doors, dusk hovered and he couldn't shake the image of a lurking, shadowy threat.

He studied Celia's face, relaxed in sleep. She'd been out for a couple of hours and he dreaded having to wake her, having to watch her face the reality of Cicely's death again. He understood all too well the pain of losing someone intensely loved.

Damn it all, if he'd understood that fucking dream, Cicely

might be alive. Here was the reason he'd hated the flashes of foreboding, the dreams, all his life. What good were they? He'd never been able to understand them enough to really stop anything from happening.

What had Celia called it, a Gift?

Like hell. More like the curse he'd always known it was.

The doorbell rang and he jumped. The adoption papers scattered to the floor and he left them, hurrying to the door before Celia woke. A quick look through the peephole revealed Rhett standing on the stoop.

Surprised, Tom swung the door open. His face set in lines of concern, Rhett stepped forward into the foyer area. "Tom, man, what is going on?"

"Keep your voice down." Tom cast a glance over his shoulder. Celia slept on, hidden from Rhett's view by the back of the couch. "What are you doing here? You're supposed to be with your family."

Rhett looked at him, askance. "Raquel called me and then I saw the news reports about Celia's murder...um, her death. They said you were a suspect. I figured you might need me down here and Mariah agreed I should come back."

Tom shook his head. He looked outside, where shadows waited beyond his driveway lights. With a tight motion, he closed the door and threw the lock. "Everything's under control. Amarie needs you right now; you should be in Atlanta."

Rhett eyed the banker's boxes and files littering the living room. "What are you doing?"

He strode forward into the living room before Tom could stop him. "Rhett, wait, you need to—"

"Holy shit." Shock reverberated in Rhett's deep voice and Tom swallowed a curse. He'd seen her and one more person would have to be in on their secret. A swallow moved the line of Rhett's throat. "She's alive."

"Keep your voice down." Tom waved a hand toward the stairs. "Come upstairs."

They went up to his office and Tom closed the door. Rhett shot him an accusing look. "What's going on, man? Why didn't you tell me she was alive?"

Tom pitched his voice low, despite the closed door. "Because she could still be in danger and we were keeping this on a need-to-know basis."

Rhett's eyes narrowed. "So I get to think a colleague's been murdered and my best friend's a suspect in that murder? I don't need to know differently? Thanks a lot, Tom."

"Someone wanted her dead, Rhett. Keeping her safe was my first priority."

Rhett passed a hand over the smooth surface of his scalp. "So who was the woman killed?"

Tom winced, remembering Celia's tearing sobs. "Her sister."

"Shit." Rhett shook his head. "That's a hell of a note."

"Yeah."

"Well, I'm here. What can I do to help?"

An echo of his earlier disquiet shivered over him. Tom shrugged. "I—"

His cell phone, plugged in on his desk, rang. Leaning over, he saw Tick Calvert's name displayed on the caller ID screen.

"I have to take this." He picked up the phone. "McMillian."

"We may have something." Excitement colored Tick's words. Tom's skin prickled.

"What's going on?"

"Alton Baker's daughter is in the emergency room at

Chandler General. She ran out in front of car over on Delta Pine Road."

"On foot?"

"Yeah. Layla called it in. The girl is traumatized, became hysterical when they started talking about calling her father. Anyway, I thought you might want to meet me there."

"I do." Tom's thoughts went to Celia, downstairs. He couldn't leave her alone. "Hang on." He covered the phone and looked at Rhett. "I need to meet Calvert at the hospital. Can you stay with Celia?"

"Sure."

Nodding a thanks at him, Tom lifted the phone to his ear again. "I'm on my way."

He clipped the phone on his belt. Rhett followed him downstairs. "What's going on?"

Where had he put his keys? "Alton Baker's daughter is in the ER. I'm just going to go check it out."

Rhett perched on the chair Tom had vacated earlier and began picking up the scattered adoption papers. "You think she's linked to Jessie?"

He snagged his keys from the foyer console table, almost knocking his golf bag over. "I don't know. But something's going on. I don't know how long I'll be gone."

"Take your time." Rhett glanced through one of the files.

Tom paused, his gaze falling on Celia's tousled hair. His chest tightened. "Take care of her."

A half-grin lifted Rhett's mouth. "You got it, my man."

Keys clutched in hand, Tom opened the door. The shadows hovered beyond the lights and the wave of disquiet hit him hard. Stiffening his spine, he stepped outside and locked the door behind him.

He'd left the Mercedes in the driveway for once and he walked around Rhett's Lexus SUV. He sank into the driver's seat and fired the engine. With a glance over his shoulder, he backed down the drive.

Darkness danced at the corner of his vision. He blinked, memories of his dream melding with the reality of seeing Cicely dead in Celia's bed. A cold lump of dread settled in his gut.

What the fuck was wrong with him?

On the highway's straightaway, he gunned the motor, pushing the speedometer needle higher.

He couldn't breathe. His lungs cramped and his foot faltered on the accelerator. The dread and shadows filled the air around him, almost as though something evil sat in the car with him.

God, he was losing his damn mind. He had to be.

Go back.

The soft words whispered through his head.

They weren't his thoughts.

The voice was quiet, female, vaguely familiar.

Go back.

More urgent this time, almost like fingers prodding his brain. Startled, he swerved, hit the brakes. The rumble strips bumped under the tires, grass rustled along the undercarriage as he pulled to a stop on the shoulder. His head pounded, the darkness looming around him, lights dancing before his eyes.

Head bent, he pinched the bridge of his nose, trying to catch his breath, trying to pull himself together. God, he was really losing it. His lungs constricted, seeming unable to draw air.

Go back.

Fuck, this was ridiculous. He could go back and everything

would be fine, just as he'd left it. He should pull into the light traffic, go on to the hospital, where surely Tick was waiting impatiently.

What if everything wasn't fine?

He stilled. *That* was his brain, the logical prosecutor's thought process, questioning everything. What if he went on, ignored the way his senses were screaming and it was the wrong choice? He dragged a hand down his face. He had to go back.

If anything, the sense of breathing evil grew stronger, his head pounding harder. He ignored it and pulled across the median, going back the way he'd came.

The soft voice came again, an almost inaudible pulsing under the shadows.

Hurry.

Celia dreamed.

A bright, sunny day, with sunbeams coming through the leaves of a sheltering oak tree. A butterfly skipped over tall grass. Her feet tucked under her on an old quilt, she leaned against the tree and stared up at the pattern of light and dark among the limbs.

Peace pervaded her, sinking into the depths of her being, wiping out the ravages of her grief.

A rustling caught her attention. Two women dressed in gauzy white walked toward her, similar in height, the sun bouncing off their blonde heads. Recognition shimmered through her.

"Mama." Her lips parted on an awed whisper. "Cis."

Her sister smiled and spoke, her lips moving without sound. The air wavered between them, and when Celia tried to scramble to her feet, rough, unseen hands held her prisoner. She struggled, her lungs hurting. "Mama!"

"Wake up, Celia." The familiar, beloved voice whispered over her. "You have to go back."

She struggled harder against the hands holding her, the darkness suddenly looming and pressing in on her, stealing the air from her body. "But—"

"Go back. Now, Celia. Wake up."

She jerked awake, fear and a sense of panic trying to kick her in the chest. She blinked, once, twice, centering in on her surroundings. The vicious dreamlike hands were gone, and Tom's living room came into slow focus around her. Levering up against the sofa arm, she glanced around for Tom.

Instead her gaze trailed over Rhett High, seated in Tom's armchair. He flipped through a handful of papers from the piles stacked on the coffee table. An instinctive roll of tension tightened her body and she compelled herself to relax. This was simply Rhett, the ADA and Tom's friend.

Pushing sleep-tangled hair from her face, she shifted to a sitting position. Rhett straightened and looked up from his reading, inscrutable gaze flicking over her. "Hey."

"Hello." She rubbed burning eyes and glanced around once more. Her pulse still wanted to flutter under her skin with aftershocks of adrenaline. "Where's Tom?"

Rhett cleared his throat. "He left a few minutes ago."

She nodded but he offered no additional information. A taut silence stretched between them while questions tumbled through her mind. Why was he here and not in Atlanta? And where had Tom gone?

He made an uncomfortable sound that rumbled from his chest. "I'm sorry about your sister."

She laced her fingers, pressing until the bones ached. "So am I."

The hush fell once more, each silent moment further straining her nerves. She jumped to her feet and paced to the tall windows facing the lake. Darkness lurked outside, a shadowy fog obscuring the houses across the water. She tapped on the glass, jitters skittering through her. Jesus above, she couldn't remember the last time she'd been this edgy, this ready to come out of her skin.

She sucked in a calming breath, using one of Cicely's yoga techniques, and pain sheared through her with the memory of the two of them stretched out on the floor in those wild poses, finally dissolving in laughter.

How was she supposed to manage without her sister, the one person who'd been the other half of herself?

This was too hard. On a torn swallow, she turned to find Rhett still watching her. "Where did you say Tom went?"

A key scraped in the lock. Rhett's gaze flashed in the direction of the door moments before it swung open.

"Celia?" Intensity vibrated Tom's voice. He skidded on the slick tile, a wild expression in his blue eyes as he scanned the room. He paused at the edge of the living area, lids falling, chest heaving with a deep breath. "Thank God."

What was going on?

Rhett stared at him. "Man, what the hell is wrong with you?"

Opening his eyes, Tom ignored him. Shaking himself free of whatever gripped him, he strode forward, attention focused solely on Celia. Still wearing that fierce look, he cupped her face with shaking hands. "You're all right."

"I'm fine." She frowned. His hands were all over her,

touching, checking, desperate, almost as if he needed to convince himself she was real. "What's wrong?"

He shook his head, his eyes intent on her face, and the line of his throat convulsed. "I had to come back."

She shook her head, tears threatening. Come back? What was he talking about?

"I was supposed to meet Calvert at the hospital. Rhett was here and I left because he said he'd watch over you. Except it didn't feel right and the farther away I got, the worse it was. Then there was that damn voice…"

"Voice?"

"In my head." His hands gripped her arms, almost bruising in his intensity. Fine tremors traveled through him, transferring into her body through his forceful touch. "Telling me to come back. I had to."

He wasn't making any sense, but nothing today did. Cicely dead. Tom coming back to her because of a voice? The unreality of it all crawled under her skin.

His face closed on a flare of chagrin. After one more pass over her arms and shoulders, he dropped his hands. "Fuck."

"Tom." She reached for him, laid gentle fingers on his arm. "It's all right."

"Yeah." He passed a hand over already disheveled hair. "A Gift, Cee? Fucking useless is what it is."

The need to comfort swamped her and she took a half-step toward him. Remembering Rhett's silent presence, she halted.

"You're wiped out, man." Curiosity lingered in Rhett's tone, overlaid by a heavy dose of sympathy. "Why don't I go meet Calvert? You need to crash."

"Why were you meeting him?" Celia cut across what she suspected was a denial forming on Tom's thin mouth.

Tom gave a quick jerk of his head, some of the remaining fear draining from his features, although the self-derision hung on. "Alton Baker's daughter is in the ER."

Avenues of opportunity opened before her. Celia drew herself up and prepared for battle. "I'm going with you."

"No, you're not. You're staying here. I want you safe."

"You can't make me—"

"I will do whatever it takes to keep you safe." He took her chin in a firm grip and leaned down, eyes locked on hers. "Do you understand me, Cee? Whatever it takes."

She shrugged free of his hold, the memory of Cicely's body pulsing in her brain. "There's nothing to keep me safe from. They've accomplished the one thing that could hurt me most by taking Cis. What more can they possibly do?"

"What more...?" He caught her chin once more. "Celia—"

"I'm going."

His cell phone rang, forestalling his reply. He jerked it from his waist and lifted it to his ear. "McMillian. I was delayed." He listened, features tightening into a thunderous expression. "Shit. How did that...all right." He darted a look at Celia. "Yes, she wants to come with me. In a few minutes."

He snapped the cell shut and returned it to his belt. Frustration twisted his mouth into a tight line.

"What's going on?" Rhett asked.

A harsh sigh shook Tom's shoulders. "A reporter from WALB called the crime lab to verify Celia's death and a lab clerk 'corrected' the misidentification. They broadcast the correction during the midevening news, just a few minutes ago."

"So whoever killed Cicely knows I'm alive." Celia wrapped her arms over her midriff. Just saying the words hurt. "I'm going with you."

He gazed down at her a long moment, then gave a brief nod. "Come on."

"I'll follow." Rhett pulled his keys from his pocket. "I'm here so I might as well see if there's any way I can help."

Tom gave him a quick glance. "Thanks, but you really should head back up to Emory. Celia, let's go."

Chapter Thirteen

Tom placed his own body securely behind Celia as they hurried up the hospital steps. A ghost of the lurking threat he'd sensed earlier remained, trying to wrap fingers of dread around his brain. Frustration slammed into him all over again. Gift, his ass.

A hand at the small of her back, Tom ushered Celia into the ER. The antiseptic smell invaded his senses, making his screaming tension even worse. For once the area was devoid of patients and family members, although Mark Cook cooled his heels against one wall, his gray eyes fixed on the doors marked "No Admittance". He straightened at their approach. Heavy with concern, his gaze flicked over Celia's face.

"St. John."

A glimmer of a tremulous smile curved her mouth and disappeared. "Cook."

The doors swished open, admitting Tick Calvert to the waiting area. Tom straightened, aware of Cook coming to attention as well, inquiry all over his face.

"Is she talking?" Cook asked.

"Holy hell, is she." Excitement glittering in his dark eyes, Tick pulled them to the side. "Tori's with her now. Get this—she said she had a baby and her daddy took it away."

Cook's gaze sharpened. "When?"

Tick grinned, a cat-got-the-canary smile. "Tuesday. And it was a girl."

With a triumphant smile, Cook smacked his hands together. "That's our dead baby."

"Did she say why Baker took the baby?" Tom rubbed a hand along his nape, aware of Celia's quiet withdrawal next to him. Damn it all, he should have gone with his first instincts and made her stay at his place. She was hurting and didn't need to be involved in this.

Tick shook his head. "Just that she'd basically been a prisoner in that house since she got pregnant. Seems she wasn't off at school like he told everyone she was. She broke her window to get out tonight, slipped down the rose trellis. Tore her hands all to hell, even before the car knocked her over."

Tom narrowed his eyes. "Bring Baker in. Charge him with unlawful imprisonment. We'll come up with the rest later."

Cook lifted his chin in Tom's direction. "You want in on that questioning?"

He folded his arm around Celia's hunched shoulders. "Hell yes."

"Want some company?"

Her hands wrapped around a cup of squad-room coffee long gone cold, Celia glanced up at Cook. She shrugged.

His holster creaking, he dropped into his desk chair. Sipping his coffee, he eyed her own cold cup and the greasy film atop the dark liquid. Finally, he lifted his gaze to hers. "So, you okay?"

Okay? She smothered an inappropriate laugh. At this

point, she wasn't sure she'd ever be okay again. "I'm alive."

A half-grin tugged at his mouth. "That counts."

The laugh emerged as a rusty, disbelieving chuckle. "Yeah."

He rubbed a finger around the bottom of his cup. "I'm sorry about your sister, St. John. Sorry you had to go through this."

She smiled, the roughness of his genuine sympathy easing the knot in her chest somewhat. "Thanks, Cook."

"Baker won't talk, unless screaming obscenities counts. Tick and McMillian are throwing him in lockup."

She nodded, but none of the excitement of chasing a case emerged. What did it matter who did what? Baker's daughter's statement, her implication of her father, being closer to the truth...none of it would bring Cicely back.

She'd still be alone.

Cook lifted his coffee. "So what are you going to do?"

"Going to do?" she echoed, frowning.

He waved a hand at the deserted room. "You gonna sit here all night?"

She glanced at her watch. After midnight. "Maybe."

"I didn't know if you needed a place to crash." He coughed uncomfortably. "Figured you didn't want to go back to your place."

A place to crash? Hell, she hadn't even thought that far ahead. She was simply putting one foot before the other, trying to get through the remains of this awful day. Waking in Tom's bed, close to his side and warmed by him, seemed a lifetime ago.

"You should have seen the look on McMillian's face the whole time we were in with Baker."

Cook's words finally penetrated the fog of her brain. "What

look on McMillian's face?"

"Like he wanted to take Baker apart. Slowly, with his bare hands." One corner of Cook's mouth quirked. "I think he could too."

"No doubt." She set the foam cup aside. She was tired, a soul-deep weariness that hurt all the way through her bones. "He's a tough son of a bitch."

"Yeah."

Familiar male voices wafted from the stairwell, Tom's cool tone blending with Calvert's deep drawl.

"...subpoena Baker's financial records, see if there's any way to link him to Jessie or Blanton." Tom zeroed in on her, concern darkening his eyes.

"I'll call the lab in the morning, see if I can get them to put a rush on our DNA results." Calvert rubbed a hand over his shadow of stubble. "If he fathered that baby, you'll have a hell of a motive argument."

Cook leaned back in his chair. "You want to finish going through Grady's financial records tonight?"

"Yeah. No reason for me to go home with Cait down in Florida so—" Music cut him off and he glanced at his cell-phone display. "Excuse me a second."

He disappeared into the hallway, his murmured conversation mixing with the hum of radio transmissions from dispatch. Celia rested her head against the chair back and let her lids slide closed. Immediately, regret gripped her as the freeze-frame images of Cicely's body flashed against the backs of her eyelids. She jerked upright, lashes flying up, to find both Cook and Tom watching her with anxious expressions.

"Celia, you need to rest." Tom tucked a stray strand of hair behind her ear. "Let's go."

He extended a hand. For a split second, she thought of refusing, of insisting on going through records and reports, but all she really wanted was to be away from here, somewhere dark and quiet where she could face the agony.

All she wanted now was to be alone, with him, losing the pain and grief in the steadiness of him.

She laid her palm in his and warm fingers closed about hers.

"That was Cait." Calvert strode back into the room. Fuzzily, Celia realized he wasn't talking to her, but Cook. "Get this—they found the body, right where the psychic told them to look."

Cook's eyes widened in surprise. "For real?"

"Yeah. The guy drew them a map; the local cops recognized some of the landmarks on it and that led the team straight to the area where the remains were recovered." Calvert chuckled. "I told her to make sure she got his number, in case we ever need it."

A tiny frown furrowed Tom's brow. "You believe in psychics?"

"All of them? No." Calvert shrugged. "But I've worked with a couple who were invaluable. If someone's intuition can turn up a solid lead, I'm not going to ignore it."

"Interesting." Tom tightened his hold on her hand. "Celia?"

She let him draw her nearer to his side. "I'm ready."

Outside, the air hung cool and damp in the still night. Tom wrapped an arm around her shoulder and she tucked her face into the curve of his neck. As they walked to his car, he dropped a kiss atop her head. Her eyes burned with a renewed wave of tears, a shaky sob pushing up from her chest.

Beside the passenger door, he turned, pulling her fully into his embrace. Arms folded about her, he rocked her side to side in a slow, soothing rhythm and brushed periodic kisses over her temple, cheek, hair.

"I can't do this." The whispered words hurt, tearing at her throat. "Not without her."

"Yes, you can." He murmured the assurance into her hair. His arms tightened. "I'll help you."

"Tom." She wrapped her arms about his neck and buried her face in his shoulder, tears scalding her eyes. "God, it *hurts*."

"I know. I know, baby." He swayed with her once more, one hand smoothing up and down her spine. "I'm so sorry." He pulled back enough to look down at her, one thumb brushing wetness from her cheek. "Let me take you home with me."

She nodded, more tears slipping free. He kissed one away and moved to open the door. She sank into the passenger seat and stared across the empty parking lot. He came around the hood to the driver's side. Behind the wheel, he lifted her palm to his mouth for a moment before firing the engine.

Town faded as he drove into the suburban area around the lake. Celia rested her forehead against the cool glass, willing her mind to wander anywhere but over and over the actuality of Cicely's death, what agonies and indignities she'd suffered.

In her place.

She squeezed her eyes closed, trying to draw up the memory of her dream, the peacefulness of the meadow Cicely shared with their mother. Her sister had been beautiful and content there, none of the pain of her death evident in her face or eyes.

Jesus above, how Celia wanted to believe that had been more than a dream, to believe it was a message...

Remembrance of the dream's shift into something dark and ominous slithered over her. She shuddered, seeking anything to take her mind in a different direction.

She traced a random pattern on the window. "What is Rhett doing down here, anyway? Why isn't he in Atlanta with Mariah and Amarie?"

Tom cleared his throat and she sensed rather than saw the glance he cast her. "He thought he would have to step in for me, if I were under suspicion in your...he thought it was you."

Because it should have been.

Things could have been so different, if she'd been there. She'd been trained to protect herself physically, she could have—

"Cee, don't." Warm fingers covered her wrist. "You can't change it. What you're doing...it only makes the pain worse."

Memories tinted his voice. She turned to look at his profile as he swung onto the lakefront road. She swallowed against the ever-present lump in her throat. "Was it this hard for you?"

He slowed for his drive but didn't speak until he drew the car to a stop before the garage. He killed the engine, rubbing his palm over the steering wheel, gaze trained on the house. His audible inhale shook his frame.

"Losing him was the hardest thing I ever had to face."

She reached for his hand and laced her fingers through his. "I'm sorry."

Wrapping his fingers around hers, he drew her to him and whispered his lips over hers. Their mouths clung, separated, and he released a low breath. In the dimness, his eyes gleamed down at her. He traced the back of one knuckle along her jaw.

"You need to rest."

A shuddery sigh escaped her. "I'm afraid to close my eyes. Every time I do, I see—"

"Sshh." He feathered his lips over hers once more. "Come

upstairs and let me hold you. Let me comfort you."

Her lashes fell and she nodded.

Sleep eluded Tom.

Celia had wept in his arms again and now dozed behind him. Standing at the window, he could see her reflected in the glass. She clutched the comforter like a frightened child in the throes of a nightmare, silvery blonde hair spread across the golden pillowcase, a small frown wrinkling her face.

Something wasn't right.

He couldn't get his mind centered on what exactly niggled beneath the surface of his thoughts, but *something* was off. He passed a hand over eyes burning with weariness. He was missing a fact, a nuance...an item of utmost importance.

It fucking pissed him off. He needed to be at the top of his game, needed to fit all the pieces together, to give Cicely the justice she deserved.

To give Celia that justice.

She shifted, murmuring. He spun. Her lashes fluttered, giving him a glimpse of pain-filled blue eyes. "Tom?"

"I'm right here, baby." He crossed to the bed and sat beside her. He stroked tangled hair away from her cheek.

Her eyes closed, a tear trickling across the bridge of her nose. "Please don't leave me."

He caught the tear on his thumb and pressed his mouth to her temple. "I'm not going anywhere."

She sucked in a tremulous breath. He shifted, sliding beneath the comforter, pulling her into his arms. She rested against his chest, fingers clutching at him with a desperation that tore at his heart.

"I keep dreaming of her." Her ragged whisper seemed pulled from deep in her throat. "She's with my mother, in this meadow, and I'm happy there with them, but...but there's this darkness and she's gone and I'm alone."

He pressed her closer, willing her pain into him, wanting nothing more than to take it away. It washed over him in smothering waves, a grief as thick and choking as his own for Everett. Memories of how lost he'd been, of being adrift and separate, needing to connect with Kathleen over the loss of their son, being refused that comfort, deluged him.

He'd be damned before he'd leave Celia lost and alone like that.

He rubbed his fingertips down the side of her neck in an easy caress. Her hold tightened at his shoulder. Turning his head, he rested his mouth against her brow.

"I love you, Celia."

She stilled in his embrace, even her uneven breathing seeming to stop. A tsunami of fear slammed over him and he waited for her to withdraw from his touch, his comfort, his loving her.

Like Kathleen all over again.

He suppressed a shudder, a cold hard knot sitting in his chest. He wasn't going there. It wasn't fair and it wasn't true.

Celia wasn't Kathleen. He needed to remember that. Knee-jerk reactions based on his failed marriage would only fuck up everything. He wasn't the same man he'd been in his twenties. Pushing hadn't worked with Kathleen. He was smart enough now not to make the same mistake with Celia.

He couldn't afford to, couldn't handle the thought of ending up pushing her away.

If she pulled away, he'd turn loose. If she spurned his

declaration, he'd step back and give her all the time she needed, and somehow, at the same time, he'd find a way to be her source of support in her grief.

She rested a hand against his chest and levered away, to rest on an elbow and gaze down at him. "You—"

"Shhh." He brushed his mouth over hers again, then her cheek, temple, jaw. "I said it too soon, after everything you've been through."

"No." She laid a finger against his lips, her gaze, dark with grief, fixed on his. "Don't be sorry."

Hope unfurled within him, stretching out tentative tendrils within his chest.

She sank white teeth into her bottom lip, her eyes troubled. "I don't think I can give you...my head is so messed up—"

"Not now." He laid a finger against her lips. "It's not about me." He tucked her head into his shoulder and sifted his fingers through her hair. "Rest, baby. I won't leave. I promise."

"What do you mean, you're not going to the office?"

Tom glanced up to meet Celia's gaze in the mirror. She stood behind him in the bathroom doorway, frowning. Sunlight streamed in the windows behind her, gilding her hair.

She folded her arms over her midriff. "Of course you're going to the office."

He wiped a smudge of shaving cream from his chin. "No, I'm not. I have no intention of leaving you alone today."

She leaned a shoulder against the doorjamb and fixed him with a steady look, her eyes swollen and red. "You're an elected official, one who took a hefty shot to his professional reputation yesterday, and you can't afford to not be in that office."

"I don't give a rat's ass about my reputation. I'm not leaving you."

"Bullshit, McMillian—"

"Tom."

"Fine. Bullshit, Tom. You worked too hard to get where you are to not give a rat's ass."

"Celia, I didn't have anything but the position and the politics before." He swallowed, hard, and turned to face her. "That's not true any longer." He cleared his throat. "I meant what I said last night, about loving you."

A wistful smile didn't quite banish the ravages of grief from her expression. "I know. I believe you. But that doesn't change the fact you need to be in your office today of all days."

"Celia—"

"Tom. There's absolutely nothing you can do here today." A sudden wash of tears shimmered in her eyes. "It will be days before the crime lab releases...before I can make any plans. But I'm still going to be a mess all day and I'd rather you didn't see anymore of that after last night. I'll work on those financial records downstairs or something and—"

He stepped forward to stop the flow of words with his mouth. "A half day at the office, then I'll be here for you this afternoon. And if you need me, for anything, you call and I'm on my way. Deal?"

She pressed her forehead to his cheek on a trembling sigh. "Deal."

"You could come with me." He murmured the words against her temple.

"No." A palpable shudder traveled through her body. "I can't face that yet."

He nodded, rocking her against him. He kissed her cheek.

"A half day. And I'll see you at lunch."

The office area buzzed—questions and sympathy for Celia, speculation about the reasons behind Cicely's death, murmured conversations about his own involvement with Celia. He ignored the latter, aware his late-for-him arrival had only fueled the gossip inferno. Let 'em talk. All that mattered, really, was Celia.

Standing behind his desk, he flipped through the gargantuan stack of phone messages from the day before. The volume of emails in his inbox was bound to be twice as huge. Concerned with Celia, he'd not checked in from home, ignoring even his personal voice mail. Maybe Celia was right. Maybe coming in, even for half a day, was the smart thing to do. He'd never dig out from under this if he...

What the fuck?

He flicked back three messages. Mariah High. He frowned at the blue message slip. Considering the story flying yesterday, the news of Jessie's death over the weekend, Rhett's wife calling wasn't unusual—he and Rhett had been together a long time and he considered Mariah a friend as well. Other than mothering Amarie, Mariah had seemed to make it her life's purpose to introduce Tom to any and all single women after his divorce. How often had she ragged him about wanting to see him as settled and happy as she and Rhett?

Hell, she'd introduced him to Jessie in the first place. She liked Celia, had teased him about hiring her. If she thought Celia was dead, that he was a suspect, he'd expect her to be on the phone, looking for him, even with Amarie starting treatment.

Still, something about the message slip sent unease skittering through him, echoes of the darkness that had shrouded his mind and car the evening before.

Darkness that had turned out to be absolutely nothing.

Shit, he was losing it. Chilly discomfort flitted up his nape, taunting him, poking him with tormenting fingers.

A sharp knock on his open door split the relative quiet. Startled from his musings, he fumbled the slips, managing to dump them on the desk rather than the floor before turning a narrow-eyed gaze at the doorway.

"Sorry about that." Cook managed to exude genuine contrition for a half-second. Just behind him, Tick stared down the hallway with a speculative twist to his mouth.

As Tom waved them in, Rhett's deep voice rumbled from the hall. Tick closed the door and jerked a thumb over his shoulder. "I thought High's daughter was at Emory, getting prepped to undergo chemo before a bone-marrow transplant. At least, that's what the church's prayer list said."

"She is." Tom settled into his chair. Cook took one of the leather seats facing the desk.

Tick ambled to the other chair. "And he's here?"

Tom shrugged, the muscles at his shoulders and neck screaming with tension. Mariah's message slip stared up at him from the desk. "He thought yesterday he'd have to step in for me."

"That was yesterday." Tick shook his head. "Why isn't he in Atlanta today?"

Hell if I know. Ask him yourself. Tom swallowed the words. Irritability flowed around him in waves, worsened by the disquiet flooding him in quiet rivulets. He tapped his thumb on Mariah's name, then sighed and pinched the bridge of his nose. "I don't know. Last night, I thought he was driving back."

Tick's grunt bordered on disparaging.

"You're a judgmental son of a bitch." Cook lounged in the chair, a mocking gleam lighting his gray eyes.

Tick heaved a rough sigh. "Shit, Cookie, quit looking at me like that. You agree with me. We both know if you had a kid and she was sick, you wouldn't be sitting here, anymore than I would."

Their exchange grated on Tom's already jangling nerves. "Is there a reason you're here now?"

"Yeah." With one final glare at his partner, Tick extracted a paper from the folder he held and pushed it across the desk. "We found that in Jessica's financial records this morning."

On the credit card statement, Tom underlined the charge from an Atlanta-area women's clinic with his finger and glanced at the date. June of the previous year. "It's too early to be for prenatal care."

"It's an abortion." Tick straightened the knife-edge crease of his slacks between his knee and ankle. "The same clinic performed a CVS test a week before."

"CVS?"

"Chorionic villi sampling. Prenatal testing for birth defects. I couldn't get her medical records without a subpoena, but once the nurse heard she was a murder victim, I did get her to tell me what she remembered."

Tom frowned at the statement. So those weeks when Jessica had kept him out of her bed early last summer hadn't been about her period and a yeast infection. Instead, it had been about recovery from an abortion. He rubbed his thumb over the VISA symbol at the top of the paper. He'd been through all of her credit card transactions the night before. Why hadn't he seen this one?

He *hadn't* seen this one. He was sure of it. Without looking up, he reached for the phone and punched in the auto dial for

Celia's cell phone.

She answered on the second ring. "Hello?"

Her tear-roughened voice quavered and his heart contracted. "How are you?"

"Okay." Her tremulous sigh carried over the line. "I just got off the phone with Jarrod O'Shea at the funeral home."

He closed his eyes, pinching the bridge of his nose again. "Are you downstairs?"

"Yes, why?"

"Look through Jessie's stuff, find her VISA transactions for me."

"All right." The sounds of rustling papers filled the connection. "I've got them."

"Pull the July statement, the one showing her charges from June."

A long pause, more rustling. "It's not here. It skips from May to August."

"Thanks, baby." He cleared his throat against a sudden lump. "Take care."

"I will." With the soft words, she was gone.

He looked up in time to catch the knowing look Tick and Cook exchanged. He shrugged it off and frowned. Why was this statement missing from the ones he'd taken home? He'd specifically asked Raquel to pull all of Jessie's financial records.

Reaching for the phone again, he buzzed through to his secretary's line, verifying that yes, she *had* pulled that particular month and placed it in the file for him.

Which meant he *had* had it and somewhere along the way it had vanished.

Or been made to disappear? The pulsing sense of agitation

grew stronger. Where had that thought come from, anyway? No one had had access to those records except—

"I don't get it." Cook's low voice cut through his ruminations. Across from him, Tick and Cook engaged in a quiet conversation, tossing around ideas the way he'd heard them do on several occasions before. "So what would this CVS testing tell about a baby?"

Tick shrugged, a negligent roll of his shoulders. "Chromosomal defects, blood type, maybe some DNA markers?"

Eyes closed, Cook rubbed a forefinger over his brow. "So she aborted the fetus for a defect? Afraid it wouldn't bring the big bucks if it wasn't perfect?"

"Maybe." A grimace twisted Tick's features. "People can be crazy about stuff like that. During our last round of in vitro, the tech got us mixed up with another couple who were choosing donor sperm. She made it sound like shopping for a car with options. You know, picking out tall, athletic, intelligent, musical talent, hair color, eye color. I guess in some situations knowing your kid had the perfect blood type could be important too, especially if you're willing to throw fifty grand to—"

"Shit." Tom stared at Mariah's name on the message slip.

Perfect blood type.

His gaze tracked to the time and date, written in Raquel's neat script.

"What did I say?" Tick leaned forward, intrigue saturating his voice.

Eleven thirty-five. Mariah had called at eleven thirty-five. Before he'd left Celia's with Tick under a cloud of mock suspicion. Before the news had broken on the local news and certainly before it had made the Atlanta-area stations. Before he'd instructed Raquel to call Rhett.

I figured you might need me here and Mariah agreed I should come.

Because only something massively important would have induced Mariah to agree that Rhett should leave their child.

And once the secret truth about Celia's "death" was revealed, Rhett would have needed an equally massive incentive to stay.

The facts clicked into place: Rhett's appearance on scene, Mariah's early phone call, the missing credit card statement, Rhett's continued presence.

"McMillian?"

Fucking son of a bitch.

"Who?"

The simultaneous realizations that he'd spoken aloud and was on his feet sank in together. Fury spiked up his spine, exploding in his brain with pulverizing strength.

"McMillian, what's up?" Apprehension colored Cook's voice, but Tom ignored him, throwing the door open with enough force to send it slamming into the wall. He strode down the hall. The cubicles in the hub area fell silent, except for the chime of an unanswered phone. A law clerk and a paralegal moved out of his way, eyes wide, faces curious and apprehensive.

He halted in the open doorway to Rhett's office and narrowed his eyes at the man he'd considered his best friend.

"Why'd you do it, Rhett?" For the first time, he really heard the quiet deadliness others had described in his courtroom voice.

Rhett looked up from the folder he held. "Tom—"

"I fucking asked you a question."

He sensed Cook and Tick behind him, tensing. What did the investigators think, that he'd attack his former friend? He glowered at Rhett. Better to send him to rot in prison among the very men Rhett had put away.

Eyes closed, Rhett exhaled, a long, pain-filled breath. "I had to."

The rage tried to consume him and he smothered it under icy calm. "You had to? That's a bullshit answer, High. What the fuck does that mean?"

"You were too close. I had to do something."

"Kill Celia, you mean?"

"You don't understand." Rhett licked his lips and opened his eyes, wild emotion burning deep in them. "You can't."

"You're right. I sure as hell can't."

"McMillian. Stop. Don't ask him anything else." Cook clapped his shoulder in a firm grip. Tom shook him off. "He's not been Mirandized, remember?"

Tom slanted him a contemptuous look. He hadn't forgotten anything.

"I'll waive my rights." Rhett slumped into his chair, bearing a cloak of defeat Tom had never seen on him. "I understand them and I waive them."

"Why, Rhett?" He ground his teeth together hard enough to send waves of pain radiating down his neck. "Explain it to me."

Grimacing, Rhett shook his head. His hands rested in his lap, palms up. "All she had to do was give us the baby like she promised."

"She?" Cook leaned against the doorjamb. "Allison Baker?"

"No. Jessie." Rhett's gaze shot to Tom's. "I didn't want to hurt her."

Memories detonated in Tom's brain, the gaping wound on Jessie's abdomen, the broken cheekbone, the skin split over it, the paralyzing fear and agony frozen on her face. She'd suffered the most horrific death Tom had seen in almost twenty years of criminal law, and Rhett sat here, saying he hadn't wanted to hurt her? Tom curled his hands into fists. The fucking bastard.

Cook leaned forward. "Are you saying you killed Jessica Grady?"

"I went with him." Rhett's voice lowered to a pained whisper. "I helped him. For Amarie."

"Him?"

"Amarie?" Tom and Cook spoke together. Cook frowned at him and Tom waved him on.

"Who is 'him'?" Cook asked.

"Alton Baker."

"Baker killed Jessica?"

Rhett nodded. Nausea settled in Tom's gut. "For the baby."

"We had to have that baby, for Amarie."

"What do you mean, for Amarie?" Tick asked, his voice firm and quiet.

"They needed the baby for a marrow donor." Tom pushed out the words. Now he understood, on some level, why Jessie's baby had been worth so much. To a father, nothing was worth more than a child's life. He caught Rhett's pain-filled gaze. "Jessie was Amarie's birth mother, wasn't she?"

Rhett nodded again. "We'd graduated law school together, and she'd known Mariah since high school, you knew that. We...all Mariah wanted was a baby. When Jessie found out she was pregnant, Mariah convinced her to give the baby to us."

"Was Baker Amarie's father?"

"Yes. When Amarie got sick, when none of the treatments worked, we needed a sibling donor. Our chances were better for a match. Jessie said she'd do it, for a price."

"Fifty grand."

Rhett shook his head, a long roll against the back of his chair. "Fifty upfront, paid in installments so it would be easier to hide. Another fifty when she delivered. But then she started asking for more."

Cook tapped his thumbs on the jamb. "Baker killed her for it."

"She'd been trying to blackmail him, had a film of them together."

"Which one of you killed Cicely St. John?"

"He sent someone to do it." An aggrieved expression twisted Rhett's face. "That's how it got fucked up. He didn't realize it wasn't Celia."

"Fucked up?" Fury shot through Tom once more. "She was tortured before she was killed. The bastard strangled her, let her wake up, then slit her throat. You planned for someone to do that to Celia and you call that fucked up? You son of a bitch."

"Tommy, I had to. You gotta understand that, man."

Tom clenched his hands, so he wouldn't wrap them around the other man's throat. He spun and stalked to the hallway.

"Tom, man, you gotta believe me. I had to save my daughter. I had to." Rhett's anguished voice stopped him mid-stride, for a half-second. "I had to!"

"Go to hell, Rhett."

I love you, Celia.

Frustrated, Celia pushed the pen and notebook with her list of ideas away and rested her elbows on the coffee table. Tom's declaration bounced around her head, completely killing what little concentration she had left. What was she supposed to do with those words? They frightened her.

She wasn't good with the whole love thing. Look what had happened with the last man who'd claimed to love her.

Fingers pressed to her closed eyes, she let out a strangled groan. She couldn't deal, couldn't handle this right now—

And that was such bullshit. She had to deal with it because this was *Tom*, putting himself out there for her, risking rejection. Because he hadn't put himself out there for it to happen again, after his divorce, and that more than anything convinced her of the veracity of his avowal.

I love you, Celia.

Oh, Jesus above. He'd put himself out there in the biggest way possible for her.

She was making herself insane. He wasn't asking her for anything. She could just let it be for now. But worried about being alone without Cicely, and yet wanting to push away the man she loved, keep herself safe—

The man she *loved*?

No way. Loving meant getting hurt, ending up alone.

With a confused moan, she buried her face in her hands. Tears burned at her eyes. His "I love you, Celia" scared her freaking silly because she *couldn't* just let it be.

"Celia? Are you all right?" Concern laced Tom's deep voice. He knelt behind her on the carpet and strong hands took her shoulders in an easy grip.

"I'm fine." She lifted her head and swiped at her damp lashes. "I didn't hear you come in."

He shifted her hair to one side and rested his face against her nape. A shudder moved through him as he wrapped his arms around her waist. "Cook and Calvert arrested Baker's accomplice this morning."

The quiet words sank into her consciousness, along with the tension hanging about him. She spun in his arms. "Who?"

He brushed her hair back and trailed his knuckle along her face. A shaky exhale escaped him. "Rhett."

Shock stole her breath. She gaped at him, then swallowed hard, trying to get her lungs and brain to work. "What?"

His throat moved and he licked his upper lip. "He confessed when I confronted him."

She scooted away from him, breaking his easy hold. She pressed her spine against the coffee table. "Rhett High killed my sister."

"Baker had it done. Rhett knew about it." Tom looked away, his expression bleak. "He helped Baker kill Jessie."

"God." She shoved her hair away from her face, digging her fingers into her scalp. Images tumbled through her brain, the horrific death inflicted on Jessica Grady. *Rhett* had taken part in that? "Why?"

"Because her baby was conceived to be Amarie's marrow donor." His raw, audible swallow made her throat hurt. "Jessie got greedy, started asking for more money from Rhett for the child and blackmailing Baker as well. So they went and...took it."

"Where's the baby now?" She covered her mouth with both hands as another thought slammed into her. "Did Mariah know?"

"No." He shook his head, rubbing a thumb along the seam at his thigh. "Baker had one of his lackeys take the baby to Atlanta. Obviously, he had a doctor on the payroll up there. They concocted some story about finding a donor. My bet is they planned to put the baby up for an illegal adoption once the marrow was extracted."

Another transaction. Another problem to be disposed of.

Like Jessie. Like Cicely.

She closed her eyes, heart aching now for Mariah and Amarie. So many lives destroyed.

Pain nudged at her mind and she instinctively recoiled. That wasn't her emotion. Her lashes lifted, in time for her to catch a flash of naked agony on his face.

No, not her pain. His. Tom's hurt and sense of betrayal. His anger and confusion.

Moving on intuition, she bracketed his face with her hands. "I'm sorry," she murmured and leaned forward to feather her mouth over his, to smooth kisses along his jaw. "So sorry. I know he was your friend, how much this has to hurt you."

His arms came around her with crushing force, clutching her to him as though he feared she'd disappear if he let her go. Celia buried her face in the curve between his neck and shoulder and sucked in a deep breath, fortifying herself. "I love you, Tom."

He froze but she sensed the relieved shudder that traveled through him.

"I can't make you forget any of this, Cee," he whispered into her hair. "Not what happened to Cicely, what Rhett did, but I can promise you new memories, good memories, baby."

"Memories of us." She trailed a hand down his back, a touch of connection and comfort rather than desire, a connection she felt all the way to her soul. "For both of us."

He held on tighter. "I'm so sorry, baby. I know she was all you had—"

"I have you." She murmured the words against his throat, and when he pressed his face to her temple, she felt the dampness of tears on her skin. "I just didn't know how much I needed you."

"I'll always be here for you. As long as you need me."

She leaned back and tilted her face so their gazes met. "It could take a long time to make those memories, McMillian. A lifetime, maybe."

"Definitely a lifetime, if that's what you want, Celia." He cupped her face, catching her tears on his thumbs and rubbing the moisture away. Frustration twisted his mouth. "Damn it all, I have to go to the sheriff's department. Tick is going to make a statement to the press and I want to be there. I wish I could stay with you and be—"

"It's okay." She smiled, although her lips trembled, the same sense of connection and comfort unfurling between them. "I'll come with you."

"I'm going to put them away, both of them, baby, for as long as I can, for what they did. I swear it to you."

"I know you will. You're a tough son of a bitch." She lifted his hand, brushed her lips across the inside of his wrist. "That's what I love about you most."

Epilogue

The steady flow of icy water did little to soothe her burning skin. Celia lifted her face from the stream spilling from the hose. She blinked, her eyes still blurred and watering. Jesus above, she hated recertifying for pepper spray.

"I'm really sorry." Cook spoke somewhere over her head.

She straightened and handed the hose off to a waiting deputy, also a fellow victim. She brushed wet hair from her face and fixed a decidedly unrepentant Mark Cook with a glare. "Sure you are. Just wait. I'm going to pay Calvert off so I can hold the canister when you have to do this."

"I'm good for two more years." With a smug grin, he folded his arms.

She narrowed her eyes at him but squashed the desire to stick out her tongue. "I'll wait."

His soft laugh rumbled between them. She lifted the collar of her T-shirt and rubbed water from her face with a gingery motion. Hell, even touching her capsicum-abraded skin hurt. She gazed across the parking lot behind the Chandler County Sheriff's Department, where the training exercise was going on. Tick Calvert sat on the back steps, scribbling on a clipboard. He looked as withdrawn and dejected as he'd been all day, the normally straight line of his shoulders slumped.

Celia nudged Cook's side. "What's with him?"

Cook rested his hands at his gun belt. "His wife's pregnant again. They just found out last week."

"That's not a good thing?" Celia frowned. "I thought they wanted kids."

"They did. They quit trying after her third miscarriage last year. Hurts too bad, I guess." Cook's mouth tightened. "This one was a total surprise for both of them and I don't think it's a happy one. More a wait-and-see-what-goes-wrong one, you know?"

"Yeah." Sympathy swirled through her. The sorrow apparent in Tick's posture she understood. It mirrored Tom's over the loss of his son so long ago. Losing a loved one lingered, the grief rising to torment when least expected. Celia tugged at her chain, where the small ring Cicely had always worn on her right hand now shared space with a tarnished button from an Air Force dress blue uniform.

"You don't have to hang around here." Cook pulled her from the melancholy reverie. "We're going to debrief as a department. Don't think you have to suffer through that just to get your certificate renewed."

"Thanks." She lifted a hand in a wave. "See you."

This late on a summer Saturday afternoon, traffic was sparse, not that it was ever too heavy to begin with. Within minutes, she was zipping along the lakefront, the warm breeze whipping in through open windows and soothing the sting from her skin. After pulling into the drive, she parked the Xterra in the garage beside the Mercedes and entered through the laundry room.

The house lay quiet and she wandered through the kitchen to the living area. She needed a shower as the biting smell of pepper spray still clung to her clothes and hair. Sunlight slanted in through tall windows. She stopped, smiling at the sight of Tom napping on the wide leather couch, a recent law journal on his chest, reading glasses perched askew on his nose.

His bare feet were propped on the sofa arm, and she tweaked his big toe and watched his tall body come to alertness. Dark lashes lifted to reveal sharp blue eyes.

"Hello, Counselor." She moved closer to lean down and remove his glasses. She'd barely set them aside on the coffee table when he grasped her wrist and pulled her down atop him. The glossy journal slid to the floor.

"Hello, Mrs. McMillian." Still holding her wrist and with one arm clamped around her waist, he nuzzled her ear. Shivery anticipation tingled over her.

"You get a serious jolly from saying that, don't you?" She melted into him, rubbing her hands over his chest. Under her palm, his heart thudded a steady rhythm.

"Yes." He nipped at her earlobe. "I like knowing you belong to me, that I belong to you."

She liked it too, liked knowing that even when things went pear-shaped, she could count on him to be there. He'd proven it over and over in the last year, from Cicely's funeral to Rhett High's and Alton Baker's trials for her sister's murder.

And through everything, she'd been right with him too.

With his mouth doing wicked things to her senses, she fiddled with the placket of his golf shirt, freeing the buttons so she could slide her fingers across warm, hair-roughened skin. The hand at her waist slipped down, dipping beneath the waistband of her jeans to caress the small of her back and lower.

"Know what I think we should do, Mr. McMillian?" She caught her breath as those marauding fingers found intimate flesh.

"What's that, Cee?" Near her ear, his voice lowered to a sinful growl.

"I think..." She tiptoed her fingers down his chest. "We should go upstairs and make another memory."

His teeth flashed in the shark's smile she loved and he pressed her to him, drawing her mouth down to his. "My pleasure, Mrs. McMillian."

Two lazy hours later, after they'd showered together, she'd managed to weaken his knees and leave him moaning, and he'd returned the favor, Tom set about putting together shish kebobs for the grill. A glass of pinot noir in hand, Celia perched on a stool at the island, chatting to him about her training mishaps while he sliced peppers and a red onion. The spicy scent of marinade filled the air.

Tom set the strips of pepper aside, warm contentment spreading through him. This part of each day he liked best— well, second best, since life didn't hold anything better than waking with Celia rumpled and drowsy in his arms each morning, knowing she'd be there again when night fell. But he treasured the simple pleasure of their evenings, sharing the task of preparing a casual supper while they indulged in conversation punctuated with laughter and love.

The memories they made got him through even the toughest days.

Celia flipped through the day's mail lying atop the granite countertop. She tapped a short, neat fingernail on a flyer from the Alabama Shakespeare Festival. "They're showing *The Count of Monte Cristo* next month. We should go, maybe spend the night..."

She let the thought trail away as the front bell rang. "Were you expecting someone?"

He dumped wedges of onion next to the pepper. "No."

"Wonder who it is?" Twirling her wine flute, Celia slid from the stool and sauntered through to the foyer, bare feet whispering against the tile.

Tom reached for the skewers. Voices wafted down the short hallway, Celia's blending with two familiar male tones. An ominous prickle started at the base of his spine, radiating through his lower back to become a nagging pain. He stilled, a familiar and hated sensation of prodding darkness invading his brain.

Fuck. He dropped the damp wooden spits and spun to follow his wife. He almost collided with her in the doorway as she entered with Cook and Tick on her heels. The throb in his back pulsed into a low agony; the looming danger tried to cloud his mind.

He gritted his teeth against both. "What's wrong?"

"Nothing." Surprise flared in Celia's blue gaze, followed by concern. She held aloft a sheet of paper. "I forgot my training log and they dropped it by." She cast the paper aside and laid a gentle hand on his forearm. "Are you all right? You're pale."

"Fine." He stepped backward into the kitchen, fighting the waves of sensation that didn't belong to him.

"I'm going to get you some water." Celia moved away. Pain speared across his chest, right to left, at a downward angle, taking his breath. Shit, psychic awareness was supposed to be a good thing? Like hell. Every single book he'd read on the topic which tried to put a positive spin on it lied. This was not good. Darkness crowded his vision and he tried to catch his breath.

"McMillian, you need to sit down." Tick took his arm in a firm grip and steered him toward the dining set before the tall windows. Nausea pushed up in Tom's throat; he laid a palm over the agony burning his torso. "St. John, you got any aspirin in the house?"

Cook flipped open his cell. "I'm calling for an ambulance."

It was one of *them*, he was experiencing what would happen to one of them and they thought he was having a fucking heart attack. If he didn't hurt so damn bad, it would be funny.

"Don't need an ambulance." He'd be fine as soon as whichever one of them he was feeling was out of the house. "I'm all right."

"Sure you are." Grim humor colored Tick's words. His fingers rested on Tom's wrist in a firm grip. Taking his pulse, Tom realized.

"He'll be okay in a minute." Celia knelt beside him and pushed a cool glass into his hand. Grateful, he lifted it to his mouth.

"Pulse is normal." Surprise vibrated in Tick's voice. He released Tom's wrist.

"I'm not having a damn heart attack." He let more of the cold water trickle down his throat. The weird pain subsided somewhat. He looked up in time to see Tick shrug and mouth "anxiety" at Cook. Yeah, that was one word for it—knowing something terrible was looming, but not being able to tell where or when it would strike. Sounded like anxiety to him.

"He needs to rest." Celia stroked the inside of his forearm. "Why don't you two take off?"

"You're sure?" Cell phone still in hand, Cook frowned.

"Yes." She curved her hand along Tom's jaw, warmth and peace spreading out from the simple contact.

"We'll let ourselves out." As they left the kitchen, the discomfort eased, evaporating when the front door closed behind them with a quiet snick.

Celia glanced toward the foyer then back at him. "Better?"

He blew out a less-than-steady breath, icy sweat peppering his upper lip. "Much."

Her eyes troubled, Celia continued to touch him in easy, soothing caresses. "Don't you think we should tell them?"

He flinched away from the idea before he could stop himself. A scornful laugh escaped his lips. "Yeah. What am I going to say? I think something catastrophic is going to happen to one of you, but I don't know which one, I don't know when, and I don't know exactly what that something is. Hell."

"At least think about it."

"I will." Frustration made his voice sharp. Like he'd think about anything else the rest of the evening.

"Oh Tom." She enfolded him in a close embrace. "I'm sorry."

He wrapped his arms around her and rested his chin atop her shining hair. "So am I."

"I'd take it away if I could," she whispered into the curve of his throat. "I'd make it better."

"I know." He managed to smile. Pulling back, he touched her face. "You make everything better."

She laid her forefinger in the center of his bottom lip. "Oh yeah?"

"Yeah." He kissed her fingertip. "You're the one thing I'm always certain of, Cee."

She leaned forward to whisper against his mouth, her words wrapping welcome warmth around him. "It's mutual, Counselor."

About the Author

How does a high school English teacher end up plotting murders? She uses her experiences as a cop's wife to become a writer of romantic suspense! Linda Winfree lives in a quintessential small Georgia town with her husband and two children. By day, she teaches American Literature, advises the student government and coaches the drama team; by night she pens sultry books full of murder and mayhem.

To learn more about Linda and her books, visit her website at www.lindawinfree.com or join her Yahoo newsletter group at http://groups.yahoo.com/group/linda_winfree. Linda loves hearing from readers. Feel free to drop her an email at linda_winfree@yahoo.com.

Their passion rivals the fires they battle.

Hot Shot
© 2008 M.J. Fredrick

Peyton Michaels expected her assignment to be simple—write an article about everyday heroes. Heroes like Hot Shot firefighter Gabe Cooper. She never expected to find herself running up a mountain, a wildfire nipping at her heels, her life in his hands.

And she never expected to be drawn to Gabe. After the loss of her husband in the line of duty, the last thing she wants is to fall in love with yet another man who routinely puts his life at risk.

Gabe has had enough of women who want to make him into someone he's not. Women like his ex, who couldn't handle the heat of his job. Like Peyton, who sees him as a hero when he's just a man doing a job. Except time after time, the pesky reporter proves her mettle. And gets deeper under his skin.

But there's an arsonist at work, and danger is closing in with the speed of a raging brush fire. Peyton and Gabe have to dig deep for what it takes to be a real hero—to find the courage to reach out and grab a forever kind of love. Before it's too late.

Warning: sexy.

Available now in ebook and print from Samhain Publishing.

Love is the last line of defense.

Still Mine
© 2008 Mary Wine

Jolene Benate has spent six years keeping a vow to herself to never again be that weak woman weeping at her young husband's graveside. Now she's a deputy marshal on the elite warrant squad, as physically and mentally tough as they come. But moving on isn't as easy as it looks.

Especially when the husband she thought was dead suddenly reappears. And, even in the face of his betrayal, she still wants him.

Paul Benate's gifted mind was groomed from a young age to serve the military and its top-secret projects. His one youthful act of rebellion was to marry Jolene, only to discover a terrorist could use her to force him to give up his classified secrets. For her own safety, he had to let her go.

But the safety he thought was assured by his "death" was only an illusion. Secrets have a way of surfacing, and once again Jolene is the perfect target. There's only one thing left to do…reclaim the woman that he has always loved.

Even if she's mad as hell at him.

Warning: Hot and flammable. Sometimes they just don't make it to the bedroom.

Available now in ebook and print from Samhain Publishing.

Will her need to do the right thing cost them everything?

Anything But Mine
© 2008 Linda Winfree

Book Four of the Hearts of the South series.

Public Defender Autry Holton, honor-bound to defend an accused serial killer, is in a "shunned if she does, disbarred if she doesn't" position. To complicate matters, she's pregnant and hasn't yet told her ex-lover he's the father. The reason? She's pretty sure he won't want the baby.

After raising one family and suffering a failed marriage, Sheriff Stanton Reed never believed he was the right man for Autry. Then an attempted break-in at Autry's home highlights the real danger she faces, and all he can think of is protecting her. When she tells him the truth about their baby, the past doesn't matter. He wants both her and their child in his life.

But just as Autry dares to hope there's a future for them, an act of homegrown terrorism shatters her trust—and threatens their lives.

Available now in ebook and print from Samhain Publishing.

GREAT cheap FUN

Discover eBooks!

THE FASTEST WAY TO GET THE HOTTEST NAMES

Get your favorite authors on your favorite reader, long before they're
out in print! Ebooks from Samhain go wherever you go, and work with
whatever you carry—Palm, PDF, Mobi, and more.

Samhain
publishing
LTD

WWW.SAMHAINPUBLISHING.COM

Printed in the United Kingdom by
Lightning Source UK Ltd., Milton Keynes
137748UK00001B/319-321/P